Jake Arnott

Jake Arnott was born in 1961, and lives in London. His debut novel, *The Long Firm*, was published in 1999 to great acclaim. It was subsequently made into a television series by the BBC, and was followed by the equally praised *He Kills Coppers* in 2001 and *truecrime* in 2003. *Johnny Come Home* is currently being adapted as a television drama for Channel Four.

Jake Arnott

Johnny Come Home

SCEPTRE

First published in Great Britain in 2006 by Hodder & Stoughton
A division of Hodder Headline

A Sceptre Paperback

3

A CIP catalogue record for this title is available from the British Library

ISBN 978 0 340 81859 6

Typeset by Hewer Text UK Ltd, Edinburgh

Printed and bound in Great Britain by
Clays Ltd, St Ives plc

Hodder Headline's policy is to use papers that are natural, renewable
and recyclable products and made from wood grown in sustainable
forests. The logging and manufacturing processes are expected to
conform to the environmental regulations of the country of origin.

Hodder and Stoughton
A division of Hodder Headline
338 Euston Road
London NW1 3BH

Johnny Come Home

I

as good a time as any

O'Connell came back to the squat and went up to his room. The house was empty, so now was as good a time as any. He started to rifle through the papers on his desk. There were a few things to be sorted out. He was thinking ahead. Soon he would be dead, he mused. There were plans to be made for the promising future.

He started to gather up all that was on the worktop and dump it into a plastic bag. He would get rid of everything, he decided. There was nothing that he wanted to leave behind. Should he write a note? What would be the point of that? Out of politeness perhaps, but that was never his style. He had never liked goodbyes, after all. He knew that if he delayed any longer he would lose his resolve. It was time to go. He knew that he should have said something to Pearson. Too late for that. He had treated him pretty shabbily but the poor fucker would have to fend for himself now. Pearson would be better off on his own.

As he stacked up a pile of notes for the bin he came across a file that contained his last story. He picked it up and looked at it. It was an absurd and pretentious piece of work. Embarrassing. Everything was so bloody embarrassing, even his death. He wanted to get it over with. The sooner the better. The story, well, it said it all. There was some sort of meaning to it: humiliation. He would leave it behind, he decided; it might explain things. He lifted up his typewriter and put the file underneath it.

O'Connell took the bag containing the other papers to put downstairs with the rubbish. There was a vague sense of relief in chucking it all away. Time for a new start, he thought with a grim satisfaction. So much to look forward to. So much.

He went back upstairs and took out the wrap of heroin. There was enough here to do it properly. He fixed it up with a teaspoon and the little paraffin burner he had taken from a chemistry set that he had bought in a second-hand shop. Back when this habit was just an experiment in self-medication. He drew the hot liquid into a syringe, tied off his arm with his belt and tapped along his forearm for a vein. He broke into a sudden sweat. There was a moment of panic. He made himself concentrate. He needed to get all this done quickly. If he messed it up and was somehow resuscitated people might say that it was a 'cry for help'. He couldn't bear that. No. He would have to do this right. So many things he'd fucked up in life but please God not this. The sweat cooled on his brow and his hand steadied itself. The needle went in and he pressed the plunger slowly. The drug surged through the tired blood, seeping into the weary flesh. He felt the hit. Yeah. He sighed. It was going to be all right.

He drew a bath and took off his clothes. He ran the water until it nearly reached the top of the tub then gently eased himself into its warmth. He felt the junk rush through him, enveloping him with a deep yawning drowsiness. He let his head slip under the surface and a little wave of bath water slopped noisily on to the floor. *Eureka*, he thought. Maybe it was his last thought, he thought. It wouldn't be a bad last thought, but then he had another. Just at the moment that he was about to forget everything for ever, as his last breath bubbled out of him, he thought of something he had left behind.

2

monday, 29 may 1972

Nina couldn't come.

She reached down to gently push Jan's face away from her cunt. Jan looked up from the end of the bed, her elfin face crowned with a shock of short feathery blonde hair, her green eyes wide with concern.

'What's the matter?'

'It isn't happening,' Nina said.

'What do you want me to do?'

'It's all right. It doesn't matter.'

'But I want it to be good for you.'

'Look, it just doesn't work, that's all. It's OK.'

Jan sat up and looked away with a sullen pout.

'It never has.' She shrugged. 'I'm not any good for you, am I?'

Nina sighed. This was always the way. It was always her that had to do the reassuring. It didn't seem fair that she had to worry about hurting other people's feelings over sex. It was as though they felt that she was holding something back from them by not coming. But she couldn't help it.

'Look, it's not you,' she told Jan. 'It's me. We've been through this before, Jan. It just doesn't happen for me, that's all.'

Nina couldn't come. Not with Jan nor with anybody else. She could make herself come when she was alone but not with another person. When she masturbated by herself she would always imagine somebody else there. A woman or a man. She

3

would even dream of lovers that she had had in the past and be able to orgasm to a fantasy that had never actually happened for her. When she was having sex with another person, she would try to block out their presence from her mind and desperately concentrate on her own solitary pleasure, but it didn't work. It was ridiculous, she concluded. She had tried so hard to join in with life, to connect, but her own desires seemed to float out into an unsubstantial space, always out of reach.

She had faked it back in the sixties. It hadn't been hard. The supposed 'sexual revolution' was really all about what men wanted while women would just lie back and pretend most of the time. It still seemed like it was a joke being played on her. She had been so optimistic when she had first arrived at college, with all the talk of liberation and permissiveness. She had met Kevin in her first term. He was good looking and had seemed so groovy in his shoulder-length hair and Chelsea boots. But he was a terrible disappointment. Kevin had thought of himself as a real hipster, brandishing Wilhelm Reich and talking loudly about 'free love', but in reality he just wanted hippy domesticity, for her to roll his joints and cook his brown rice. He wanted to be mothered, really – he even called her his 'old lady'. Nina eventually gave up simulating climaxes when she made love with him. She'd had enough of it. It had made her feel false and empty and it was exhausting. But this became an affront to Kevin's precious sense of his own sexual technique. His fucking prowess. She spent so much time and energy telling *him* that it was OK. When they finally split up at the end of the first year he accused her of being 'hung up' about sex. Whatever that was supposed to mean.

She met an American called Martha at a party in Notting Hill Gate a week later and went home with her. It was her first time with a woman but she didn't feel it changed her or gave her a new definition. It just made her more like herself, she thought. She had always known that she could love men and women, it had always seemed a natural thing to her. She didn't feel she had to declare herself. But still she couldn't come.

She tried so many things yet nothing did the trick. She sometimes felt that there was a great party going on while she stood on the edge. Watching it all happen but unable to really be part of it. In her mind there was an orgy of desires and pleasure that she could imagine. She just could never attach these feelings to anything real.

She thought that it might work with Jan. She had really fallen for her when they first met. It was at the Gateways club in 1970, and Jan was the shy student with long blonde hair shocked by the sight of women kissing each other openly. Nina rescued her from the attentions of a butch dyke who was clearly scaring her. She went over and asked her to dance. Jan had looked so innocent then. They started seeing each other and for a while Nina thought that they were in love. She didn't worry so much about the sex, she thought that she had met a soulmate. But then Jan became serious – not about their relationship, but about herself. It wasn't just love any more for her, it was a political act.

She soon changed from the wide-eyed girl Nina had kissed on the dance floor. She became militant and cut her hair. A year later and she was picketing the Gateways with the Gay Liberation Front because they wouldn't let them distribute GLF leaflets inside. She declared herself a lesbian separatist and went to live in a women-only commune.

Nina could never be that determined about herself. She got involved with sexual politics but she had never been able to fit in, or feel comfortable with a fixed identity. What had once been liberation became just another orthodoxy. Her desires had always meant more than that. She had once considered herself to be bisexual, now she just felt ambivalent. Lesbian feminists accused her of betraying the cause. People on the scene called her 'Betty Bothways'. Straight men just thought that she was weird or got some twisted thrill out of their surreal fantasies of women having sex with each other. Her polymorphous desire didn't seem to give her much choice, just multiply the opportunities for failure.

She had tried to make things work with Jan but it always came back to the same arguments. She wished that Jan didn't have to be so serious. She had discovered radicalism later than Nina and had all the fervour of a convert. Nina had grown up with politics, she felt that she could be less strident about them.

Today she had gone around to Jan's to talk about the Women's Liberation Street Theatre Group that they had both been involved in. Nina hadn't been to their meetings for a while and wasn't sure whether she was still interested. The fact was that she needed company. O'Connell was dead and she needed the warmth of a living body near her for a while. She hadn't expected to end up in bed with Jan again but there was some comfort in it. She took pleasure in making Jan come even if she couldn't make it herself. It was an act of protest against death, an affirmation of life.

They got up and dressed. Jan looked beautiful, lit up by the noonday sunlight that strafed into the bedroom. She still loved Jan, even the newly serious and intense Jan. But Jan wanted her to commit to the cause, to be pure in mind and body. Nina had wanted their love to be something special, defined by its own terms, not collectivised into some sort of manifesto.

'So how are you coping?' Jan asked. 'With O'Connell dying and everything.'

'I'm OK.'

'It must be awful.'

It was Nina who had found O'Connell dead in the bathroom a fortnight earlier, and who had had to deal with it all. Pearson had been hopeless. She couldn't blame him, he was in a state of shock. It was all too much for him. He had taken to wandering the streets for hours on end, leaving her to sort out the arrangements. O'Connell had family but he had broken all contact with them a long time ago. It had been a bloody time.

'Nina sighed. 'Yeah.'

'You want to talk about it?'

'Not now. Tell me about the theatre group. What's happening?'

'Well, we're calling ourselves Red Rag now,' Jan had said.

Nina laughed. 'You're kidding.'

'Like a red rag to the bull of patriarchy.'

Like a jam rag, Nina thought to herself, but kept quiet. She often felt the urge to make an inappropriate joke at the expense of some earnest proclamation but she didn't want to goad Jan. Not just now.

'We bleed,' Jan went on. 'But that is our strength. Men are jealous of that, you know? That's why they make war. You know what war is?'

'Go on,' Nina said. 'Tell me.'

'War is menstruation envy.'

Nina suppressed the urge to laugh again.

'That's a pretty good slogan,' she offered.

'It's not just a slogan, Nina. You should get involved, you know. You have to decide which side you're on.'

'It's not about sides, though, is it?'

'Come on Nina. It's about power.'

'Yeah, of course.'

'Well, men don't just have the power. Men are the power. It's as simple as that.'

Nina shrugged. She wished that she could be that certain, that she could hold on, as Jan did, to a clear and unambiguous idea.

'You can still move in, you know,' Jan told her. 'There's space here.'

'I wouldn't fit in.'

'Look, Nina, why don't you make up your mind?'

'What?'

'Give up on men. They're a waste of time. Come live with women.'

'I'm happy where I am,' Nina said, knowing that it wasn't entirely true.

'What, in that death house?'

'Yeah, well, that's one way of putting it.'

'I'm sorry. But you see how self-destructive they are.'

'I can't just leave Pearson on his own.'

'That's just an excuse.'

'Come on, Jan. That's not fair.'

'Look, Nina, I know you have a problem with sex—'

'Please don't start that again—'

'But maybe the problem is that you won't commit yourself.'

'I can commit myself to you.'

'But it has to be more than that.'

'Does it?'

'Of course. You need to commit yourself to being a lesbian.'

'Really, Jan, I didn't come here for a consciousness-raising session.'

'Well, you should think about it. I do feel a bit exploited, to tell you the truth.'

'I thought you enjoyed being with me.'

'I do. But then you leave. You use lesbian space and then you desert it. It's not enough for me.'

8

'Can't we just love other?'

'You know it's not as simple as that, Nina.'

'Yeah,' Nina sighed, 'I know.'

Jan was right in a way, she knew that. There had to be some sort of alternative to patriarchy. She was impressed by sisters who had strived to be apart from it. She liked the idea of living in a women-only space. In practice it seemed fine. It was the theory that worried her. There was so much of it, and she doubted that she could ever aspire to such high ideals.

'And what about the theatre group?' Jan asked. 'Don't you want to get involved in that?'

'Well, I'm involved in something else at the moment.'

'What?'

'The Stoke Newington Eight Defence Committee. There's a meeting tonight.'

'Oh. Right.' Jan shrugged. 'Well, that's a good thing, I suppose. One of the defendants is a lesbian.'

'I'm not getting involved just for that, you know.'

'Well, you should. It should be about supporting the sisterhood.'

'Not everything has to be defined by that.'

'Why not?'

'Look, Jan, let's not argue. Please?'

'I just think—'

'Please?'

Jan sighed.

'OK,' she said. 'But look, there's a place for you here, you know that?'

Nina looked at Jan's serious little face and smiled.

'Yeah,' she said.

'Then think about it. And let me know soon.'

'Yeah,' Nina nodded, 'I will.'

They hugged each other and Nina left and made her way

home. It was already afternoon when she got back. Nobody was in. The house was cleaner and more well ordered than she had ever known it. She had gone through it from top to bottom after O'Connell's death, mindlessly scrubbing away as Pearson stood for hours in his bedroom staring out of the window. Only O'Connell's room was left untouched.

The cat was mewling insistently, demanding to be fed. Nina found a half-empty tin of cat food in the fridge and spooned it out into a bowl. They had once called the cat Chairman Miaow. It had been O'Connell's joke so naturally he had soon grown sick of it. Then they all did and everyone took to simply calling the cat 'the cat'. The cat quickly finished its slimy meal and came and rubbed itself against Nina. Nina scratched its head. It purred expectantly, like a dialling tone.

She had been sharing Pearson and O'Connell's squat for only a few months but had first met them at the Sombrero club in 1971. She could hardly recall what was said but she could clearly remember their demeanour. They had stood slightly apart from everything, making casual or intense comments to each other, finishing each other's sentences. It seemed more like a conspiracy than a relationship. She couldn't imagine how Pearson was going to cope without O'Connell. Things had been bad between them in the last few months but there had still been a deep bond right up until the end. Ever since, Pearson had been dazed, constantly going over reasons as to why his lover had killed himself. Nina didn't know what to say – perhaps they would never know. And the fact was that she had found O'Connell easier to talk to, even though he could be a difficult bastard. She felt awkward with Pearson. She had found him hard to engage with at the best of times, and now he was completely dislocated. But she worried about him; he just kept wandering off.

She would have to go out again soon, to the Stoke Newington Eight Defence Committee meeting. She would wait for
a while: she had no idea what she could say or do but she
wanted to know where he was.

3

playland

Pearson was in Playland.

AMUSEMENTS, declared the sign above the door, inviting all in to a dissolute arcadia. Roll up. Amidst the cacophony of mechanical bells and electric buzzers, the clatter of the flippers on the pinball machines, Capital Radio distorted on a cheap PA system, Pearson noticed a seraphic boy tilting at a pintable, thrusting his little body against the machine. Flashing lights, rattling scoreboard – there was a voluptuous Amazon on the painted display above, which announced FIRE QUEEN in gaudy fairground calligraphy. The boy's beatific wide eyes flickered as the tumblers clicked and the numbers rolled. Trying for the bonus ball. More than a game of chance – not the fruit machine or the one-armed bandit, there's no solid currency to be gained, only the pleasure of winning. A rarefied skill that could only be developed in the inverse work ethic of Playland. An industrial trade of sorts, a mystery if you like. Like all skilled work it permits the human to imagine that he is working the machine, not the other way around. It's more than sport and less than life but something is registered: the score. Numbers click away into oblivion when the next player sets up; but the score will add up to eternity. Roll up. Playland, the most notorious slot machine joint in the West End. Rent boys and runaways, strung-out junkies on the tap, the dirty-mac brigade leering. All drawn down the Dilly to Playland. But what was Pearson doing here?

Pearson had walked along Regent's Street down towards

Piccadilly Circus. He was lost. He knew where he was going, all right, the direction he was headed, but it couldn't matter now. Not now that O'Connell was dead. He walked aimlessly in a futile gesture of following. He always used to follow O'Connell. Pearson had looked to him as someone who could lead him through the world. Even near the end, when O'Connell cut himself off from Pearson, he still had an instinct to go after him. It was as if he was still following him now. Keeping on the move seemed the best way of coping with his grief. He felt it best not to be standing still for too long, not to present himself as a target for further calamity. Sorrow hovered somewhere above his head, ready to swoop down at any moment.

He wanted to hold on to what was left. He still hadn't cleared out his room. He was even wearing O'Connell's jacket. He had put it on for comfort. It hung loosely around his thinner frame. He tugged at it and fished out a card from the top pocket.

PEARSON & O'CONNELL
FUNERAL DIRECTORS

it read. It had been one of O'Connell's jokes. They had always called each other by their surnames. They had become Pearson & O'Connell, a partnership expressed with an intimate formality, aloof from the fashionable casualness they encountered outside their *folie à deux*. 'We sound like an undertaker's,' O'Connell had declared, and had ordered a set of business cards printed up. He had always liked to joke about his occupation. He would say that he was a gravedigger or a rat-catcher when asked what he did for a living. FAMILY BUTCHERS was a retail sign he always laughed at. 'Like their speciality is butchering whole households, I can see the demand there.' He made a point of not taking work seriously. The fact was that O'Connell had pursued a variety of peculiar jobs but had spent most of his adult life unemployed. He had been an artist's life model when Pearson had first met him.

Pearson looked at the battered card. Some joke now, he thought. He had once felt a little thrill at the sight of the ampersand that had bound them to each other with its delicate bow. Now the '&' was untied for good. Cut through like the Gordian knot. Rendered apart for ever. He tore the card up and threw it in the gutter.

What was he going to do? What did it matter, what could it matter? His own existence seemed determined only by an absence. He felt the dread that every move, every gesture he made, could merely be elegiac. Part of him hated O'Connell for having killed himself. For leaving him behind.

He had first seen him as the subject of a life drawing class when he was a first-year student at the Slade School of Art. O'Connell told him later that he liked life modelling because he could become invisible. It would take about seven minutes, O'Connell reckoned, for the semicircle of art students to stop seeing him as a person at all and instead to concentrate on the form and proportion, the light and shade, of the space that he occupied. The crescent of heads would bow modestly, peeping up from behind the veil of the drawing boards. It was not his flesh that would then be exposed but the rectangles of white skin stretched out on the pads of the undergraduates. Then he would begin to vanish, transformed into graphite or charcoal, as they desperately tried to cover the nakedness of the paper in front of them.

A studious calm would descend upon the room and O'Connell could then escape, slip away without anybody noticing. All he had to do was to stay still and he could disappear, leave his body behind and let his mind wander off. Occasionally he would notice a stare that was less than aesthetic in purpose. But he liked that too, it fed his narcissism, he was proud of his lean and tightly muscled body, which he exercised daily at the University Union swimming baths in Malet Street. He liked this excuse to show it off. He had caught Pearson at it that morning before Pearson had even realised that he was looking at him in that way. O'Connell held his gaze for a second and Pearson blushed, quickly looking down at his work then busying himself with his pencil once more.

O'Connell had loved that blush but hadn't imagined that the skinny little student would still be waiting in the room when he had dressed and come out from behind the screen after the class was over. He was perched on a stool, a portfolio under his arm. He looked distracted, watching the patterns of light on the floor in front of him. He had light brown hair and bright naive eyes, a nervous lack of focus that O'Connell found endearing. He went up to him and beckoned.

'Let me see,' he demanded softly.

Pearson looked up with a start, nearly falling off his stool.

'What?' he replied.

'What you've made of me.'

'Oh,' said Pearson, and gingerly handed over the drawing.

O'Connell studied it. Pearson had tried to be bold, roughing out O'Connell's form with thick lines of graphite. But here and there O'Connell detected tiny flecks of rubber that clung to the paper like dead skin on bath enamel. Erased lines still showed through and marred the shading that tried to cover them. Pearson had really wanted to sketch freely and sponta-neously but had become too meticulous, too tentative. He had idealised his form too, O'Connell noticed, his musculature and features slightly too classical. That was promising, he thought to himself.

He handed the portfolio back to Pearson and offered to take

him for a drink. He told him that he knew a pub where Francis Bacon sometimes went and that he could introduce him. Pearson suspected that O'Connell was just trying to impress him, but he liked that. He wanted to be impressed.

In the bright late afternoon of a nearly deserted pub on Tottenham Court Road, O'Connell held forth. He said things that sounded extraordinary and provocative to Pearson, who giggled as he started to get drunk on light and bitter.

'Life is a practical joke,' O'Connell declared.

'What do you mean?'

'It's a trick that's played on us. A dirty trick, if you ask me.'

'Yeah?'

'Yeah. And the only thing to do is to get your own back. Play a few tricks yourself.'

Pearson wasn't sure what this meant but it sounded interesting, exciting. He found out that O'Connell was only four years older than himself, but there seemed such a distance between them. A lifetime of discovery and adventure beckoned, and Pearson felt an intoxicating sense of anticipation in the slanting light of the saloon bar. He desired experience. O'Connell's. And his own.

He went back with him, to the squat where the older man lived in Somers Town, just to the north of the Euston Road. And O'Connell watched that beautiful blush once more. Later, as they lay together in the darkness, Pearson realised that although he had introduced himself as Stephen, he hadn't caught O'Connell's forename.

'Declan,' O'Connell told him. 'But, please, call me O'Connell. In this modern age we're all supposed to be on first-name terms with the whole fucking world so it strikes me that you're only really intimate with someone when you know their surname. And I surely like being intimate with you.'

He kissed Pearson on the cheek.

'So?' he went on.

'What?'

'What's your name?'

'Oh,' said Pearson, 'um, it's Pearson.'

'Pearson. Right, then. That's fine. Pearson and O'Connell it is, then.'

This had all happened on the night of 3 June 1968. Pearson could always remember the date because when he crept back to his student digs in Gower Street the following morning he took out the journal he had been keeping since he had started college. He had looked at the blank page for that date. He leafed back through pages past. There were long entries for times where not much had really happened in his life and yet there seemed so much to record. He had once felt so proud of being accepted by the Slade, believed that he was on his way to becoming a real artist. He had meticulously jotted down interior thoughts, reflections on his own feelings, outpourings of angst and attempts at existentialism, opinions about art and culture. All useless now. Now something had really happened he didn't have any idea what to write. His mind was numbed with this new knowledge. He realised that, up until that point, he had just been a suburban middle-class kid with a few clever ideas that he'd picked up on the way. He'd known hardly anything of the world, nor even of himself. Now life was going faster than his thoughts, he could not express the exhilaration that he felt. So he simply wrote *Declan* in his diary, then crossed it out and replaced it with *O'Connell*. And he never wrote in that journal ever again.

And now he was in Playland. *What the hell am I doing in Playland?* he thought. Then he saw the boy at the pinball machine and he knew.

Sweet Thing knew how to play this machine. Fire Queen was his, his bitch. He had tickled her flipper buttons many times and was intimate with all her features and bonuses. He had habitually followed its shuddering labyrinth day by day, finding out its tricks and rewards. Fourth ball. He pulled back the spring with his right hand. Gently. Opening his hand in a hidden gesture, he let the steel ball catapult slowly around the table to bounce off the side bumpers back home to the flippers. He lowered his posture as he felt it slide down to the edge of the right open flipper and then clicked the button once to slingshot it out on to the targets at the top. If he hit them all he would get the bonus ball. Another goes down. Yes. But now the ball rolls down, chugs against the circular bumpers in the middle, *bam-bam-bam*, clugging up tens and hundreds. Not enough. His squint eye hoped for more, for thousands, for hundreds of thousands. The ball cannoned free, the metal sphere rolling quickly beneath the glass slope, straight down, between the flippers, between the hopelessly clattering rubberised electric limbs. Lost. The ball dropped into the guts of the machine and the relays began to clatter. Binary switchboard computation chattered away in a moronic algorithm, the machine code that he had learnt to understand instinctively. Figures appeared on the scoreboard, the tumblers rolling, a high score already but not enough yet. Their percussive rhythm his own anxious heartbeat. *Da-da-da-da, di-di-di-di, da-da-da-da, di-di-di-di.* The big numbers he had manipulated with his own nimble digits. He had one ball left. It appeared, clunking up from the bowels of the pin-table. Last ball on the plunger. Sweet Thing played with the stopper, teasing the spring as he glanced around. Looking to see whether anyone's watching. Checking the trade. Not much business about today. He sees a guy in his twenties with long hair staring over at him. Hippy looking, doesn't look much like trade, but then you get all kinds in Playland.

*   *   *

Pearson stared at the boy. He looked like a degenerate angel. Blond hair in a feather cut framed a smooth, cherubic face. Pale blue eyes dark-rimmed with kohl, a light dusting of glitter on his cheeks, a lipsticked pout. He wore a tight silver blouse over sequined jeans and a pair of red vinyl platform boots. Black varnished nails tapped nervously against the side of the machine.

It should have seemed ridiculous but it worked. He looked dangerously beautiful. Far more effective than the radical-drag get-up that some of the Gay Liberation Front queens put on to try to shock the public. This was more provocative, more real.

This was the sort of thing kids were wearing now, thought Pearson. Fashion had gone all queer again. Glam rock, they were calling it. It had started about the time that the Angry Brigade had bombed the Biba boutique in May 1971. That had blown things apart, split the scene right down the middle between popular and progressive, fashion and politics. This glam thing seemed to explode out of that with glitter ballistics of its own. The kids wanted glamour, and who could blame them? Dismal times needed some adornment, some sparkle.

The boy noticed Pearson looking at him and the bright blue eyes pulsed automatically. Pattern recognition, the machine language of hustlers. He's on the game, thought Pearson. But at least it was a sign of life, something bright amid his gloom. The kid looked beautiful, desirable. Pearson felt all his grief surge into a single stab of lust. There was a sad solitary impulse, a feeling of want, of need, a desolate hunger for contact. He found himself moving across the arcade. Another man approached the boy from the other side of the pinball machine.

'Hello, Sweet Thing.'

Sweet Thing turned to see Berkovitch at his elbow. A middle-aged man in a shabby plum-coloured mohair suit.

'What do you want?' Sweet Thing muttered.

'Johnny wants to see you.'

'So?'

'Come on. Don't fuck me about. I'm parked around the corner.'

'If Johnny wants to see me why doesn't Johnny come down here?'

'Don't be fucking stupid. Johnny's a household name now. He's recognisable. He can't come down here.'

'So he sent you to do his dirty work?'

'That's what a manager's for.'

'Well, I'm busy.'

'You what?'

'I ain't finished my game, have I?'

Sweet Thing had learnt from his time on the street to always try to keep the upper hand with a punter. Not to let them push you about if you could help it. To be a good rent boy you had to exploit your clients and not let it go the other way. He turned away from Berkovitch and launched his final ball up the alley of the machine.

Joe Berkovitch was short and fat but he was still tough. As a teenager in Stamford Hill in the late forties he had joined the 43 Group, a Jewish street-fighting gang that attacked fascist meetings in Whitechapel, Kilburn and the West End. He'd also spivved around spielers and kalooki games and had learnt to hold his own. Through the late fifties and early sixties he had set himself up on the cheap end of Tin Pan Alley, managing second-division rock 'n' roll acts and beat groups, sending them off to Hamburg, holiday camps and the working-men's club circuit. He had had to deal with no end of shirty little snot-nosed kids. And he had developed a very firm policy: never to take shit from any of them.

He gently pushed Sweet Thing from the machine and slammed the end of the table hard enough for the TILT sign to light up and the power to cut out in penalty. Fire Queen died on him. The last ball trickled down to the bottom. Game over.

'There,' said Berkovitch. 'You're done. Now let's go.'

'You cunt!' Sweet Thing spat out at him. 'I nearly had the bonus ball!'

'Come on,' Berkovitch tried to insist, taking the boy's arm.

'Get your fucking hands—'

'Don't make a scene,' Berkovitch sing-songed through gritted teeth.

'Leave him alone!' came a command from nowhere.

Sweet Thing and Berkovitch looked up to see Pearson standing on the other side of the pinball machine. There was a furious look in his eyes. He glared at Berkovitch. The older man shrugged.

'Who's this, then?' he asked Sweet Thing, all the time sneering at Pearson. 'Your ponce or something? Doesn't look the type to me.'

Sweet Thing frowned at Pearson.

'Never seen him before in my life,' he said.

'Well then,' said Berkovitch, cocking his head. 'What's all this about?'

'Fuck off, you!' Pearson declared sharply.

Berkovitch gave a flat little laugh and a dismissive huff.

'Oh, right, then.' He shrugged and started to turn away.

'Wait a minute, Joe,' Sweet Thing began, suddenly realising that he was losing much-needed business.

'No, you forget it, son,' said Berkovitch, looking briefly over his shoulder. 'I'll tell Johnny you're too much fucking trouble. I ain't being fucked around in Playland by some bit of trash and his hippy boyfriend.'

And he walked out of the arcade.

'What did you want to go and do that for?' Sweet Thing demanded when Berkovitch had gone.

'He was hassling you.'

'It was fucking trade, mate. That's fifty quid down the drain.'

'I'm sorry.'

'Well, that doesn't help, does it?'

'He was pushing you around.'

'Look,' Sweet Thing suddenly announced, looking fierce, black-traced eyes a blaze of blue. 'I can look after myself, all right?'

'Yeah, all right.' Pearson shrugged. 'I was only trying to help.'

He turned to go, and once again Sweet Thing felt an opportunity slipping away from him, but he wasn't quite sure what this one was. Not a regular punter but there was always an opportunity. Always something you could work if someone showed an interest. *Trying to help*, he had said. Maybe there was something there. There were the ones you could tap for money with guilt rather than sex. The ones that wanted just to talk. The ones that wanted to save you, they were the easiest to fool, and you would never have to do a bloody thing. Maybe he was one of them. These hippies looked scruffy but most of them were middle class and some were drop-out kids from rich families with some confused sense of social conscience. Sweet Thing made a quick scan of Playland. A couple of young tourists on the shooting range, that Chinese guy who was always playing the one-armed bandits, a nasty-looking old bloke in a grubby raincoat. The place was dead.

'Wait a minute,' he called after Pearson.
Pearson turned around.
'What?' he asked.
Sweet Thing flashed a smile.
'Buy us a cup of tea,' he suggested.

4

king mob

Pearson watched as the boy shovelled four heaped spoonfuls of sugar into the steaming mug and then took a bite out of a big sticky cake.

'What's your name?' he asked.

Sweet Thing swallowed and smacked his lips.

'Sweet Thing,' he mumbled.

Pearson chuckled.

'That figures.'

The boy took a slurp of tea, frowned and nodded.

'Yours?'

Pearson wanted to say 'Pearson' but he knew it wouldn't make sense any more. Certainly not to this kid. It would seem trivial to someone with a street name, an alias, a real *nom de guerre*. He was condemned to be on first-name terms with the rest of the world once again. He sighed. It was a brutal intimacy.

'Stephen,' he admitted.

'Right,' said Sweet Thing.

He eyed up Pearson, trying to work out what advantage he could take of him. The day had started badly. He had lost the bonus ball, that was a bad omen. Now he needed to score something back.

There was a dab of cream on the corner of Sweet Thing's delicate lips. Pearson watched as a pink tongue snaked out and licked it off. The kid smacked his mouth provocatively, his milky blue eyes widened into an alert stare. Pearson looked away. He didn't really have any idea what to do or what to say. He felt awkward but he didn't care. A moment of distraction in having an abstract sense of desire for the strange-looking kid. That he could feel anything to do with life was hopeful.

The first few weeks that he had been seeing O'Connell had been filled with promise and possibility. He had been glad that O'Connell was older than him. It made him feel special, chosen. Before O'Connell, Pearson had been frightened of what he was, but it suddenly became sophisticated for him, romantic.

It was two o'clock in the morning of a hot, muggy Midsummer's Day, after a party in Hampstead, when O'Connell took Pearson up to the Heath. He led him to the men's swimming pond and began stripping off by a wooden jetty.

'Come on,' he told Pearson.

O'Connell's naked body glowed pale with moonshine. Beneath his shock of black hair a grin flashed and green eyes sparkled.

'Come on,' O'Connell said again, and turned to run along the wooden boards.

Pearson looked on as O'Connell loped along the jetty, jumping up to land on both feet at its far edge and launching himself into the air with his arms stretched out towards the purple sky. His body piked and he dived headlong into the water. As he watched O'Connell's legs disappear beneath the surface, Pearson began to take off his own clothes. He padded gently up the walkway, feeling the coolness of the night air on his skin. O'Connell emerged with a splash and an exultant exhalation a few yards out. Treading water, he panted and looked up at Pearson expectantly.

Pearson couldn't dive; he could hardly swim beyond an inelegant thrashing stroke. For a second he wasn't sure what to do, knew just that he wanted to follow O'Connell in. Then he laughed and ran. He leapt up, gathered his knees in his arms and bombed into the pool.

Later they stood on the bank in an embrace. Their glistening bodies shivered together, finding warmth in each other. Pearson's teeth chattered slightly as he kissed O'Connell on the mouth.

'I . . . I . . .,' he trembled. 'I really . . .'

'What?'

'. . . love you,' Pearson whispered.

'Mmm.' O'Connell nodded and stared at him through the gloom. 'Do you now?'

Pearson suddenly felt vulnerable. His flesh tensed slightly with the chill.

'Yes,' he hissed, certain of it, frightened of it.

O'Connell gave a soft laugh.

'Then why don't you do something about it?' he demanded.

'What?'

'Why don't you move in with me?'

'You?' Pearson mumbled.

'Yeah, me. Come live with me.'

'Yeah?'

'Yeah. If you want to.'

Pearson kissed him again.

'Yeah, I do,' he said.

They made love beneath a gnarled oak tree. Pearson remembered the fecund woodland scent, the taste of pond water on O'Connell's skin. It felt pure, stark, elemental.

He moved in with O'Connell the same week. There was protest and agitation in the air. A lot of clever talk at art school about 'liberation', 'revolution', 'free love'. Pearson felt that he was really doing these things, not just talking about them. Their love was a rebellion in itself and he felt free for the first time in his life. Not completely free. He belonged to O'Connell, O'Connell belonged to him. It was a conspiracy of two.

Pearson lost some of the timidness he had felt when he had first started college. His work became bolder, more daring. He found himself involved in the radical student politics. The demos, the sit-ins, the occupations. His lover taught him to be wary. 'Don't join anything,' he cautioned. O'Connell had a romantic notion of the organised masses but always managed to avoid including himself in any kind of collectivisation. He remained detached, aloof even. Though he needed an audience. Sometimes Pearson felt that O'Connell saw him as a mere confederate in his campaign against the world, but it gave him a sense of belonging. Pearson & O'Connell was his organisation, his party apparatus.

And they set about some activism of their own. Direct action. O'Connell showed him shoplifting techniques, insisting it was a political act. 'The only real choice in consumerism is a refusal to pay,' he declared. And there were the practical jokes. They made prank phone calls, let off stink bombs during church services, planted pornographic books on the shelves of public libraries, released a live rat on to the floor of a fashionable Kensington restaurant. They waged their own private war against society.

Pearson started to go with O'Connell to the University Union swimming baths. O'Connell tried to teach him front crawl. Pearson felt clumsy and awkward at first but regular exercise gave him a fledgling confidence in his body. O'Connell was a strong swimmer. He cut fiercely through the turquoise water, twisting with each stroke, his torso a taut breastplate of muscle. Pearson found it hard to resist reaching out and touching him when they were in the changing rooms. Once, when they were alone by the lockers, he brushed his lips against the rack of O'Connell's ribcage, tasting the astringency of the lightly bleached flesh.

'No petting,' O'Connell chided him.

There was a notice bolted to the wall by the foot bath that read: WILL PATRONS KINDLY REFRAIN FROM: RUNNING, PUSHING, ACROBATICS AND GYMNASTICS, SHOUTING, BOMBING, PETTING, DUCKING, SWIMMING IN THE DIVING AREA, SMOKING, THANK YOU! Each commandment had a corresponding illustration, a line drawing showing people acting out the forbidden activities. The picture next to PETTING showed a spiv-like man with his arm around a blonde pouting woman; cartoon hearts surrounded them. O'Connell had joked about the sign. 'Petting?' he had commented. 'Isn't that something that you do with animals?' But they were constantly aware of how furtive and cautious they had to be in displaying affection for each other.

When the Gay Liberation Front started to hold meetings at the London School of Economics in 1970 they were among the first people to attend, but O'Connell was belligerently contrary and found it impossible to sit through a meeting without starting an argument. They soon grew tired of discussion. They decided that they would only get involved with organisations that took direct action. And these actions would be co-opted by them, they would become part of their own campaign.

One Christmas, a group calling itself King Mob entered Selfridges toy department led by a man dressed as Santa Claus. They started grabbing items from the shelves and thrusting them into the surprised but eager hands of children. The security staff, unable to control the situation, called the police, and very soon these same children witnessed Father Christmas being arrested and suffered the indignity of having their 'presents' confiscated. Flyers were handed out declaring: CHRISTMAS: IT WAS MEANT TO BE GREAT BUT IT'S HORRIBLE. LET'S SMASH THE GREAT DECEPTION. LIGHT UP OXFORD STREET AND DANCE AROUND THE FIRE.

Pearson loved the playfulness of these reprisals. Most of all he loved being O'Connell's accomplice. The actions were proof and evidence of their bond as partners in crime. 'You're my cause,' he once told his lover. But he soon learnt that mischief was not enough for O'Connell. He was always saying: 'We should do something serious'. Pearson never quite knew what he meant. He thought that the whole point was not to be serious.

'But they're just practical jokes, aren't they?' he asked O'Connell. 'You said so yourself.'

'Practical can mean merely demonstrative,' O'Connell replied. 'Or it can mean something useful.'

'Useful?'

'Yes. Practical can mean something with a purpose.'

'What purpose?'

'Revenge.'

'Revenge on what?'

'What does it matter?' O'Connell replied with an impatient edge to his voice.

'I don't understand.'

'Well, try. I can't explain every fucking thing to you, you know.'

He began to realise that it wasn't all fun and games for O'Connell. He could be clever and playful but it was a sense of humour that came from despair, a black comedy. He was dogged by depression and melancholia. Pearson found out that he had spent some time in a psychiatric hospital in Ireland when he was a teenager. O'Connell didn't say much about it but Pearson could tell that he was very bitter about the past. And despite his apparent flippancy, O'Connell despised the pettiness of life.

O'Connell could be encouraging and generous in his praise for Pearson's art but he couldn't apply any of those qualities to his own endeavours. He was trying to write but was never satisfied with whatever he managed to get down. He had a few articles accepted by the underground press but he was so resentful in what he expected from life that any gain could quickly become a loss. He could appear confident, arrogant even, to the rest of the world, but Pearson knew that he was deeply insecure and profoundly unhappy.

Sweet Thing tried to figure out the angle on Pearson, he looked for clues. He noticed a purple badge on the lapel of Pearson's coat. It had an upright clenched fist on it with four interlocking circles and some lettering in a semicircle on its upper rim.

'What's that?' asked Sweet Thing, pointing at the badge.

Pearson leaned across the table so Sweet Thing could read it.

'Gay, Liberation, Front,' Sweet Thing read out slowly. 'What's liberation?'

Pearson shrugged. 'It means to become free.'

'Is that what you want, then?' Sweet Thing demanded indignantly.

'Er, yeah.'

'You want us to do it for free?'

'What?'

'You're gay, right?'

'Yeah.'

'Well, I ain't.'

'No?' Pearson frowned.

'No. I'm not bent, I'm rent. I only do it for the money.'

'Right.'

'You think just because I dress like this I'm a poof? This is fashion, mate. It's smooth. And the punters love it.'

'So you're straight?'

'Yeah. But this Gay Liberation thing, you'd want all the rent boys to do it for free or something?'

'Er, not exactly.'

'Well, what, then?'

Pearson shrugged and sighed. He'd had easier and less complex discussions on sexual politics with the hardline militant feminists that Nina knew.

'Well, we'd make it legal, I suppose,' he reasoned.

But he didn't really know. Prostitution was one of many problems that were going to be solved by the revolution, but nobody quite knew how.

'And how would that work?' Sweet Thing went on.

Pearson laughed and shook his head.

'I really don't know,' he admitted. 'You're a sharp kid, you know. How old are you?'

'What's that got to do with anything?'

'I just—'

'I'm seventeen,' Sweet Thing declared.

He had been seventeen for a long time, ever since he had run away and come to London. It was what he told the police or social workers or an official so he wouldn't be taken back into care. He had been seventeen for so long now he had almost forgotten what his real age was.

Sweet Thing's bright blue eyes glowered fiercely. They had seen too much, too soon. They burned into Pearson, cutting into his grief, challenging him to do something.

'Where do you live?' Pearson asked him.

'You've got a lot of questions.'

'Well, do you have somewhere to stay?'

'Here and there,' Sweet Thing replied, and took another gulp of tea.

'But nowhere permanent?'

'It's all right. I know plenty of places to kip.'

Then Pearson had an idea: Sweet Thing could have O'Connell's room. He would have to sort out all the stuff but it would force him to deal with it. He could clear it out and start over. And it made sense. The squat scene was always going on about tackling homelessness, and what better case was there than this street kid? Pearson suddenly felt inspired by the thought of doing something, changing something.

The only problem was Nina – he would have to get her to agree to it. He hesitated for a second, envisaging for a moment all the complications and difficulties this idea would bring. *This boy is trouble*, came a thought. But it was from a part of his brain that he wasn't really using and it merely reverberated there, a distant echo of the urgent compassion that he suddenly felt. Instead of presenting a warning, it rather augmented the reckless and liberating feeling of desire that had overcome him.

'There's a room going at my house,' he offered.

'Yeah?'

'If you want it.'

Sweet Thing squinted at Pearson, trying to work out what the catch was.

'What's the rent?' he asked.

Pearson smiled.

'Oh, it's rent free.'

Sweet Thing frowned. Nothing was rent free, at least not on his side of the bargain.

'I don't know,' he said.
'Well, come and have a look if you like.'
The boy shrugged and nodded cautiously.
'All right.'

5

johnny chrome

Joe Berkovitch pulled up on the driveway of Johnny Chrome's house with a rent boy he had picked up from the meat rack on Glasshouse Street, just around the corner from Playland. He ushered the boy up the drive and rang the bell. Johnny came to the door and squinted at the daylight with pained incredulity. His eyes were bloodshot and puffy, his face pale and flabby beneath a ruined nest of blue-black dyed hair.

'You got the kid?' he croaked to Joe.

'Yeah, well,' replied Joe, pushing his procurement forward. 'This is Stevie.'

Johnny Chrome frowned at the boy.

'That's not the one, Joe,' he protested. 'I want Sweet Thing.'

'Yeah, well, I had a spot of bother with that one. But look, I brought you someone to keep you company. Say hello to Johnny, Stevie.'

'Hello, Johnny,' said Stevie with a tight little smile.

'No, no, no, no,' Johnny mumbled. 'He's not the one.'

'I know but—'

'Get rid of him. Pay him off, Joe.'

'Me pay him off? No, you pay him off.'

Johnny sighed.

'I ain't got no money, Joe.'

'Right,' said Berkovitch, pulling out his wallet. 'But this is coming out of expenses.'

He handed the boy a sheaf of notes.

'Off you go, son,' he told him.

'And how am I going to get home?' the boy demanded.

'There's enough there for a taxi.'

'Wait a minute—'

'Go on,' Berkovitch insisted. 'Sling your hook.'

Stevie sighed petulantly and walked away.

'I better come in, Johnny,' said Berkovitch. 'We need to talk.'

Johnny nodded slowly and led him into the front room.

'I ain't got no money, Joe,' he complained once more. 'I've had a fucking hit record and yet I'm skint.'

He collapsed on to the white leather sofa. He looked dazed. *He's on the downers again*, thought Berkovitch. Johnny had developed a big Mandrax habit since his success.

'You just need to organise your finances a bit better,' said Berkovitch.

'I don't understand. I should be getting more.'

'It's a fifty-fifty split, you know that.'

'Yeah, but the company is expanding, new offices and everything. I should be getting half of that.'

'But you don't have a share of Diamond Music, Johnny.'

'Yeah, like you said, it's a fifty-fifty split.'

'No, look, I already explained this to you last Tuesday. Diamond Music is your management company. You're entitled to fifty per cent of the profits.'

'Yeah, fifty per cent.'

'Fifty per cent of the net profits, that is. And that's after expenses.'

'But—'

'And there's been a lot of expenses, Johnny. Besides that we're investing funds for your future successes. We've got to keep it going. That's why you really need to get back in the studio and record the new single.'

Johnny sighed.

'I feel so empty,' he said.

Johnny felt a yawning gravity in the pit of his stomach. A vertiginious sense of falling. It had been like this ever since his number-one hit. Success had come too late for him and, after a brief moment at the top, all he seemed to have to look forward to was descent. And it was a fall that promised no coming down to earth. Just a long, slow, decaying orbit.

He had been born Johnny Evans in Swansea in 1941. He had sung in chapel as a child, with a sweet, clear soprano tone that had brought him much praise and attention. The promise of his talent broke with his voice – he acquired an unremarkable tenor, though he could hold a tune and belt it out well enough. He formed a skiffle band with some schoolmates. Johnny Rebel and the Rabble Rousers, they called themselves. They went up to London in 1958, even got a slot on *Saturday Night Skiffle* on the BBC Light Programme. But the skiffle boom was over and nobody seemed interested any more. As the money ran out, one by one the group drifted back to Wales. But Johnny Rebel stayed. Something new was happening. Rock 'n' roll. He took his guitar and tried to get spots in the coffee bars and clubs in Soho.

And his dream came true, or so he thought. He was discovered. Larry Parnes came up to him after he'd done a couple of numbers at this espresso bar and had invited him to his house. Larry Parnes! The biggest manager in the whole of Tin Pan Alley. He had it made, he thought. When he went around to Parnes's house there was some sort of party going on. Lots of teenage boys and older men. No women. Larry spotted him and came over.

'Put this on,' Parnes said, handing him a white cotton T-shirt.

'Why?' Johnny asked.

'Just want to see what you look like in it.'

It was a simple enough request so Johnny went to the bathroom and changed. When he came back to the party things had livened up a bit. Some of the older men were acting in a predatory way towards the youngsters, but no one tried it on with him. Larry Parnes appeared and started paying him a lot of attention. Johnny felt so special; at that moment he felt the whole room was watching him. And they were, of course, they knew what the white T-shirt meant. When Parnes invited him upstairs it seemed a perfectly sensible thing to do, to go to bed with him. Johnny had no aversion to having sex with another man. He got a hard-on thinking about what it might get him.

Afterwards, Larry Parnes handed him a black T-shirt. This time he gave no explanation but hurried back to his duties as host. They'd discuss things later, Johnny reasoned. He went back downstairs. The party was thinning out. Those who were left looked at him differently now. He found himself being chatted up by a short and queeny restaurant owner in a hideously informal manner. Parnes was nowhere to be seen. Johnny got very drunk. He staggered out into the cold night air.

It was explained to him in the Giaconda Café on Denmark Street a week later. If Larry wanted to have a boy he would give them a white T-shirt to let everybody know, so they wouldn't get in the way. If he gave a boy a black one it meant he'd had them already, they were up for grabs, have a go if you want.

Johnny was distraught. It wasn't the assault on his sexual self so much as that his integrity had been fucked with. How could he have been that stupid? he railed at himself. A simple lesson: don't put out until you've got what you want because, otherwise, they've got what they want from you already. He felt heartbroken, his dreams of stardom shattered. And he felt frozen from intimacy. He couldn't even trust himself.

He got a day job. He worked as a porter at the Middlesex Hospital. He strummed his guitar in his bed-sit at night and tried to dream again. One night he gazed at *6.5 Special* on his tiny TV and saw Gene Vincent limp into the light in black leather. A beautiful, wounded creature howling 'Be Bop A Lula'. He was inspired once more. He started wearing that dark hide himself. He loved the way the cured skin encased him, protected him.

He began touting around again. The ton-up look was in, he found. He met up with Joe Berkovitch after coming second in a talent contest at a pub in Bermondsey. Joe was looking for a group to send out for a three-month season at the Kaiser Keller club in Hamburg. Joe had put together a band and he auditioned Johnny as front man. Johnny had the leather threads, the rocker demeanour and the rebel-yell twang. He got the gig. He and Joe Berkovitch discussed nomenclature. Johnny had a new name for himself. He could be born again and forget the humiliations of the past. He had just the thing. Something hard and brutal that would go with his new leather image.

'Johnny Savage?' Berkovitch enquired.

'That's right.'

'Hmm,' pondered Joe. 'I don't know. We've got to have a band name too. It could be the Savages. What about Johnny Noble and the Savages?'

'Nah.' Johnny shook his head. 'I don't want to be Noble. I want to be Savage.'

'So what do we call the band?'

'Johnny shrugged'. 'I dunno.' 'The Wild Boys?'

'Heinz has already got them.'

'Heinz?'

'Yeah. You know, that bottle blond Joe Meek is boosting.'

'The Barbarians!' Johnny suddenly exclaimed.

'What?'

'Johnny Savage and the Barbarians.'

'Yeah.' Berkovitch nodded slowly. 'Yeah. That'll do.'

Johnny felt lost in Hamburg. He couldn't connect with the rest of the band. They were just in it for kicks, on a three-month bender, sustained by amphetamines and penicillin. Hammering out standards, going through the motions. Johnny wanted more; like Eddie Cochran, he wanted something else. He was a performer, they were just musicians. They didn't take him seriously. He wanted to project something, something that they could never understand. He was so alone. Like Ruth amid the alien corn. He found a leather bar in the Reeperbaum, got taken back home by a kind and friendly queen called Ernst. But it didn't work. He couldn't get a hard-on. He still felt the awful failure of being had over for sex. He needed some sort of success for it to work. He could wank himself silly on his own on his flea-pit hotel bed but he felt awkward and anxious when he was close to another soul.

Sometimes he'd burn himself with a cigarette end, just to feel something other than desolation. He wouldn't stub it out on his arm or anything. He'd do it lightly, touching himself gently with the glowing end, turning half a circumference of burning ash against his trembling forearm. The pain would make him feel alive, real. He'd make little half-moon scars, silken crescents of regenerating tissue.

The contract ended and he got back to London to find that the rock 'n' roll thing was all but over. It was rhythm and blues now. Young men were brushing their hair forward. He could never quite bring himself to do such a thing.

'Johnny Savage just isn't working,' Joe Berkovitch finally declared in 1965. 'You need a change of image.'

'What?'

'How about Johnny Flower?'

'Joe!'

'Come on. Drop the butch thing. Grow your hair.'

Joe Berkovitch had long since resigned himself to the fact that he'd never be a first-rank manager because he was far too heterosexual. He'd tried to cultivate queer instincts but always found himself second-guessing. And he also knew that ironically, in performance terms it was the straight boys that could always do the queer thing better than the homos. But he had a strange soft spot for Johnny; their roles were reversed in such a messed-up way. He got him work all through the sixties. Hamburg, summer seasons, cabaret residences, holiday camps and working-men's clubs. In the meantime Joe found himself dealing with long-haired rock bands with their college-boy notions of authenticity. Their idealistic and educated ethics of non-materialism and anti-capitalism only meant that they were sharper when it came to contracts and royalty agreements. They were a pain in the arse.

Johnny was always grateful for any work that came his way. He had become reliably kitsch, an act that could be slotted in here and there without too much trouble. There was a sort of lull at the end of the sixties – nobody was really sure what was going to happen next. The hairies just got hairier and the only alternative, for the time being, seemed the skinheads. Then the seventies came and something else was going on. Something was happening, and Joe knew, for once a little ahead of the game, that something flash was needed to brighten up the new grey decade. As the acid dream faded, bubblegum pop came back. Then glam. And Joe saw that it was stripped down and over-produced rock 'n' roll. Boogie-woogie in a bit of make-up. It was just like the old days but tarted up. And Johnny was retro in just the right timescale: the lost years of British vaudeville. Joe was perfectly positioned to make a killing. They just needed another naming ceremony.

Johnny Chrome was the moniker they finally agreed upon. Johnny wanted to keep that tough image which had already become so camp. Red vinyl jump boots with stacked heels poked out of flared leather jeans, tight at the crotch, held together with a wide belt clasped by a biker badge buckle. Silver lamé bomber jacket, heavy chain necklace, black pompadour hair. It was the make-up they disagreed on.

'It's just rock 'n' roll with lipstick on,' Berkovitch suggested.

'I ain't wearing lipstick.'

'Well, a bit of eyeliner. Come on, Johnny, don't try and tell me you've never worn make-up before.'

'Yeah, but –'

'A bit of glitter, then, on the cheeks. It's show business, for fuck's sake.'

'But I wanna be butch, Joe.'

'Glitter is butch, Johnny. It's powdered metal. Think of it as the shavings of heavy machinery.'

'What?'

'It's industrial.'

'Yeah?'

'Yeah,' Joe assured Johnny. 'A bit of rouge too.'

'What?'

'Just a bit of day slap.'

Joe had found a song by a couple of guys that had once worked for Mickie Most. 'Hey You (Wotcha Gonna Do?)', it was called. It was recorded with a tribal reverb drum pattern, over-dubbed guitar power chords on delay, buzzsaw saxophone and soaring backing vocals. Johnny belted out the

41

anthemic lead vocal; the chorus was like a terrace chant. They had only one day booked in the studio so the producer did an instrumental version for the B-side and called it 'Hey You (Part Two)'. It sounded sparse and spasmodic, with Johnny's echoing 'heys' like lonesome howls in an urban wasteland. They released it as a single in the spring of '72 and it somehow made it on to a Radio One DJ's playlist. Only, for some reason, he turned the record over and played 'Hey You (Part Two)' instead of the A-side. It soon acquired a sort of cult status. It sounded so strange and minimalist and, quite by accident, far more avant-garde than anything that Bowie or Roxy Music were doing at the time. Requests for it came pouring in; it charted and Johnny had to go on *Top of the Pops* with scarcely anything to mime to. But he pulled it off. He delivered a strange twitching pantomime, full of unconscious camp and kitsch that just caught the feeling of the moment. With the lack of any discernible lyrics the empty song became flooded with meaning. It seemed an arch parody of all the dichotomies of music, culture, sex and style of that time. Pure music hall futurism. It went straight to number one.

Johnny never got over the confusion of what had happened. This new look had worked but he couldn't comprehend it. He had no idea what he meant. People kept telling him all sorts of things about himself and none of it made any sense. *New Musical Express* called him a 'sci-fi Liberace'; there were photo spreads and profiles of him in *Jackie* and *Disc* magazine. He was locked into an image that he didn't understand. Crowds of teenage girls attended his public performances, full of frightening adolescent hysteria. *What are they screaming at?* he thought, with growing anxiety. He was a success, that much was certain, but he didn't know how to celebrate it. He started taking tranquillisers to calm himself down. He drove around the West End in the back of a hired limousine. He picked up Sweet Thing in Piccadilly and took him back to his new home. As he pushed his cock into the boy's mouth he thought: *Yeah, this is what success is.* Suck. Sessss. Yes. He could relax for a moment, the panic subsided. He had Sweet Thing stick around for a while afterwards. He hoped that the glam kid might be able to tell him what he was doing and how he might keep doing it. And although Sweet Thing didn't say much Johnny liked him being there, just so that he could watch him.

Berkovitch had been planning Johnny Chrome's follow-up single. Another song had been written: 'Hey, Hey (The Gang's All Here)'. It was just a cash-in on the first hit. Joe had no real illusions about Johnny's long-term future but instead concentrated on capitalising on the diminishing returns of a novelty act. Johnny played it straight, not realising how camp his Chrome persona came across as. It was the alchemy of the moment. But they had to move fast. This glam thing could be over by the end of the summer. Joe had booked studio time and got a backing band together. He needed to get Johnny to cut another record and get out on tour. But Johnny looked like he was cracking up.

Berkovitch handed him a cassette tape.

'This is the demo for the next single.'

Johnny held it up and stared at it blankly.

'What am I supposed to do with this?'

'Listen to it, of course. Work on the vocals. We need to cut this single. The record company are waiting.'

Johnny sighed heavily. He dropped the tape on the coffee table.

'I want Sweet Thing,' he announced, forlornly.

Berkovitch realised that he shouldn't have brought just any boy around for Johnny. Johnny needed this particular boy for some reason, which was a lot of trouble, but if it could keep him together, get him back into the studio, back in some sort of shape for live appearances, well, it was worth it.

'Don't worry,' he assured him. 'I'll find him for you.'

6

the tenant of the room

Shit, thought Sweet Thing when they got to Pearson's house, *it's a bloody squat*. A waste of bloody time – this guy wasn't a rich hippy, he was just a hippy hippy. He froze on the doorstep as Pearson opened up. He thought about turning around and getting the 73 bus back to Soho. Pearson beckoned to him.

'Come on in,' he said, cocking his head in invitation.

Sweet Thing wandered in and was amazed by the interior of the house. Pearson smiled as he noticed the black-lined eyes widen. He was still proud of all the time and effort they had put into fixing the place up. O'Connell had picked up all sorts of skills from the various times he had worked as a builder's labourer. Pearson's forte was decoration. They had scoured junk shops and antique markets for objects of ornament, raided empty premises for architectural features, fixed the plaster mouldings and cornices. They had sanded down, stained and varnished woodwork here and there, gilded other fixtures with cheap gold paint. There were wall hangings from Morocco and India and elaborate light fittings with coloured bulbs. They had created a deliberate elegance as a rebellion against the crash-pad squat ethic that surrounded them. They had taken such pleasure in transforming the house. And, in counterpoint, all over this ersatz splendour were radical posters, montages of newspaper headlines and press photographs, even graffiti sprayed or painted directly on to the walls. The overall effect was one of baroque anarchism. Sweet Thing instantly loved the cheap rococo glamour of it all.

'Nice,' he admitted, nodding up at the stairway.

'Yeah,' Pearson agreed. 'Well, let me show you where you can stay.'

He and O'Connell had spent the whole summer after they met on the house. They could live cheaply, content, at first, with each other's company and the easy routine of the days – going for a swim at the Union pool, shoplifting in the West End, browsing the second-hand book shops in Bloomsbury, constantly talking of new strategies of attack. Grandiose ideas that came to nothing. They would poison the pigeons in Trafalgar Square, spike the municipal water supply with a huge quantity of LSD, creep into Regent's Park Zoo at night and break open the cages of the dangerous animals. When a new academic year began at the Slade, O'Connell started to write a novel. Two years later, Pearson had graduated but O'Connell's book remained unwritten. By then they had lost enthusiasm for the practical jokes they had played together or planned. Once they had felt that the fervour and radicalism around them merely reflected their own rebellious passions. It had been their revolution. But it was a revolution that had failed. Darker days lay ahead.

Sweet Thing followed him up the stairs. Pearson and O'Connell had occupied the two bedrooms on the first floor of the house, while Nina had the top storey all to herself. Pearson's room was at the front, and this had been where they had slept together in the beginning. O'Connell's room had served more as a kind of study, its walls lined with books, a bureau in the corner by the window and a single bed. It was here that O'Connell retreated in the end. He had even fitted a lock to the door.

As Pearson tried to find the key, Sweet Thing wandered into the front bedroom. Whereas O'Connell's room was spartan, Pearson's was voluptuous. This had worked for the time they had been sleeping together, but when they reverted to their separate quarters it only exacerbated a feeling of disjunction. The contrived luxury of the room began to mock Pearson's loneliness. The heavy velvet curtains, the gilt-framed mirror, the now-too-big brass bedstead – all the things that had once made the space comfortable conspired to make him uneasy. At nights he had lain awake and listened to O'Connell stumbling about in the next room, so close, so distant.

He caught Sweet Thing gawping at it, taking in the four walls, the large balustraded windows, and he remembered how it had once seemed. A place full of warmth, of love and passion. Not just an over-furnished room with too much red in it. Sweet Thing nodded and gave a cautious smile.

'Yeah,' he said. 'This is all right.'

Pearson coughed awkwardly.

'This isn't the room.'

'No?'

'No. This is my room.'

Sweet Thing shrugged. 'So, where's my room?'

Pearson had found the key. He unlocked the door and gestured inside.

'Here we are,' he said.

There was a dank and musty smell. Sweet Thing wrinkled up his face and peered in. The dirty windows made the space look gloomy and forlorn. Pearson had forgotten how much clutter O'Connell had accumulated.

'What's all this stuff?' Sweet Thing demanded.

'It belonged to the guy that used to live here. We'll clear it out.'

'Where's he now?'

'Don't worry. He's dead.'

Sweet Thing's eyes flashed with shock and he all but jumped out of the room.

'You've got to be fucking joking!' he exclaimed.

'What?'

'A dead man's room.'

'It's just a room.'

'I ain't staying in there.'

Pearson smiled.

'You afraid of ghosts?' he taunted him.

No matter how hard headed Sweet Thing had become in most matters, he observed certain objects and occurrences in life as signs and portents, in a systematic though completely irrational way. Like most people exposed to misfortune from an early age, he was deeply superstitious. The odds had been against him from the start, an awful unluckiness that had compelled him to believe in chance. Ladders, black cats, single magpies, the funny little hopscotch shuffle he found himself doing on the street sometimes to avoid the cracks in the pavement. Even bad luck gave him a feeling of possibility. Better bad luck than no luck at all. Some of it was a desire for divination, the urge to make sense out of the chaos of his life. Some of it was simply a craving to get something back from nothing. Like a compulsive gambler who, having lost his first ever bet, spends the rest of his life trying to get even.

Pearson briefly enjoyed Sweet Thing's sudden vulnerability. The boy had backed out on to the landing with a look of fear in his eyes. It amused him that Sweet Thing seemed to have no consideration for the living person who had once occupied the room, just an absolute terror of the transmigration of his soul. O'Connell would have found this funny. *You didn't half scare this kid*, he reminded himself to tell O'Connell, then in the next second realised that this was impossible, would always be impossible. O'Connell was no longer there, would never be anywhere ever again.

'Look,' he went on, 'it's all right.'

'No, it ain't all right,' Sweet Thing replied indignantly.

He started to walk down the stairs.

'Wait a minute,' Pearson called after him.

Sweet Thing turned around and looked up.

'What?'

'You can have my room.'

'What?'

'Yeah, you can have it. I'll have the other one.'

Pearson felt a reckless decisiveness overwhelm him after so many long days of useless brooding. Without thinking, he convinced himself that this arrangement made sense. He wouldn't have to clear it with Nina – it was *his* room he was giving up, after all. And he would still clear out O'Connell's stuff. It would be even more of a new start.

Sweet Thing frowned and thought: *Christ, this is an easy punter*. He could get what he wanted from this one without having to give much in return. Make him feel like he's doing good but don't let him think that you owe him a favour, he told himself. He'd never asked for anything, after all.

'Yeah,' he shrugged, 'all right.'

He came back up the stairs and into Pearson's room. His room now. Yeah, he thought, looking around. Not bad, not bad at all. He sat on the bed. He could bring trade back here. It was walking distance from King's Cross and Euston stations. Maybe he could start working those areas instead of Soho and Piccadilly. They even had a telephone. And he'd have to find Johnny Chrome. He was good money. He'd written the address down somewhere. He sighed, kicked off his platform boots and lay on the bed.

'Are you OK?' Pearson asked.

Sweet Thing yawned.

'Tired,' he whispered, and closed his eyes.

Pearson had wanted to explain everything about the house,

about Nina, about how it was all going to work out, but Sweet Thing was soon fast asleep. The feather-cut blond hair fanned out on to the pillow to frame his face. His lips quivered, half open. Darkened eye sockets, mottled with tiny creases, the closed lids fluttering gently, like insect wing cases. REM sleep – he was already dreaming. Pearson leant over him and gently touched his cheek. A tiny constellation of glitter smudged on to his fingertip.

Sweet Thing murmured something and turned slightly on the bed. Pearson backed away; he didn't want to wake him. He stood and watched him for a while, then crept out of the room. He looked in at O'Connell's room again, loitered in the doorway. O'Connell's space, his smell. All that was left of him. They had cremated the body at Golders Green but there would be particles of him in the house dust. Pearson sighed and closed the door. He thought about the sleeping boy in his room and felt sick with desire. Stillness made him anxious once more. He had to get out. He padded down the stairs, opened the front door and walked out on to the street again.

Sweet Thing would be a handful, he felt sure of that, but he didn't care. Maybe that was what he was looking for: trouble. Something to distract him from thinking about O'Connell. He had spent so long trying to figure out what happened to his lover. O'Connell had become depressed but that had just been part of it. He had also become secretive and distant. Pearson had been suspicious when O'Connell began to go out more on his own, and was vague and evasive when Pearson asked him where he had been. O'Connell withdrew more and more into his own space. They started to sleep apart on a regular basis. Pearson had thought that maybe O'Connell was having an affair. There was a guy called Phil that they had come across back in the days when they were out together. He was something to do with the underground press. O'Connell always behaved in an elaborately casual manner with this man. It was as if he was trying to act cool, but there was something forced about it. He couldn't hide a certain furtiveness between them. As if they shared a secret. Pearson had confronted him about it.

'Look, I'm not having sex with anybody else,' O'Connell had insisted.

'Well, you're not having sex with me. We haven't done it for ages.'

'Yeah, well.'

'Just tell me if there is somebody else. It's not supposed to matter, is it?'

'What do you mean?'

'You know, a liberated, open relationship – we're all supposed to be doing that now, aren't we?'

'Don't be so pathetic.'

'I'm not being pathetic.'

'Yeah you are.'

O'Connell was right. That was exactly how Pearson had felt. Pathetic. But he had been loyal. *Faithful.* The old-fashioned word caused his eyes to prick with tears. He had followed O'Connell, lost touch with friends at college to devote himself to him. Yet O'Connell had frozen him out. When the police began rounding up suspects in the Angry Brigade bombings, O'Connell seemed paranoid. At first Pearson didn't think that this was unusual. The whole of the underground was on edge as the squats and radical bookshops were raided, the premises of alternative newspapers turned over. People were facing serious charges. It all came to a head with the Stoke Newington bust, by which stage O'Connell had cut himself off from Pearson almost completely. Pearson started to suspect that his lover had been involved somehow. It would make sense of all his talk of 'doing something serious'. But if this was true it meant that O'Connell had never really taken him seriously. He had merely been a convenient foil for the harmless pranks of the past but a liability when it came to real acts of sabotage. He had then felt a jealousy as keen as his fears of physical infidelity: O'Connell had been conspiring with someone else all along.

7

hungry

The Stoke Newington Eight Defence Committee had been set up to support the defendants in the Angry Brigade trial. There were witnesses to be traced, transcripts to be prepared, articles to be published and, of course, banners to be made. A vigil was planned outside the Old Bailey once the trial had begun. There was a sober atmosphere at the meetings; the trial really did seem to signal that the party was finally over. NOW WE ARE ALL ANGRY! read one of the placards in the room. All the hope and optimism of the sixties seemed to have burnt out into bitterness and powerless rage. The committee was trying to organise something constructive around the trial, but it was a plan of defence, a rearguard action. It felt as if they were on the run now.

There was a growing sense of confusion about what was to be done. Nina came back from the meeting, her head still reeling with the arguments that had been thrown about. Everyone could agree on what they were against but nobody seemed able to agree on what they were for any more. That's what had happened.

When she was very little it had all been certain. She had grown up in Finchley, her father a pharmacist and a Communist Party member, her mother too. There had been a portrait of Stalin in the living room, beaming down at her with an avuncular benevolence. It was her Uncle Joe, Great Friend of the People. It had been as simple as that.

Then when she was five Dad had taken the picture down

and exiled it to the back room. Propped against the skirting board, it leaned forlornly against the wall and collected dust. Nina hadn't known that Stalin had been denounced at the 20th Party Congress of the Soviet Union, but gathered that something was amiss.

'Has Uncle Joe done something wrong?' she had asked her father.

Dad had muttered words at her that she didn't understand. He seemed confused, and Nina began to feel a sense of uncertainty herself. It had been a normal childhood. They were communists but essentially they were an ordinary, respectable household. There were jumble sales and outings with other families; it was just that they were organised by and for the Party. She had played with Jessica Mitford's children one summer afternoon on a trip to Hampstead Heath. It seemed clear in her young mind back then. The world would be a better place once everyone was like them. Daddy was a good man who gave medicine to cure the sick. But then the doubts came.

Later in the year during which Uncle Joe's picture had been taken down she overheard quarrels between her father and friends of the family that had come to visit. Raised voices that talked of Hungry. She tried to understand what they were saying. Hungry, that gnawing emptiness in the stomach, was a place, she now imagined. A land where hunger came from. Something bad was happening there. Then there were arguments about another place where trouble was. Suet, it sounded like – there was much talk of Suet. A land of pudding, she decided. The heavy-bellied stodginess of Suet offset the rumbling starvation of Hungry. They seemed like opposite states in her imagination.

One night she heard her father rowing with a woman she knew as Auntie Mavis.

'Hungry is as bad as Suet,' she thought she heard the woman say to her father, who loudly contradicted her.

She would discover later that they were talking about the Soviet invasion of Hungary and the British intervention in Suez. At the time she simply felt that 1956 was when the world became complicated. Something was wrong. There always seemed to be arguments now. Lots of people they knew left the Party that year. They were no longer friends of the family, her father decided.

She was eight when her mother got very ill. It was breast cancer, though she wasn't told that at the time. There was nothing they could do, no medicines that could cure her. Only morphine near the end, something for the pain. Her father felt betrayed by the failure of the very drugs that he had once put all his faith in. He became hardline in his views with a cold decisiveness that came out of his despair.

Nina was an only child. While her mother was alive she had been close to her father. With her gone and only the two of them in the house their relationship had become awkward, antagonistic. An easefulness they had once shared was replaced by anxiety. He was over-protective and authoritarian towards her. They began to quarrel – that was what they became good at. She had learnt to be argumentative from him, after all.

As a teenager she started to rebel properly. Her father despised the very things that excited her about the sixties. Pop music, youth culture, new fashions – he loudly expressed a hatred for them all. But he reserved his most bitter bile for recreational drug use. It was as if he was being deeply mocked, as a pharmacist, by the misuse of his trade. When Nina was fourteen his chemist's shop was broken into by youths looking for amphetamines.

'Is this what you young people are doing now?' he railed at

her, as if she herself were implicated by the action. 'Stealing this stuff to poison your minds with?'

She would lie to him, saying that she was off to a Communist Youth League meeting when she was really going to a dance hall in Finsbury Park. Changing at a friend's house into clothes he would never approve of. But she still worked hard at school. She wanted an education.

He was very proud when she got into university, but it was then that they started to argue seriously about politics. She had an instinctive flair for debate in the endless campus meetings of 1968. New ideologies on the left were emerging. She began seriously to question her father's values.

For many that year, it was the May events in Paris that had been so absorbing. For her it was the Soviet invasion of Czechoslovakia in the summer. It reminded her of Hungary, when she had been a little girl, desperately trying to make sense out of confusion. Hungry. She realised that her father had been wrong all along. She felt a vehement sense of liberation from him. She had shown him a newspaper clipping with the photograph of the immolated body of Jan Palach, a young Czech who had set himself on fire in protest at the Russian occupation. He had pushed it from him and turned his head away.

'I don't want to look at that imperialist propaganda,' he had muttered, and she had stormed out.

When she dropped out of university it was the last straw.

'Well,' he said, looking at her coldly, 'you've thrown your life away.'

She tried to explain to him that there were more important things than passing an English degree, but he wouldn't listen. He saw her involvement in libertarian politics as just another rebellion against his authority. She dismissed his views as Stalinist and patriarchal. They stopped talking to each other.

She joined in with the anti-Vietnam War movement, women's liberation, the Gay Liberation Front. She signed on the dole and participated in the Claimants Union. She got involved in radical theatre. There was a great sense of excitement for a while, all the demonstrations and occupations, a heady sense of fervour. Once the excitement had died down there was a growing feeling of disillusionment. Nothing much had really changed. There followed a descent into in-fighting and rancour among all the factions on the left. Nina found as much frustration in radical politics as she had in her personal life. And she wasn't alone. People who had once tried to Ban the Bomb started making their own and setting them off. She couldn't agree with their methods but she understood their motivations. They were acts of desperation.

Like most people involved, she saw the Defence Committee as a way of holding on to what little gains they had made. The tide of the sixties had receded and left some of them high and dry. They couldn't just leave these brothers and sisters behind. They had to do something. It was a cause worth fighting for, even if it was a lost one.

Nina got back to the squat and looked around for Pearson. She went upstairs. His bedroom door was ajar. She called his name and wandered in. Someone was sleeping in his bed.

For a moment she thought that it was a girl lying there, a delicately slumbering nymph. A fairy-tale princess. Then she looked closer and realised that it was a boy. She smiled. Pearson had got lucky, she thought. She shook the boy gently by the arm.

'Hey,' she whispered. 'Wake up.'

Sweet Thing awoke with a start. A woman with short dark hair and bright green eyes was standing above him. She stepped back as he raised himself on to his elbows. He blinked and looked at her again. A tightly curved body in jeans and a T-shirt.

'Who are you?' he mumbled.

'Well, I could ask you the same question.'

'I'm a friend of, er—' He paused. He'd forgotten the name. 'The bloke who lives here.'

'Of course you are. Where did he find you?'

'What do you mean?'

'Where did he pick you up?'

'He didn't pick me up,' Sweet Thing countered.

'Sorry, I just thought—'

'He said I could stay here.'

'Did he now?'

'Yeah.'

'So you're moving in with him?' Nina asked incredulously.

'No, no. Nothing like that. He just said there was a room going here.'

'Oh yeah?' She smiled and folded her arms.

'Yeah.'

'And where is he? "The bloke who lives here."'

Sweet Thing looked around.

'I don't know.'

'Well, I'm the woman who lives here. And I don't know anything about this.'

'He never said anything about you. Just said I could have a room.'

Sweet Thing stared at her indignantly, already proprietorial. *Great*, thought Nina. *Pearson has gone and made a house decision without even consulting me.* It was always the bloody same, same as when O'Connell was alive. Jan was right – male

58

behaviour was so predictable. They were gay but in the end they treated women just the same as other men did.

'So . . .' She caught his gaze. 'Like I said, where did he find you?'

Her eyes were glaring straight back at him, like she could see right into him. *I'll have to be more careful with this one*, Sweet Thing decided. She stared him down and he had to look away for a moment. She gave a little laugh. *Bitch*, he thought.

'We met on the street,' he muttered, grudgingly. 'I ain't got nowhere to stay'.

He looked up at her again, smudged lashes flickering. His eyes shone, filmy from sleep. Nina noticed again how pretty he was. A moody little bastard full of hurt. A tough little cherub. He sighed and swung himself around to sit on the edge of the bed. His bony frame hunched over itself, his shoulder blades jutting out like unformed wings.

'He asked me, you know,' Sweet Thing insisted. 'He offered me the room. I didn't ask for nothing.'

'This room?'

'What?'

'You're staying with . . . oh yeah, you've forgotten his name already, haven't you? "The bloke who lives here." '

'No. He's moving into the other room.'

'What other room?'

'You know, next door, the bloke who . . .' Sweet Thing's shoulders tensed. '. . . died,' he said with a shudder.

'Well, you know everbody's name, don't you?'

'Look, I didn't ask.'

'My name's Nina.'

'What?'

'Nina. Think you can remember that?'

Sweet Thing nodded sullenly.

'Yeah, sure.'

They heard the sound of the front door closing. Sweet Thing and Nina looked at each other.

'Well, make sure that you do,' she said.

8

the bomb squad

Does the eagle know what is in the pit? thought Walker as he made his way along the corridor to the commander's office, *or wilt thou go ask the mole?* It was the motto from *The Book of Thel* by William Blake. He had to find his mole, his informer. He had lost contact with him; maybe he had lost control of him too.

It was Walker who had first noticed quotes from Blake among political graffiti. He knew that it wasn't something that Special Branch officers were exactly trained to look for. But he saw the Proverbs of Hell daubed on the hoardings and railway bridges: THE ROAD TO EXCESS LEADS TO THE PALACE OF WISDOM, THE TIGERS OF WRATH ARE WISER THAN THE HORSES OF INSTRUCTION. They were coded messages of some kind, prophesy for the counter-culture. Their interpretation could have an operational value. So he took time to study the poetry, to understand what Blake meant to the freaks and radicals. There were visions that he had to try to see.

Detective Sergeant Walker was a thin man who wore a mournful expression on his hollow and cadaverous face. He looked and moved like a ghost. He had haunted the underground – he was the Bomb Squad's 'hippy specialist'. He was going to miss this beat now that the trial was about to start. There was something about the passion of these people that had inspired him. They were idealistic, romantic, with dreams beyond his cold reason. But they had become dangerous. He had needed to know what was in the pit, the world beneath the surface. Where was his mole? He knocked on the commander's door and was called in.

'You still here, Walker?' asked the commander as he entered.

'Yes, sir.'

'Haven't you got a home to go to?'

Walker forced a laugh.

'No wife waiting up for you?' the commander continued.

'No, sir.'

'Single?'

'Divorced, sir.'

'Lucky man.'

'Quite, sir.'

'Well, I'm glad you're still here. I wanted a word. I want you with the watchers outside the court tomorrow.'

Walker looked dolefully at his boss.

'Do I have to, sir? There's something I need to follow up.'

'What?'

'One of my sources, sir. I've lost touch with him.'

'A witness?'

'No. An informant.'

'Well, does it matter now? The trial's just about to start. He's not due to testify, is he?'

'No, sir. Not for us anyway.'

'Christ, Walker, you don't mean that he might come forward for the defence?'

'No, sir. Well, I don't think so. He's just been a bit unpredictable recently.'

'Unpredictable?'

'Yes, sir. And, well, he was in possession of some incriminating evidence.'

'Shit. I thought we had all this tied up.'

'Sir.'

'The defence is going to accuse us of planting stuff, you know that.'

'Sir.'

'Well, where is this informer of yours?'

'I don't know, sir. I had a rather unusual exchange with him three weeks ago and then I lost touch.'

'If he's one of yours, well, they're all a bit strange, aren't they?'

'This was more than usually unusual, sir.'

'What did he say?'

The last communication Walker had received was a phone message: *Tell Walker I have purchased a field of blood*. Could he tell the commander that? He had no idea what it meant. He decided instead to refer to an earlier conversation.

'He wanted to return some money to the information fund, sir.'

'What? You're joking.'

'No, sir.'

'Well, that is fucking weird. I've never heard of a snout who wanted to do that. What did you tell him?'

'That there was no official procedure for such a thing.'

'And you haven't heard from him since?'

'Well, he phoned me, but I haven't been able to find him.'

I have purchased a field of blood. What could it mean? At first Walker thought that it might be a Blake reference, but he had checked and it wasn't. Perhaps it was something biblical.

'Well, anyway, I need you with the watchers tomorrow morning. There's going to be some sort of demo and we want the best surveillance we can get. You know who all these weirdos are. It's your speciality, for fuck's sake.'

'Sir.'

'I mean, we really value your analysis.'

'Thank you, sir.'

Walker allowed himself a thin smile. He hadn't always been so well regarded. For a long time he'd been seen as a bit of a joke in the department. Most Special Branch officers were simply content to do MI5's dirty work. Break-ins, phone taps, surveillance on suspect trade union officials and Communist Party members. 'F' Branch, the counter-subversion department, was obsessed with Moscow-backed enemies within the state. Hunting for moles within its own organisation. Red scares that went right to the top. But they were aloof in their analysis, they had lost touch with how things were changing politically. *Does the eagle know what is in the pit?* They were convinced that Wilson was a Soviet spy. They were stultified with Cold War madness. MI5 had been compromised itself so many times that it had become deranged with paranoia.

Walker was one of the few officers who questioned these simple assumptions. He took his job seriously, involved himself in philosophical study. He saw that times were changing. The cold war was getting warmer. Subversion wasn't just reds under the beds, it was becoming something else. 1968. Paris, the Events of May. London, Grosvenor Square. Riots, demos, university occupations. There was a move from simply monitoring the CP and the unions to cultivating informers in the anti-Vietnam movement and the Trotskyist left. There was an urgent subversion threat assessment ordered for a chief of staff's report on 'The Security of the United Kingdom in the Pre-attack Phase of General War'.

Walker became Special Branch's expert on anarchism and libertarian socialism. It was a brief no one else wanted. He was drawn to its obscure and eccentric nature. He could work alone, without much interference. He enjoyed his homework. Along with Blake he read the fashionable French radicals Herbert Marcuse and Guy Debord. They spoke of alienation in modern life – it was something he could understand very well. He went down into the underground, moving quietly through its lower depths, stalking the demos and embassy pickets. Browsing the obscure bookshops and checking on political meetings. He had to try to make sense of their *demi-monde*. Happenings, poetry performances, art-house films – there were clues everywhere. He read and tried to decipher the pamphlets churned out in basements on small offset-lithograph printers. Slogans on T-shirts and badges, rock 'n' roll lyrics, arcana that required divination. It was laborious work but he had to try to look for meaning. That was what his colleagues could never understand. They scarcely noticed what he was doing until the bombs started going off.

The hopeful dreams of the sixties had begun to evaporate. Peace and love had failed. War and hate ruled. Days of Rage. Bringing Vietnam Home. Getting warmer. Going deeper. Below zero. In the USA: Black Mask, Weather Underground, Up Against the Wall Motherfuckers. In Italy: the Red Brigades. In Germany: the Red Army Faction. In the UK: a couple of small explosions, shots fired at the Spanish embassy. Strange notes signed 'the Wild Bunch' or 'Butch Cassidy and the Sundance Kid'. A press blackout at first. Then the bomb at the house of the minister of employment and communiqué number four from the Angry Brigade: *Robert Carr got it tonight. We're getting closer.*

'So I'll see you tomorrow, then.'

Walker sighed.

'Yes, sir,' he said, and moved along the corridor.

'Oh, and Eric,' the boss called after him. 'Good news. There's to be an official announcement but you might as well know. We're not going to be disbanded after the trial.'

'No?'

'No. We're not going to be the Bomb Squad, though. We'll be designated C13, Anti-terrorist Branch.'

The Bomb Squad was meant to have been a temporary operation. Set up as a reaction to the Angry Brigade. An ad hoc grouping of Flying Squad detectives, Special Branch officers, army bomb disposal experts and Home Office scientists. Walker had been assigned to it, now an important expert on the counter-culture. The Bomb Squad. The name seemed quaint now, like the old habit of calling explosive apparatus 'infernal machines'. *We're getting closer*. Terror, that was the future, thought Walker. The bombs would come and go, but terror would hang in the air like a dust cloud. It was a state of mind. The squad wasn't being disbanded because this was the beginning, not the end. Walker had seen the words on the hoardings, the slogans on the walls, heard the battle cries and shibboleths. It was coming. Getting warmer. *We're getting closer*. An endless war of attrition. An intimate dance. Both sides would feed off each other. It was all there in Blake, *The Marriage of Heaven and Hell*: *Without contraries is no progression*. Terror and anti-terror, insurgency and counter-insurgency, shadowing each other with nightmare images of what was to come. The vision of Urizen: *the dark power, divided & measur'd*. It was escalating. The Provos were bringing a bombing campaign to the mainland. Bringing the war home. Fear would bring control, repression reassurance. Terror was the future. *We're getting closer*. It would escalate for ever, spiralling upwards into a state of panic. A state of emergency. A state of continuous anxiety. A state of perpetual vigilance.

9

miss world

The second time Nina had met Pearson and O'Connell was on a demonstration outside Bow Street magistrates' court earlier that year. It had been organised by Women's Liberation and the Gay Liberation Front to protest against the trial of five women who had been arrested after disrupting the Miss World competition at the Albert Hall. Some of the GLF were performing a street theatre satire, the 'Miss Trial Competition', with queens in radical drag parading up and down the middle of the road. Chants and slogans were instigated with a shrill enthusiasm that soon diffused into mournful protestations. Cheers and laughter came too readily and trailed off too soon. There was an air of forced carnival about the demo.

There were tensions and conflicts among the demonstrators. Many of the Women's Lib lobby felt that the GLF men were sexist. There were muttered complaints about the drag queens, that transvestism demeaned women just as much as any beauty contest. The GLF itself was beginning to fall apart from within. And there were complaints that there were never enough lesbians involved. Solidarity gritted its teeth into a grim smile for the bemused public.

Nina noticed Pearson and O'Connell on the edge of the crowd. They were outsiders, she decided, just like her. She went over to talk to them. O'Connell was the talkative one, making sarcastic comments about the demonstration. There was a blasphemous spirit to his jokes that she could secretly relate to. He was edgy. Like her. On the edge. Pearson was quietly friendly, laughing in a disparaging way at his lover's comments. She got on with them almost at once. And they liked her company, though she soon realised that her role was often to mediate their intense relationship. Couples so often look for a referee.

She moved into their squat and took the top room that had just been vacated by a taciturn German student. The attic had a skylight with a ladder fixed to it. On sunny days she could climb up, open the window and sit on the ledge of its frame and look out across the city. She liked to go up on the roof to think things over or simply to daydream idly under the pattern of clouds.

At first, living there had been an ideal arrangement. She brought a new energy to the household. It was a beautiful place to live and for a while she was made a fuss of. They were both showing off to her, she knew that. Pearson with his paintings and O'Connell with his words and his plans to write. They seemed playful and full of ideas, even though they didn't seem to have actually done very much for a while. They would speak of their schemes with a desperate boldness, as if trying to convince themselves of the power of their complicity. For a while she had been almost jealous of their closeness, though there was a sense of safety in being at one remove from a relationship. It allowed her a vicarious pleasure of connected emotions. She soon discovered the ugly bitterness that stalked their partnership, the awful hidden pressures hidden beneath a veneer of calculated cleverness. O'Connell's black moods dogged the house, and Pearson simply could not cope with his lover's depression. She became the audience for a darker performance. She watched them fall apart, and it exhausted her. A horribly quiet and selfish anger descended upon the house. Pearson would talk to her plaintively, his voice full of hurt and confusion.

O'Connell confided in her in a curious and oblique way. She'd always found it easier to engage with him than Pearson but now he rambled on, strange confessions that hardly made any sense.

She had known that O'Connell had been taking heroin long before Pearson had realised. All the signs were there. Clues that her father had told her to look out for, when he had lectured her about drug addiction. The dilated pupils, the track marks on the inside of his forearms. Something for the pain, just like her mother's morphine shots when she was dying of cancer. When she confronted him about it he made her promise not to tell Pearson.

'But doesn't he suspect any way?' she had demanded.

'Oh, you'd be surprised what you can keep a secret,' he'd replied.

They had ceased being intimate with each other and O'Connell took to wearing long sleeves when Pearson was about. She knew that he would find out eventually. It was very near the end when he did.

She felt guilty about O'Connell's death. She had known about his habit and done nothing about it. But what could she have done? She felt awkward, too, that she hadn't told Pearson, that he had been the last to know. He was in a terrible state and she felt a responsibility towards him. But he would just wander off on his own for hours. Now he'd brought the first stray he had found home. A pretty little thing. What the hell was he playing at?

She heard his footfalls on the stairs. She went out on to the landing and waited for him.

'Nina,' he said.

'What the hell's going on?'

'What's the matter?'

'I've met your little friend.'

'Look—'

'So you made a decision about the house without asking me. Thanks.'

'It's my room.'

'And what about O'Connell's room?'

'I'm going to move in there.'

'Oh, right. Then it's all sorted, then.'

'The kid doesn't have anywhere to stay.'

'So we're a hostel for the homeless, then?'

'Yeah, why not? At least we'd be doing something.'

'Helping a poor innocent boy.'

'Nina.'

'He's a hustler, isn't he?'

'Yeah, so?'

'Well, I don't want my house becoming a crash pad for any passing trade.'

'Christ, Nina.'

'I mean it.'

'When did you get so fucking stuffy?'

'Pearson, you're the little innocent here, if you ask me, not that boy in there. And when did you get this social conscience all of a sudden?'

'Well, you care about all these campaigns and causes out there but when someone who actually needs help comes along you don't want to know.'

'Yeah, someone who just happens to be a pretty young man. Maybe that's why you're feeling so charitable.'

'You bitch.'

'Excuse me,' came a voice. They both suddenly stopped arguing and turned around.

Sweet Thing stood behind them in the bedroom doorway. He'd put his platform boots back on. They looked at him. Pearson coughed.

'Make up your minds,' he went on. 'I ain't staying where I'm not wanted.'

'Sweet Thing—' Pearson started.

'No,' Sweet Thing cut in. 'I didn't ask for nothing. You offered. So I don't know what she's getting on her high horse about.'

'It's Nina, remember?' said Nina.

'Yeah, yeah. Well, sort it out. I'm going out.'

He started down the stairs, his platforms clomping heavily on the bare wooden steps.

'Sweet Thing, wait,' Pearson called after him.

'I'll see you later,' he called back. 'Maybe.'

10

the whispering squad

Walker met Nick Prentice at the Pronto coffee bar in Leicester Square. Prentice was wearing a suit and looking smarter than he usually did. He had even had a haircut.

'What's with the clean-cut look, Nick?' Walker asked.

'We're up shit creek, that's what. They're breaking up the Whispering Squad and A10 are sniffing around everybody.'

The Whispering Squad was an operational team within the Drugs Squad so called because of its secretiveness and isolation. And its reputation for running a highly organised system of informers. Rumour had it that their grasses were paid off with drugs seized in raids and there was a series of dealers who could continue their trade with impunity in return for bodies. Now there had been an investigation.

'I mean A10, Eric,' Prentice went on. 'This new squad for investigating complaints is being run from A Department, not C Department. Administration, not Crime. We're not even allowed to clean up our own house any more. It's all being run by woodentops and provincials who know fuck all about the realities of detective work.'

Most of Walker's Special Branch or Bomb Squad colleagues expressed a barely concealed contempt for the Drugs Squad, but he had seen them as an opportunity to find a way into the underground. Walker had needed help, someone on the inside. The squats and the communes were impenetrable to him – he needed a way of penetrating this other world. In the past Prentice himself had been as scruffy and long haired as any bona fide hippy when he worked undercover in the dope scene. He had worn a heavy Afghan coat with an authentic goat-like tang. He had introduced Walker to one of his informers who had told strange stories of plans to blow things up when he'd been stoned. He was a burnt-out junkie that Prentice had very little time for any more. He was always desperate for a fix and willing to talk about all sorts of things, so Prentice had handed him over to Walker.

'To be honest, Eric, it all started going wrong when dope became a middle-class habit, you know what I mean? Those fucking university-educated hippies and troublemakers from Release. Rock stars with expensive lawyers. It was a lot less grief when we were just dealing with a bunch of spades from West Eleven.'

'Well, you have been a bit on the hookey side, haven't you?'

'Come on, Eric. Don't be a cunt. Everybody's been up to something. You're political. You can get away with anything, can't you?'

Some of the raids carried out by the Bomb Squad hadn't exactly been legal. Forensics tampered with, suspects verballed up. They were vulnerable to accusations of fitting up suspects. That was why he had to be sure that certain incriminating material was secure and that his mole would keep quiet. But Prentice was right, they would get away with it, it was political. Lots of squads were in trouble because of allegations of corruption: the Drugs Squad, the Dirty Squad, the Flying Squad even, but not the Bomb Squad. Because they weren't just bent for the job, they were bent for the state.

'And you owe me,' Prentice went on. 'Don't forget that.'

'Oh, I haven't, Nick. That's what I want to talk to you about.'

'What?'

'Our little friend.'

'What about him?'

'He's gone missing.'

'Yeah?'

'Yeah. Have you seen him lately?'

'I saw him with a bent script outside Boots in Piccadilly about a month ago. He looked fucking awful.'

Walker knew that his informer had become increasingly desperate. When they had first met it had all seemed like an intellectual game. He'd seen it before, that pleasure people got from playing both sides. A misplaced sense of control. Having lost his own way, his informer was drawn to the idea of secretly determining the destiny of others. He had imagined that he was the player and realised only when it was too late that it was he who was being played.

He was a loner, disaffected, which Walker could understand only too well. But his man was connected, he knew the radical scene. He clearly knew some of the people behind the bombings – maybe he had been involved in some way himself. But Walker could tell that he didn't belong to a group or even a cause. Here was someone who had always felt apart from things. There was a great deal of in-fighting and factionalism on the left, a parade of groupuscules that divided like cells under a microscope. Fissiparous, they grew by division. They often seemed to struggle more against each other than the state. Walker had once thought that he could exploit these divisions. But it was hard to keep up with their constant fission. His informer offered something more tangible, a personal insight, something more vicious. He was driven by a self-destructive egotism that Walker could charge and detonate.

He had worked him slowly. He had learnt how to disguise interrogation as casual conversation. Never asking direct questions but slowly drawing things out into the open. As in a game of chess, Walker kept to a defensive strategy, allowing his opponent to show off, with audacious moves, flamboyant gestures that would ultimately trap him. Walker had read widely and could expound obscure political theories and provoke complex arguments. He could work so that it was he who seemed the idealist and his informer the cynic. There was so much bitterness that he could work upon, so much anger.

Walker would always imply that he was sympathetic to certain principles, that he was independent of his superiors. And in a way he was. He could never have such open and stimulating discussions with his own colleagues. They had so little understanding. There was a dialectic meaning to his relationship with his informer. A Blakean energy. He thought of animal symbolism, the eagle and the mole, the horse and the tiger. Walker insisted that he was offering as much knowledge of the state as he was gaining of the underground, that they complemented each other. He believed that they were more to each other than merely cop and grass. His informer was not so sure.

'I'm sorry to disappoint you,' he told him. 'But I ain't exactly a Tyger of Wrath any more. A pussycat of Wrath maybe.'

'But I'm a Horse of Instruction, aren't I?'

His informer laughed darkly.

'Oh yes,' he replied. 'You certainly are that.'

It was true. He was harnessed to duty, yoked to dull reason. But he wanted to liberate his mind, even if it were just through the imagination of another.

'We understand each other, don't we?' he implored.

'We've got nothing in common, man.'

'Exactly. "Opposition is True Friendship".'

His informer laughed again.

'You're just trying to get information out of me, that's all.'

And he was right. Walker couldn't help doing his job. He was so fixed to laws and regulations. But somewhere in his trapped soul he wanted something more. Not just information or evidence but real wisdom. He yearned for some sort of revelation. He had once even thought of taking drugs so that he might see visions, but he knew that would never do. He suspected that they wouldn't work for him, and he'd seen what they had done to the Mole.

He watched as his informer went into decline, filled with self-loathing, self-annihilation. The Whispering Squad had used him up. He'd traded people he knew on the drugs scene so that he could secure his own supply. Heroin killed the pain but had deadened other feelings as well. By the time Walker got hold of him he was ready to sell his political associates too. When the arrests began, his informer started to realise the true gravity of his treachery and a growing sense of guilt and dread ate away at him. Walker saw less of him after that. He didn't really need him any more; the man was becoming unstable, he reasoned. He missed their talks, though, and he was determined to stay in touch. It was always the informer who would get in contact with him, never the other way around, and they had never met at the informer's home. These two rules were always part of the deal. Now Walker did need to see him.

'Can you keep an eye out for him?' he asked Prentice.

'What's it worth?'

'Oh, for Christ's sake, Nick.'

'I mean it. I need all the favours I can get at the moment. They're going to put us in the fucking dock, you know.'

'What do you want?'

'Well, I might need you to testify that some of my dealings with snouts were of a highly sensitive political nature.'

'I don't know.'
'Go on, mate. It's fucking true, after all.'
Walker sighed.
'I'll see what I can do.'

11

moonage daydream

Johnny Chrome played the demo tape of the new song Joe had given him. 'Hey, Hey (The Gang's All Here)'. It sounded stupid. Just like the first single. The paradiddle backbeat, the anthemic chorus hook. He tried singing along to it but it felt flat. He didn't know what he was supposed to do. Teeny-bopper music, that's what they called it. Stripped down and infantile, not like this progressive rock stuff the hairy great-coat and plimsoll brigade went for. Concept albums – well, he never understood all that. *This*, well, he should be able to understand *this*, he reasoned. He should be programmed to do this. *Just rock 'n' roll with lipstick on*, Joe had said. It was modern and retro at the same time. It was sci-fi, but fifties sci-fi. *Yeah*, he suddenly thought. *Like the future in the past.* A vague gleam of inspiration flickered in his weary mind for a second. He remembered watching Flash Gordon at the Saturday morning pictures as a kid. For a moment he knew what it was. What Johnny Chrome was. Then it was gone. He lost his train of thought and the anxiety overcame him once more.

He worried about the deal he had with Joe. He was terrified of the idea that Joe was ripping him off. He had trusted his manager for so long. It had been so simple when it had just been the odd gig here and there, he could understand the figures then. Now that there was real money at stake, the thought that Joe might be pulling a fast one was unbearable. He knew that he should get a lawyer and renegotiate his contract but the thought of it made him feel sick.

The sun was going down. The coming of night filled him with dread. He took a couple of Mandrax and slumped on to the white leather sofa. Whatever had happened to little Johnny Evans who had sung so sweetly in the chapel choir? Johnny Rebel, Johnny Savage, Johnny Chrome – all his personas had drained him of a sense of self. He was homesick. He mourned his lost youth, yearned for that time of enchantment when he could dream of a bright future.

He looked over at the telephone and thought of his mother. He wanted to call her, to speak to her, but he couldn't. The last time they had spoken was after he had been on *Top of the Pops*. She had been so proud and he had promised that he would take care of her. But he didn't have any money. What could he say to her? *Hello, Mam*, he mouthed forlornly, *it's Johnny here*. There were no more words that he could think of. He was all alone.

So he went to the mirror. He had once spent so much time in front of the mirror. He used to be so happy there, performing in his bedroom to his eagerly reflective audience. He'd loved the silvered surface, touching the fingertips that reached out to him, stroking the glass, pressing gently against it, making delicate birch-leaf imprints of condensation. Like Jack Frost patterns on a window. He dreamt that he could push through it, that it was liquid not solid. A mercury pool that he could dive into. When he was young the face that waited for him there was all he needed.

Now somebody else stared uncomprehendingly back at him. A stranger. He was getting old. The first streaks of grey showing through. Dark-rimmed eyes and lines on his face. He was no longer at home in the looking-glass world.

His hair was a mess. He combed it into some sort of shape. A quiff on the top and shoulder length at the sides and back. He dabbed a bit of powder on his cheeks but his face was sweaty and it smudged. He sighed. He was exhausted. The downers had begun to take hold. He had moved from a state of anxiety to one of lethargy with no respite in between. He went back to the sofa and curled up into himself. There was a warm rush as the drug diffused through his flesh. He rocked himself gently and thought of Sweet Thing.

The doorbell chimed. Johnny yawned and lifted himself up from the sofa. He staggered to the front door. He thought he must be dreaming. There was Sweet Thing standing on the step as if conjured out of his own forlorn desires. Johnny Chrome peered out at the impish figure, back-lit by the hennaed sky of twilight. It was like a miraculous vision.

'Well, ain't you going to let me in?' Sweet Thing demanded.

Johnny nodded slowly and moved back to let the boy in.

'So Joe found you? That was quick.'

'Him? Nah. I saw him earlier in the penny arcade.'

'He said you were making a row.'

'Joe was being a pain in the arse.'

'Well, it's his job, you know.'

'Anyway, I found my own way here. I remembered the address.'

'Right,' said Johnny, and led Sweet Thing into the bedroom.

They stood facing each other. Sweet Thing grabbed Johnny's crotch. Johnny groaned as he started to get hard. He felt as if he were being brought back to life. He looked at the boy's face, the bright little eyes, the lovely lips he longed to kiss. But Sweet Thing was already lowering himself, crouching then kneeling on the floor. He unzipped Johnny and took him suddenly into his mouth. Johnny gasped then sighed out slowly.

Sweet Thing had learned to do this act quickly and efficiently. To bring a punter off fast – it was good for business.

Johnny felt more delicately about what was happening. He felt powerful and vulnerable at the same time. The soft mouth, the hard jaw. The warm tongue, the sharp teeth. He held on to Sweet Thing's head and pushed at it gently. The boy tilted his face slightly to accommodate the thrust and tugged gently at Johnny's scrotum, slowly extricating it through the zip of the jeans.

Johnny started to move his hips in an increasingly insistent rhythm. Sweet Thing held on to his buttocks, at one moment pulling him in, at another controlling the movement so that it was smooth and fluid. *Yeah*, Johnny murmured. *Yeah*. He held on to the back of Sweet Thing's neck as he felt a spasm running through him. He closed his eyes and his mind darkened for a second then imploded with glittering flashes of colour. He opened his eyes and let out a guttural moan of release. He staggered back as the boy pulled his mouth away.

Sweet Thing swiftly got up and went into the bathroom. He spat Johnny's sperm out into the basin and ran the cold tap and washed out his mouth. When he came back into the bedroom Johnny was sitting on the bed, zipping up his jeans.

'Right, then,' said Sweet Thing.

Johnny got up.

'Don't go yet,' he implored. 'Come here a second.'

He put his arms around the boy and held on to him. Sweet Thing shivered and pushed him away.

'Stay for a while.'

Sweet Thing shrugged.

'It'll be extra,' he insisted.

They went into the front room and Johnny opened a bottle of sweet white wine. Sweet Thing started to browse through Johnny's record collection. It was old stuff. Elvis, Eddie Cochran, Gene Vincent.

'Got any Bolan?' he asked. 'Or Bowie?'

Johnny scratched his head. Joe had left him some records to listen to. He found a carrier bag full of singles and swung it on to the sofa.

'Have a look in there,' he told the boy.

Sweet Thing found 'Starman' by David Bowie and put it on the stero. He started to mime to it, one hand on hip, the other gesticulating. He shimmied about the room, twitching his little body. It was strange and perverse but it was sexy. Dirty and somehow romantic. He swayed from side to side as the last 'la la la's faded away. Johnny smiled and clapped.

'That was good,' he said.

'I can do Bolan, too. Wanna see me do that?'

'Sure.'

Sweet Thing put on 'Get It On' and began pouting along to the words, tossing his head back haughtily. Johnny smiled. *This is it*, he thought. *This is what it's all about.* Through a haze of drugs and sex Johnny suddenly felt a sense of realisation, of inspiration. He started to mimic the boy's movements himself. Sweet Thing laughed. The record came to an end. Johnny suddenly had an idea.

'Do me,' he blurted out.

'What?'

'Do me. Do Johnny Chrome.'

Sweet Thing looked at the older man sceptically.

'You want me to do you?' he asked.

'Yeah.'

Sweet Thing emitted an ugly little cackle.

'You sure?' he asked.

Johnny smiled, thinking he was in on the joke.

'Yeah,' he insisted. 'Do me.'

Sweet Thing shrugged.

'All right,' he said.

Johnny found a copy of 'Hey You', put it on the turntable

and carefully lowered the needle. As the music started Sweet Thing launched into a spasmodic dumbshow, flailing about the room wide eyed and convulsive. There was a shocked expression on his face, as if it had been caught in the dazzle of a light. He struck faux muscleman poses and made mincing little dance steps. At times he looked like a baby learning to walk or a drunk trying to keep his balance. Sweet Thing's performance wasn't cool or slick as it had been when he had been doing Bowie and Bolan. It was a grotesque parody of their moves. Johnny was aghast. *Is this me?* he thought with horror. *Oh Christ, is this what Johnny Chrome is really like?*

He grabbed the arm of the stereo and the record came to an end with a searing rasp. Sweet Thing froze.

'What's the matter?' he demanded.

'That's enough.'

'Well, you wanted me to do you.'

Johnny sighed.

'Do I really look like that?' he asked meekly.

'Look, I was just doing what you do.'

'I'm ridiculous, ain't I?'

Sweet Thing didn't know what to say. He didn't want to upset Johnny. He was a good customer, he reckoned. Johnny shakily poured himself another glass of wine and fumbled for his pills. *Time to go*, thought Sweet Thing.

Johnny held his head in his hands. He felt so fucking embarrassed. But, he thought, maybe the kid could help him. Sweet Thing knew more than he ever could about how to make this work. He was glam personified, he knew all the tricks of the trade and more besides. Johnny was the innocent, he could learn from the kid. Learn how to become. To become whatever he was supposed to be.

'I better be off,' said Sweet Thing.

'Wait a minute,' said Johnny.

'Yeah, well. We've got to settle up.'

'What?'

'Fifty quid for the blow-job and, let's say, twenty extra for hanging out.'

'What?'

'Seventy quid. Yeah?'

'What?'

'You keep saying "what?" You know, I just need paying.'

'What?'

'Will you stop saying that? It's getting on my nerves.'

Sweet Thing started to tense up. His lithe body became angry and began to shape up into an aggressive stance, alert and fierce, protective of its interests. Johnny noticed this change in the kid, provoked him into a bleary sense of amusement and signalled a distant glow of arousal. He cracked a smile.

'Thing is,' Johnny slurred, 'I ain't got no money, see?'

'What?'

'Yeah. Well, the thing is, I was expecting you earlier, but Joe brought some other boy around.'

'What?'

'And, like, we had to pay him off.'

'What?'

'And now I ain't got no cash, see?'

'What?'

'Now you're saying "what?" all the time. Funny, ain't it?'

'No, it ain't.'

Sweet Thing grabbed Johnny's shirt. The older man was a lot bigger but he was drugged and weary. Sweet Thing could be tough if he wanted to be. If he needed to be. He had learnt from other boys down at the Dilly. Some of them made it their speciality to roll queers. He'd done that only once, and that was as part of a gang of them. But he knew the game. You had to take the initiative. There had been times when he'd been knocked about. You had to know when to run and when to stand your ground.

Sweet Thing pushed Johnny to the floor. He felt a rage surge up inside him. He was being tricked out of what was owed him and that would not do. He slapped Johnny hard across the face.

Johnny's head spun from the stinging blow. Then there was a tingling all over his face. He felt suddenly alive, as if he were being woken up from a long slumber. It felt good. He turned the other cheek.

'Yeah,' he groaned. 'Do that again.'

Shit, thought Sweet Thing. This wasn't going to work. Johnny Chrome was into this. He'd known about punters who were into being slapped around. They usually went for the rent boys who looked butch, the ones that went for the boot-boy or hooligan look.

'Get up,' he told Johnny.

Johnny stood up and stroked his cheek. There was a glimpse of something he had always known about himself. The slap woke him up to himself. It made him feel vibrant. The pain soon drained from his face and its knowledge faded.

'How come you ain't got any money?' the boy demanded, looking around the room. 'You must be rich.'

Johnny tried to explain to Sweet Thing about his contract with Joe. But he hardly understood himself. He had thought that his agreement was for fifty per cent of the gross, not the net of his earnings. That's where it had all gone wrong. Everything had been eaten up by 'expenses' and he'd been left with nothing except a meagre allowance Diamond Music paid him. It didn't make sense to him. Sweet Thing had a more instinctive knowledge. He understood capitalism on a visceral level. His body was trade, he was business made flesh. Having no one else to exploit he had ruthlessly exploited himself. And he knew that Johnny Chrome had been had over, that he had sold himself short.

'You've been ripped off,' he told Johnny.

'Yeah.' Johnny sighed forlornly. 'I guess.'

'Well, that don't help me, does it? I want my money.'

Johnny tried to think. 'Um, I could talk to Joe. He could pay you out of expenses.'

'Yeah, well.'

Then it came to Johnny. Sweet Thing could be a more permanent fixture. He could learn from the kid about his image. He could make Johnny Chrome work. And he could get regular sex too.

'I've got a better idea,' he announced. 'We could put you on the payroll, like.'

Sweet Thing frowned. He wasn't sure about this. But all sorts of possibilities started to flood into his head. This was something new. Not just a one-off transaction. This was dealing in a future.

'So how would that work?' he demanded.

'I'll give Joe a ring,' Johnny Chrome said.

12

a pound of spikenard

'The kid might not be coming back, you know,' Nina said.

Pearson had started to clear out O'Connell's room.

'Well, I need to sort out his stuff sooner or later,' he said.

'Yeah. But we need to sort something else out first.'

'What?'

'What happens if the kid *does* come back.'

Pearson shrugged. 'Well, he can stay for a bit, can't he?'

'He doesn't even remember your name, you know.'

'So?'

'I really don't appreciate you making a decision without me.'

'Yeah, you're right,' Pearson agreed. 'I'm sorry.'

'Look, you're still in shock. You're not thinking straight.'

'It seemed like a good idea at the time.'

'Yeah, sure. But you're avoiding the issue, aren't you?'

'What do you mean?'

'O'Connell. It's no use wandering about in a daze, picking up waifs and strays on the way. You've got to deal with what happened.'

'And how am I supposed to do that?' Pearson demanded, with a sharpness in his voice.

'I don't know,' Nina replied. 'You can talk to me.'

'Right.'

They stood in the doorway in silence. Pearson turned his head away from her and looked around the dead man's room.

'So,' said Nina finally. 'This kid.'

'Yeah.'

'Sweet Thing. What kind of a name is that?'

'A street name.'

'I figured that much.'

'He does need somewhere to stay.'

Nina smiled.

'You do fancy him, don't you?'

'It's not about that, Nina,' Pearson protested.

'I wouldn't blame you. I could fancy him myself.'

'Nina, come on.'

'Why not? He is very pretty. But you be careful. Don't let him take advantage.'

'Don't worry. I can look after myself.'

'Yeah, right.'

'So?'

'So what?' Nina demanded

'He can stay? Just for a while.'

'Yeah, all right,' she agreed grudgingly. 'But he better behave himself.'

'Do you want to give me a hand clearing out the room?' Pearson asked her.

'I've got things to do, I'm afraid.'

'Tomorrow, then.'

'I can't tomorrow. It's the first day of the trial.'

'What trial?'

'You know, the Stoke Newington Eight. At the Old Bailey.'

'Oh, yeah.'

The Angry Brigade, thought Pearson. It was finally happening. The big trial. He had suspected that O'Connell had been involved, that this was the reason for him becoming so distant and secretive. But when he confronted him about it O'Connell had been dismissive. 'They're hardly urban guerrillas,' he had said. '*Sub*urban guerrillas more like. I mean, Stoke Newington.'

Nina went upstairs and left him standing in the middle of O'Connell's room. He tried to size it up, decide where to start. There were a few books and records he would keep and the rest he could take down to the second-hand shops. There were journals and magazines scattered all over the floor. They could go in the bin. There wasn't much to salvage among the clothes stuffed into the chest of drawers or left in piles. O'Connell had stopped bothering about his appearance a long time ago. Pearson had already taken his coat, which was about the only thing worth saving.

He found a cardboard box and started to stack some of the books into it. He took his time at first, checking the covers in case these was something he might want to keep for himself, even flipping through the pages of some. They had all seemed to make so much sense at one time. They had been part of his education.

'I don't want just to corrupt your body,' O'Connell had announced to him when they had first started to live together. 'I want to corrupt your mind as well.'

He had tried to learn as much as he could from the older man but he found it hard to keep up with him. O'Connell was astonishingly well read, if rather eclectic in his literary tastes.

'I'm an autodidact,' he declared.

'What does that mean?' Pearson retorted.

'Self-taught. It means I'm a bit showy and resent anyone with the proper education I never had. Pretentious. The word says it all. I mean, only someone so belligerently self-taught would come up with such a grand term as "autodidact".'

O'Connell showed him poetry and philosophy, culture and politics. Pearson struggled with it all but for a while found a nurturing warmth from his lover. He felt safe in looking up to him. There seemed so much promise ahead for them both. He was sure that one day O'Connell would write a great book himself.

But O'Connell's critical faculties were so sharp that he had very little patience with anything that he actually produced. Pearson was used to O'Connell's manic energy but he hadn't bargained for the depressive side of his temperament. O'Connell became maudlin and began to lose his enthusiasm for knowledge.

'What's the point?' he said. 'I mean, the more you know, the harder life is. I'd rather be stupid and happy.'

'You don't mean that.'

'How do you know what I mean?' O'Connell taunted him. 'I don't mean much, you know.' O'Connell's moods worsened; they even stopped arguing with each other. O'Connell seemed absorbed by a sedate melancholia, a gloomy self-sufficiency.

Whenever Pearson tried to get close to him he was warned off.

'Don't jump in after a drowning man,' O'Connell had told him. 'You'll end up getting dragged down yourself.'

O'Connell gave up on his body as well as his mind. He stopped going swimming and began to look gaunt and hollow eyed. And he was right, Pearson did begin to feel pulled down by O'Connell's bleakness. He found no joy in his art any more.

Pearson looked down at the scattered volumes, filled with dumb words. He had learnt so much from O'Connell and yet knew so little of him. He wished he could make sense of it. Something must have pushed him over the edge.

There was so much dust on the books. Pearson began to shift whole blocks of volumes, gripping either end and lifting them like a cigar-box juggler, shoving them into the box without looking at them. He was choking on the dust. O'Connell's dust, he thought as he hawked from the back of his throat.

He fetched himself a mug of water and came back into the room. Sunlight caught the myriad motes that hung in the air. He put the mug down on the desk and opened the window. A loose floorboard creaked underfoot. He looked over the worktop. It was well ordered in comparison with the chaos of the room. O'Connell hardly kept anything he had written. He threw everything out eventually. He held on to sheaves of notes, a bit of a manuscript even, until, in the end, he destroyed it all with what seemed a determined sense of frustration and disappointment, even a perverse sense of satisfaction. Pearson picked up the portable typewriter. He could sell that, he thought. Underneath it was an envelope folder. He put the machine down, picked up the file and opened it. There were a handful of typewritten pages in it. He leafed through them. It looked like a story. Something O'Connell had left behind. He shuffled back to the beginning and started to read:

a pound of spikenard

it's an ancient set-up, you know. an old story. one of the oldest. the whore and the punter. the whore is getting past it but you can tell she was once a looker, that she used to have something.

– what do you want? she asks the john.
he coughs, shrugs, nervous and embarrassed.
– well? come on, we haven't got all day.
– i want, he says, i want what you did with him.
– with him?
– yeah. you know, him.

she laughs and shakes her head.

– you think that's for sale? it wasn't a trick, you know.

– well, tell me about it then.

– it'll cost you.

– how much?

– how much? you know how much. the price is always the same. thirty pieces of silver.

– ok, he agrees and hands her the cash.

she then begins the story:

– then took a woman a pound of ointment of spikenard, very precious, in an alabaster vessel. she broke it, poured it on to his head and rubbed it into his body. she then anointed his feet and wiped his feet with her hair and the house was filled with the odour of the ointment . . .

– yeah, says the punter, getting all excited. i like the bit with the feet and the hair.

– wait a minute, i haven't finished the story.

– sorry.

– right, well, the disciples became indignant. they were suspicious of women at the best of times. this display of wanton sensuality was too much for some of them and they began to berate the woman. but he chided them.

– why trouble you the woman? he demanded. she has wrought a good work on me.

– oh yeah, someone mutters underbreath.

and another says:

– why was this waste of the ointment made? for it might have been sold for thirty shillings and the money given to the poor.

this was judas who was the bagman of the gang, the economist. and jesus replied:

– for the poor always you have with you; but me you have not always.

and this was too much for judas. the poor always you have with you? he thought. then nothing really changes. it's all just talk and gesture. he cast out the moneylenders from the temple but that was just part of the spectacle. he doesn't care about the poor, he reasoned, just his own ambition.

– for in that she hath poured this ointment on my body, jesus went on, she did it for my burial.

and the other disciples nodded gravely at this. but judas felt betrayed. and it gave him an idea. he wants to be the anointed one, he thought. the holy scapegoat. well, i can fix this, he decided, and there and then he made a plan to betray his boss, just as he himself had been betrayed. so he would sell him and he knew the price that he would put on his head. the same as the price of the precious alabaster cruse of spikenard. thirty pieces of silver.

There was a loud banging on the front door. Pearson stopped reading and went downstairs. He put his hand on the latch then stopped.

'Who is it?' he called out.

'It's me. Sweet Thing.'

Pearson opened the door to see the boy standing there.

'Where have you been?' he asked.

'Had a bit of business. You going to let me in?'

'Yeah,' replied Pearson, standing aside. 'Sure.'

Sweet Thing stepped inside.

'So, can I stay here?' he asked softly, as he brushed past Pearson.

'Yeah, well, I talked to Nina. We agreed you could stay for a bit.'

'What's it got to do with her?'

'Well, it's a shared house.'

'Yeah, but it's not your house, is it?'

'What do you mean?'

'It doesn't belong to you. It's a squat, ain't it?'

'Don't push your luck, kid,' said Pearson, suddenly feeling less charitable.

Sweet Thing smiled, slightly taken aback.

'All right, all right,' he said. 'I was only saying.'

They started climbing the stairs.

'Do you even know who I am?' Pearson asked.

'Of course I do.'

'No, I mean, do you remember my name?'

'Your name? Yeah, er . . . Look, mate, it's been a long day.'

'Hasn't it just? It's Stephen. OK?'

'Yeah.' Sweet Thing nodded. 'Stephen.'

Pearson fished in his pocket and handed something to Sweet Thing.

'That's a front-door key.'

Sweet Thing rubbed the brass token between his fingers.

'Right,' he said. 'Thanks.'

They reached the landing. Sweet Thing reached for the handle of the door to his new room. Pearson stood close to him. Sweet Thing opened the door and stood on the threshold, turning to look at Pearson. He pouted coldly at him, hooding his eyes lazily, his nostrils flaring. It was a look of flirtatious malice. Pearson put a hand on Sweet Thing's shoulder.

'Hey,' Sweet Thing purred.

He leant over, his face inches from Pearson's, his mouth opening slightly as if to take a bite of air from the space between them.

'You want it?' Sweet Thing whispered.

Pearson groaned and nodded. He made a move to kiss Sweet Thing on the lips. The boy suddenly pulled back and took hold of the hand that Pearson had laid on him.

'You'll have to pay, you know,' he told Pearson.

'Yeah,' Pearson said bitterly taking his hand away. 'Of course.'

'I did tell you. I only do it for money.'

'Well, you've made that perfectly clear.'

'Good. So,' he went on, turning his head to one side, 'do you want it?'

'No, I do not want it. Not like that.'

'Please yourself,' Sweet Thing yawned and began to close his door. 'I'm off to bed, then. Goodnight.'

Pearson shook his head and went back into O'Connell's room. He stared at the papers on the desk. He thought about continuing to read the story but his eyes were tired, smarting against the bare bulb that burned in the room. He switched off the light, sighed and collapsed on to O'Connell's single bed.

I3

the watchers

WHOSE CONSPIRACY? was the graffito on the wall of the Old Bailey. Two Corporation of London workers were scrubbing at it. It was the first day of the second Angry Brigade trial.

The Stoke Newington Eight Defence Committee protest had set up camp by the public toilets on a traffic island opposite the judges' entrance. The demo moved around the small patch of pavement holding up placards and chanting. A huge scrum of press had gathered around the Central Criminal Court, and outside broadcast vans were parked all along the kerb. Walker was with the watchers, all plotted up to the side, Bomb Squad and Special Branch keeping an eye on the protest, looking out for anything suspicious that they could report to the City of London Police, whose jurisdiction it was. It was going to be a long trial. The spectacle has begun, Walker thought.

'Anyone interesting, Eric?' asked a police photographer.

'What a fucking bunch,' another officer commented.

'Well, Eric really liked this lot, didn't you, Eric?' somebody else chipped in. 'Going to miss them once this is all over, aren't you?'

He was used to this taunting. He had once overhead an officer refer to him as the 'hippy-lover'.

'Well,' he announced to his fellow officers, 'we've really got a lot to thank this lot for.'

'What the fuck are you on about, Eric?'

'They've given us a nice little middle-class lesson in urban guerrilla warfare,' Walker replied. 'We're going to need it. It's going to get much heavier.'

'He's right, you know,' said the photographer. 'I hear the Bomb Squad is being kept together. We'll be up against the Paddies after this.'

Walker scanned the crowds. The chanting protesters, the scurrying journalists. A man stood in the road holding a microphone and talking into a television camera. The Bomb Squad were supposed to be running surveillance but what could they really see? thought Walker. They too were part of the performance.

The whole life of those societies in which modern conditions prevail presents itself as an immense accumulation of spectacles. *All that once was directly lived has become mere representation*, Guy Debord had said in his Situationist tract *The Society and the Spectacle*. Debord had been the key. Walker had used his work to guide him. He became his main theoretical grass.

The second Angry Brigade communiqué, printed in *International Times* in December 1970, had read: *Fascism and oppression will be smashed, High Pigs, Embassies, Spectacles, Property*. It was the word *spectacle* that had stood out for him. Walker knew that the word could be connected to Debord and Situationism. Maybe the Angry Brigade were Situationists.

The attack on an outside broadcast van covering the Miss World contest in November 1970 certainly fitted a Situationist modus operandi. An expression of revolt against alienation, attempts to shatter the very illusion of things. The perpetrators had an emotional idealism and a sophistication that amused Walker. Other outrages didn't necessarily follow this logic; the Carr bombing was a direct assault on a minister of state. It shocked everybody and threw the authorities into confusion. Other political experts on the newly formed Bomb Squad had been baffled by the campaign. They simply couldn't work out who the Angry Brigade were. They didn't fit any pattern that they were used to. Were they communist or fascist? Marxist? Marxist-Leninist? Trotksyist? Maoist? Special Branch had been gearing itself up for some kind of fifth column organisation funded by Moscow but this wasn't it. It seemed to have something to do with the underground but they didn't understand it. Even detectives that had worked 'B' Division, which covered groovy areas like Chelsea and the King's Road, didn't have a clue about how the hippies operated.

Walker was already ahead of his colleagues. He knew that Trotskyists weren't behind the bombings. They had been critical of the Angry Brigade. To them guerrilla activity in the Third World was admirable but they weren't so keen on it when it came closer to home. And the Trots were far too authoritarian and logical. The people they wanted were against conventional rationality. Like Blake they were anti-reason. One of the most well-known Situationist slogans was BE REASONABLE DEMAND THE IMPOSSIBLE.

There was a raid on suspects at 25 Powis Square in West London in April 1971, and among the items seized was an annotated copy of The Society and the Spectacle. Walker had felt that his theoretical instincts were being confirmed. Handwriting experts would examine the calligraphy of the scribblings in its margins, but Walker would continue to study the text with a forensic epistemology. There were other clues, too. 25 Powis Square had been used as a location for Performance, a counter-culture movie starring Mick Jagger. Walker had seen it in an art-house cinema earlier that year. Gangster meets rock star, underworld and underground collide and descend into sex, drugs and obscure metaphysics. It was tangential evidence, but nothing could be overlooked. There were signs everywhere, lines converging like sacred geometry. He was getting closer.

Then a month later a bomb was planted at Biba, the fashionable department store. *If you're not busy being born you're busy buying*, the communiqué had read. *In fashion as in everything else, capitalism can only go backwards*. This was pure Situationism. Why else would they commit an outrage against a trendy boutique? Debord had said: *behind the glitter of the spectacle's distractions, modern society lies in thrall to the global domination of a banalizing trend that also dominates it at each point where the most advanced forms of commodity consumption have seemingly broadened the panoply of roles and objects available to choose from.*

Other targets were more conventional and didn't necessarily conform to this pattern. But Walker knew that it was important to establish a theory, a conspiracy of ideas. With this they could prove a criminal conspiracy. He always bemoaned the fact that most policemen in the political sector simply weren't political enough. So often they didn't know what to look for.

He used his knowledge to control his informer. Their relationship had been a battle of wills. He had worked hard to keep ahead of him with his analysis so that he could have the edge in their dealings. He had already begun to surpass his informer in ideological insight when his superiors had started to press for tangible results. They wanted bodies, not just theories. Names had to be named, material evidence had to be found in the right places. His informer could have immunity for anything that he might have been involved with himself, but this didn't protect him from his growing sense of guilt and self-loathing. He started to become more unpredictable. Walker needed to know that he could still control him.

And he missed him. There were so many things that Walker wanted to discuss, things that only the Mole would understand.

'You're terribly repressed, aren't you?' his informer had said to him.

'I prefer to see it as self-discipline,' he had replied.

'No. It's deep-seated repression. That's why you love us.'

'What?'

'You love the freaks, don't you? You'd love to be one yourself but you don't dare.'

'Don't be ridiculous.'

'It's true. You'd make one helluva freak. You already are one, aren't you? In secret.'

The detective sergeant gazed across at the parade in front of the Central Criminal Court. The Corporation of London workers continued to scrub at the WHOSE CONSPIRACY? graffito. We all conspire together, Walker thought. Even those who criticise the spectacle become part of it themselves. He looked up at the Old Bailey; the gilded statue of Justice perched above its dome, beneath it a stone inscription: DEFEND THE CHILDREN OF THE POOR & PUNISH THE WRONGDOER. Walker thought once more of the Proverbs of Hell. *Prisons are built with stones of Law, Brothels with bricks of Religion.* Power creates an illusion of justice, of reason, the vast machinery of the fallen universe. Both Blake and Debord saw the connection between industrial production and enslaved perception. The satanic mills, the workers stupefied by the products of their own labours, eyeless like Samson chained to the grinding wheel. The world we see is not the real world; society has invented a visual form for itself, one of mere appearance. We are dazzled by the glitter of the spectacle. *If the doors of perception were cleansed everything would appear to man as it is, infinite.* Walker stood mesmerised, staring up at the glitzy statue. With sword and scales, blind-folded. Hoodwinked. What could he see, standing with the watchers? What vision might appear to him if he could properly attune his mind?

The police photographer nudged him. 'Seen something Eric?'

'What?' Walker murmured, coming out of his reverie.

'You look like you spotted something.'

'Yeah,' said Walker, focusing again on the demonstration.

'So,' said the photographer, 'anyone you want me to get?'

Walker scanned the crowd of demonstrators. He had hoped that he would see the mole among them but he wasn't there. Then he spied a girl leaning against the railings of the public conveniences, smoking a cigarette. There was a placard next to her with a feminist symbol and the slogan ANNA, HILARY, ANGIE, KATE—SISTERS WE ARE ALL WITH YOU, referring to the four women among the defendants. Walker tapped the photo-grapher's arm and pointed her out to him.

'Oh yes, Eric,' he said as he started to focus. 'Very nice.'

'Looks like a lez to me, Eric,' said the other officer.

Walker sighed.

'Well, one of them on trial's a lezza,' the man went on. 'So I've heard.'

Walker ignored him and continued to watch the girl. He had remembered something. A connection to his informant. He would need to check his files.

Sweet Thing sat in the offices of Diamond Music in Wardour Street and watched as Joe Berkovitch finished eating a salt beef sandwich. Berkovitch resented having his lunch inter-rupted like this but he wanted to deal with this kid as quickly as possible. Johnny Chrome's record company had been on the phone wanting to know where the new single was that they had been promised. He picked up a paper napkin and wiped his fingers; his tongue probed his teeth and palatte. *Too much mustard and not enough pickle*, he thought, as he crumpled up the greaseproof paper and tossed it into the wastepaper basket.

'So,' he announced to the boy. 'What was all that about?'

'What?' asked Sweet Thing.

'The other day. In the penny arcade.'

'Oh, that. That was just . . .' Sweet Thing thought for a while. '. . . a misunderstanding.'

'A misunderstanding, yeah, that's good. Because we can't afford to have any trouble, can we?'

'I don't want any trouble.'

'Fine. Good. I talked to Johnny. Maybe we can work something out.'

'You owe me money.'

Joe shrugged. 'Yeah. Sure.'

'Well, you better pay me.'

'That sounds like a threat, son.'

'Well . . .'

'I thought you said you didn't want any trouble.'

'I don't. Just . . .'

'Listen, son, calm down, for fuck's sake.'

Berkovitch dug into his trouser pocket and pulled out a sheaf of notes. He plucked out ten sheets from the roll and dropped them on to the desk in front of Sweet Thing.

'There,' he declared. 'We're quits, yeah?'

Sweet Thing glared at the money. It was one hundred pounds. Cash was a sensual pleasure for Sweet Thing – the very thought of it turned him on. Though as much as he craved the possession of it, as soon as he had it in his hands, he desired nothing more than to spend it as quickly as possible. That much money excited him greatly, but maybe there was more where that came from, he pondered. He squinted at Berkovitch.

'Quits?' he asked.

'Yeah,' replied Joe. 'Or we could come to an arrangement.'

'Johnny talked about me being put on the payroll.'

'Well, I was thinking more like a retainer.'

'A retainer?'

'Yeah, a hundred quid a week.'

'A hundred? For a whole week?'

'It doesn't mean working a whole week. It means your services are retained for that period.'

'My services?'

'Yeah.' Berkovitch cleared his throat. 'You know.'

'How do you mean "retained"?'

'Well . . .,' Joe made an open-handed gesture. 'Johnny isn't going to want you around all the time, is he? We can work out when you're needed and the rest of the time is yours.'

Sweet Thing squinted at Berkovitch again, trying to work out the catch. If what he was being told was true he could be doing business through the week as well. He could make this arrangement work for him, it could be easy money. He didn't like to give up his freedom, though, to be 'retained'; he didn't like the sound of that.

'I don't know,' he said.

Joe shrugged.

'It'll be a regular income.'

'A hundred pounds a week?'

'Yeah.'

'Plus expenses,' Sweet Thing added.

Berkovitch leaned back in his chair and stared hard at the boy.

'What?' he demanded.

Sweet Thing thought for a moment. It was something he had heard somewhere. Something his instinctive business sense had picked up along the way.

'Yeah,' he declared with a smile. 'A hundred quid a week plus expenses.'

Joe narrowed his eyes and leaned forward.

'Expenses? What for?'

'You know.' Sweet Thing pondered a moment. 'Cab fares, stuff like that.'

'I'll want receipts.'

'What are receipts?'

'Good God, son, you're learning so fast you're having trouble keeping up with yourself, aren't you? A receipt is what you get when you pay for something.'

'Oh, yeah.'

'And it has to be a legitimate expense, all right?'

'Sure.'

'So we've got a deal?'

'I ain't signing nothing.'

'What?'

'I know all about your contracts. Johnny told me all about them.'

'You cheeky little . . .'

For a moment Berkovitch thought that he was about to explode with anger but laughter came instead.

'You little bastard,' he declared. 'Maybe we do understand each other. But don't fuck with me. Now look. Johnny's due in the studio tomorrow so I want you here then, right? Nine in the morning.'

'OK.'

'Right, then. Off you go. I've got work to do.'

Berkovitch stood up and walked Sweet Thing to the door.

'You little bastard,' he repeated, ushering him out. 'You'll go far, you know. If you live long enough.'

Pearson filled the cardboard boxes with books and bin-liners with clothes, then dragged them out on to the landing. The walls were covered with a mosaic of photographs, posters, leaflets, pictures cut out of magazines. He tore them all down. He tried to hollow out a space for himself in the room, exorcise its suffocating dimensions. He opened the window to let in air and light. To let in life. But a malevolent presence still occupied it. The cloying smell of decay. Sweet Thing was right to be superstitious. It was haunted.

It was here that he had discovered O'Connell's secret. Pearson had come home one afternoon and burst in on him. O'Connell had forgotten to lock the door. Pearson caught him crouched on the bed shooting up.

'What are you doing?' he demanded.

'Just taking my medicine,' O'Connell replied in a dull tone.

'That's not the answer.'

O'Connell laughed.

'No?' he retorted. 'Then what's the question?'

'You know what I mean.'

'No I don't. I don't know what you mean. How about this for an answer: I can't fucking go on any more.'

'Please,' Pearson pleaded with him. 'You can't just give up.'

'I know,' O'Connell announced with a grim smile. 'I'm a traitor to the revolution.'

'Don't joke about this.'

'It's not a joke. There aren't any jokes any more.'

'O'Connell—'

'Oh, please,' he had said. 'Just leave me alone.'

'I won't.'

'I fucking mean it,' O'Connell had insisted.

He should have taken O'Connell's advice, Pearson thought. In the end he was the one that had been left alone. Left behind to deal with all this stuff. It was driving him mad but he had to make sense of it somehow.

He sat down on the chair. The file was still there where he had left it. He picked it up and continued to read the story.

so judas went to the authorities and cut himself a deal. all he wanted was the price of the perfumed oil the whore had rubbed in the boss's body and dried with her hair. the amount that he would not give to the poor because, he had said, the poor are always with us. the price of the chrism for the burial he himself had foretold. the cost of his betrayal. his egotism. for he was not always with the poor but considered himself the anointed one.

– is that all you want for him? they asked him.
– that's the fair price.
– thirty shekels?
– thirty pieces of silver.

so they gave him the blood money and planned when they would take him. It was a bank holiday weekend and trouble was in the air so they wanted it done quietly. all police leave had been cancelled in the occupied territories, riot gear had been issued. they didn't want a repeat of the incident at the temple which had led to widespread disturbances. it was decided that he would be arrested at night and judas would finger him for them in the darkness.

a feast had been arranged for friday night and judas intended to slip away once the party was in full swing. there would be plenty of wine and food, that was certain. you never had to worry about the catering when the boss was around, that was for sure. that wedding do at cana, that thing he'd done with the loaves and the fishes, bingo!

canapes for five thousand. but this supper turned out to be a pretty dismal affair. there was a heavy atmosphere. bad vibes. the boss seemed paranoid.

– i'm telling you, he kept saying. one of you is a grass.

well, there was a bit of a commotion about this. johnny, the one the boss loved, was kind of cuddled up to him but the rest of the crew were edgy. especially rocky. now rocky's real name was simon but the butch fisherman was always known as simon-peter. peter meaning rock on account of the fact that he was a big lad. he was shy and soft, despite this, and it was the boss that started calling him rock or rocky, which always made him a little embarrassed.

– rocky, he had once joked, patting him playfully on the chest. upon this rock i will build my church.

now the boss wasn't in such a jocular mood. rocky went up to johnny who was leaning on the boss's chest and told him to ask him who it was that would betray him. all the rest of the gang were in a commotion, asking: is it me boss? is it me? rocky declared that he would lay down his life for the boss but the boss replied:

– i'm telling you rocky, before the cock is up in the morning you will deny me three times.

the disciples laughed at this, thinking it one of the boss's jokes but rocky spoke even more vehemently. later jesus said to judas:

– that thou doest, do quickly.

everyone thought this was some errand that he had to perform and thought nothing of it but judas knew what he meant. he then immediately went out; and it was night.

Pearson heard the front door slam. Nina called up to him. He gathered up the pages and shoved them back into the file. He slid the file under the typewriter on the desk and went downstairs.

Sweet Thing went to Playland and spent an hour playing Fire Queen. When he had had enough of the game he looked around the arcade. With all the money in his pocket he hadn't even been thinking about trade. He saw Angel, a fellow Dilly Boy, standing by the one-armed bandits.

'How's your luck, Angel?' he called over.

'Shit,' the boy replied. 'It's dead in here.'

'You hungry?' he asked Angel.

'Starving.'

'Come on,' he beckoned with a nod of his head. 'Let's go and eat. I'm flush.'

Angel smiled and followed him out into the street. They found a café and they both ordered the all-day breakfast. Angel had a hard-luck story to tell. Sweet Thing thought it better just to listen and not to boast of his own good fortune. He slipped Angel a fiver after the meal. It was an investment, he reasoned. One day Angel might do a favour for him.

He came across Tony the Dealer in Leicester Square. He bought a gram of speed and, thinking of the hippies back at the squat, a quarter of an ounce of Lebanese hashish. He didn't usually smoke dope but he thought it might be a good gesture to bring some back.

'How come you sell dope in ounces and speed in grams?' he asked Tony.

'It's not me. Everybody does it.'

'Yeah, but why?'

'I don't know, son.'

'You'd think with decimalisation and everything . . .'

'What's that got to do with it?'

'Well, you know, you should have one system.'

'What do you want me to do? Call a meeting of all the dealers and sort out our weights and measures?'

Sweet Thing found an off-licence. He bought twenty Players No. 6, a packet of red Rizla papers and a bottle of white wine. He caught a number 73 bus back to the house.

'They're still swearing in the jury,' Nina explained about the trial. 'The defence is objecting to some of them.'

They were sitting at the kitchen table. Pearson had cooked a vegetable stew and brown rice.

'Why?' he asked her.

'Because we want a jury that's sympathetic. It's a political trial so we don't want bourgeois types, do we? They're trying to get a working-class jury.'

'And will they be sympathetic?'

'Well, we can only hope. You could come down tomorrow, if you want. We need all the support we can get.'

He sighed. There might be people on the demo that knew him and O'Connell. He couldn't bear the thought of all those right-on people feeling sorry for him.

'I don't think I can face it.'

'What's the matter?'

'Crowds, you know. I'm just not ready for that.'

'Yeah,' said Nina. 'Of course.'

They ate for a while in silence.

'Look,' Nina said after a few minutes, 'you should talk about it. You've not really talked about any of this.'

'What am I supposed to say?'

'I don't know, but talking might help.'

'I don't see why.'

'You blame yourself, don't you?' Nina asked.

'What?'

'It's natural, but there was nothing we could have done.'

'There must have been something.'

'He was depressed. He was an addict. He had a history of mental illness. He was . . . well, he was suicidal.'

'Yeah, well, we know that now.'

'I'm sorry,' said Nina. 'I didn't mean to sound so brutal about it. But you shouldn't be so hard on yourself, you know.'

'I just want to understand what happened.'

'But you'll end up beating yourself up about it.'

'I've got to try,' he insisted. 'Try and find a reason.'

Nina sighed. Pearson sounded so desperate.

'You've got to get on with your own life as well, you know,' she told him.

'Yeah, well, I don't know how I'm supposed to do that.'

She shrugged. 'I'm just saying. If you want to talk.'

'Right.'

There was silence again. Nina felt that she hadn't broached the subject very well. She had to try, though. Pearson didn't have anyone else to talk to. All his time with O'Connell had cut him off from the few friends that he had from college. She wished now that she could lighten the atmosphere but she didn't know how.

They heard the key turn in the door. She smiled at the sudden distraction.

'Our little friend is home,' she muttered mischievously.

Pearson's face brightened a little too as he heard the door open.

'Come on,' he entreated. 'Please. Be nice.'

'All right, all right.'

'We're in here!' Pearson called out.

Sweet Thing came cautiously into the kitchen. He shuffled towards the table, looking around at the political posters plastered on the walls.

'Want something to eat?' Pearson asked.

'Nah,' he replied. 'I had a fry-up earlier.'

'Right.'

'I got this, though,' Sweet Thing announced, placing the wine on the table.

'Wow,' Pearson said quietly with a smile.

'You have been busy,' said Nina.

Sweet Thing glared at her.

'I'll get a corkscrew,' Pearson said, getting up from his chair.

Nina caught Sweet Thing's gaze. This time she didn't outstare him. She smiled.

'Sit down, then,' she said.

Sweet Thing pulled up a chair. Pearson found some glasses and poured the wine. He stood between them and lifted up his glass.

'Cheers,' he said.

'I got this and all.' Sweet Thing pulled the dope out of his pocket. 'You want some?'

Nina laughed. Pearson picked it up and sniffed it.

'Nice,' he said.

'I ain't no good at rolling joints, though.'

He handed Pearson the cigarettes and the rolling papers.

'Fancy a smoke, Nina?' Pearson asked.

She shrugged. It had been a long, serious day on the demo and she needed to relax. It might help to take Pearson a little out of himself as well.

'Yeah,' she agreed. 'Why not?'

They went into the front room. Pearson put on a record and used the album cover to roll up on, sitting cross-legged on the floor. Nina stretched out on a battered sofa. Sweet Thing perched on an armchair. He squinted at the record cover. It looked strange. There was a painting of an island hovering in the air. The music was odd too. A slow rhythm with lots of notes crammed into it. A bloke's voice was wailing over the top; he couldn't make out the words.

The joint was passed around. Nina took a lungful and watched as Pearson began to relax, nodding his head slightly to the music. The drug seemed to have the opposite effect on Sweet Thing. He looked nervous, tensed up on his chair, his eyes twitching around the room.

Sweet Thing wasn't used to hashish. Speed he could understand. It gave him an edge. It was useful. Dope just made him feel like he was losing control. It was a hippy drug. An awkward giddiness surged through him. He leant back and held on to the arms of the chair. There was a sense of falling and a fear of something he couldn't understand. His mind raced but made no sense. His imagination was usually so well ordered; now it took him to places that he didn't want to comprehend.

'Are you all right?' asked Nina.

'Yeah, yeah,' the boy muttered.

Pearson was oblivious on the floor, lost in the reverb of a soaring guitar solo. Sweet Thing sank further into the chair, gripping the sides of it hard. Nina stood up and passed the joint to him. He snatched at it and puffed on it urgently.

'Hey,' she said. 'Go easy.'

Sweet Thing coughed and handed the joint to Pearson. The boy looked up at Nina standing above him. He looked scared and vulnerable, his shoulders hunching up defensively. He seemed lost. Nina couldn't help smiling. The dope had made her feel sentimental and it seemed to have taken some of the hardness out of him. He looked like a sad and beautiful child. A wounded little bird.

'How old are you?' she asked him.

'Seventeen,' he replied.

'That's young.'

'No it ain't,' he insisted. 'Seventeen's legal. I've been seventeen for years.'

'What?'

Sweet Thing laughed and straightened himself up in the chair. Some of the toughness came back to his demeanour.

'I mean, I've been saying I'm seventeen since I was fourteen,' he declared.

'I don't understand.'

'Well, otherwise you're a minor. Then they can take you into care.'

'You mean you've been on the street since you were fourteen?'

'Off and on. I got put back into a kids' home for a bit. I ran away again.'

'That's terrible.'

'No it ain't,' he said indignantly. 'I can look after myself.'

'No, I mean . . .' She sighed. She didn't know what to say.

Sweet Thing picked up his glass and took a swig of wine. His head swam.

'What happened to you?' Nina asked him.

He squinted at her. The question filled him with a vague terror.

'Nothing,' he insisted.

He looked away from her, staring off into space. He chewed at his lower lip.

'Hey,' she said, 'look, I didn't mean to pry.'

He turned back to her and forced a smile.

'It's OK,' he said.

He tried to give his face a fixed expression, a sign to deter trespassers. It didn't quite work. He was too stoned. He blinked. His eyes were raw and filmy, smarting with smoke particles. He watched her looking at him. He frowned.

'What?' he asked.

She wondered about him. He looked so alien and enchanting. So curious and yet so lacking in curiosity.

'You're a strange kid, you know.'

'No I ain't,' he protested. 'I'm normal.'

'Oh yeah?'

'Yeah. It's you lot that are strange.'

'How do you mean?'

'Well, this hippy thing. All this freedom.'

Nina smiled.

'What's wrong with freedom?' she demanded.

'I don't want to be free.'

'No?'

'No,' he declared. 'What's the point in being free?'

She thought about it.

'I don't know,' she admitted. 'What do you want, then?'

'I want . . .' Sweet Thing started to giggle. 'I want to be expensive.'

Nina joined in with his laughter

Pearson came out of his reverie and sat up on the floor.

'What are you talking about?' he asked.

Nina shook her head.

'I've no idea,' she replied. 'Is there any of that joint left?'

'I'll roll another,' said Pearson.

The concept album came to an end. Sweet Thing got up and rifled through the record collection. He found 'Hot Love' by T.Rex. He strutted about the room to it, teetering precariously on his platform boots. He then put on a Tamla Motown collection and started to step in time to it, moving his hips and making sharp little hand gestures. Pearson got up and tried to join in but he swayed clumsily from side to side. Sweet Thing pushed him away and did a quick turn in the middle of the room. Nina had sat back down on the sofa, watching. Sweet Thing sashayed over and reached out his hands to her. She shook her head but he held her hands and pulled her. She got up and started to dance with him. His eyes were half closed, his head nodded in time. He seemed transported by the music.

Nina followed his steps falteringly. Sweet Thing could really dance. A simple, joyful spirit came from somewhere and manifested itself unselfconciously. Hippies just couldn't move like that, she thought. They had forgotten how. Sweet Thing had brought some life into the house, that was for sure. She tried to let go and give in to the music. She felt the seriousness of the day, all the earnest gestures and fervent utterances, fall away.

Pearson slumped in the armchair and looked on. The dope infused him with a dull euphoria. For a while he could forget O'Connell. Forget himself. As he watched Sweet Thing's pert little arse shake in time to the soul music he felt himself lifted out of his own body. His senses seemed to hover in the room in a warm hum of sensual desire. He wanted the boy so much. A simple, vital lust. It could have taken him out of his grief if only Sweet Thing felt the same way. Instead it left him with a melancholy yearning. Another sense of loss, of longing for something he couldn't have. He felt jealous of Nina, the easy closeness that she had with the kid. He yawned and started to roll another joint.

Nina pulled away from Sweet Thing and went back to the sofa. After a couple of tracks Sweet Thing stopped dancing and took the record off. Pearson lit the joint and they passed it around. Sweet Thing yawned and stretched.

'I got to go,' he said, standing up.

His head was spinning. He swayed about the room a bit.

'Are you OK?' Nina asked.

'A bit stoned,' he said. 'Better go to bed. I got to work tomorrow.'

'Oh yeah?'

'Yeah. Got a rich punter.'

'Right,' said Nina.

Sweet Thing staggered out of the room and clomped up the stairs. Pearson pinched the stub of the joint between his thumb and forefinger and sucked the last out of it.

'Are you OK?' Nina asked him.

He shrugged.

'I guess.'

'Well, I'm off to bed too.'

Pearson sat alone in the front room for a while. He didn't want to go up to O'Connell's room just yet. He rolled himself another joint and finished off the wine as he smoked it, wrapped up in a dull sadness. His head felt heavy. He had cleared out the room but his mind was cluttered with sorrowful remains. He had been trying to find something in what O'Connell had written. Something that might be addressed to him. A few words, was that too much to ask for? O'Connell had been so cold to him at the end. He had hoped he might leave something behind that might make sense and allow Pearson to feel something. A message of some kind, that's what he wanted. The real reason why his lover had killed himself. But it was just a stupid story. O'Connell loved being irreverent, it was a reaction against a strict Catholic upbringing. Pearson stubbed out the joint and sighed out the last of the smoke. He would have to go back to the room.

He climbed the stairs. He stood on the landing and looked out of the window on to the street below. There was a car parked by the kerb opposite the house. There was someone in it. For a moment he thought it might just be the dope or that he was finally losing his mind and starting to imagine things. He looked again. Someone was definitely watching the house. He moved back from the window, for a second relieved that he hadn't been hallucinating, then was gripped by a cold sobering fear. He crept down the stairs and opened the front door. The hall light spilled out on to the front steps. The cat mewled and rubbed against his legs. The car started up and drove away into the night.

14

the chromosomes

'Johnny tells me that you know a thing or two about this glam thing,' Joe Berkovitch said to Sweet Thing in the back of the car on the way to pick up Johnny Chrome.

The boy shrugged. 'Yeah, I guess.'

'Well, that's good. It's about image, isn't it?'

'Er, yeah.'

'And, well, glamour, of course.'

'I suppose.'

'When I was a kid,' Berkovitch went on, 'there wasn't much glamour about, you know. A bit thin on the ground, you might say. There was a war going on, for Christ's sake. Rationing, clothes shortages. A mug of cocoa and a fucking sing-song around the piano, that was fucking glamour in those days. But I always wanted it. I scarcely even knew what it was. I only had a glimmer of what it might be. I remember watching the beams of the searchlights cutting through the clouds during the blackout, fingering the sky. I thought that looked beautiful, and you know, I had no idea of the word at that time, but it must have been, what? Theatrical? Yeah, I guess. Pretend magic, that's what I thought of it then. I must have been nine or ten. I thought the lights were to dazzle the German pilots so they couldn't see where they were going. Later on I was evacuated out to the sticks. One night I was out playing and there was an air raid. On my way back home I got caught short. I had to take a shit in this bean field as the bombers started to drone overhead. There I was, crouched down with my trousers around my ankles, when these para-chute flares came slowly drifting down, lighting the whole place up. They were the pathfinders, you know, marking the targets for the bombers that followed. They must've been well off course but there I was lit up like the star of the show. At first I felt embarrassed because it was like being caught out taking a shit. Then I felt scared because I knew these flares would be seen from above, and that's where the bombers would start dropping their bombs. But as these bright hissing magnesium stars came gently down to earth spilling out with this strange ghostly light that made everything around me look magical, I felt something else as well. It was a feeling I would never forget. You know what it was, son?'

'No,' muttered Sweet Thing.

'It was when I knew for certain that I wanted to be in show business.'

'Oh yeah?'

'Yeah.'

'So what happened?'

'I pulled up my kecks and legged it as far away from that field as I could go.'

'No,' Sweet Thing went on. 'I mean about show business.'

Berkovitch glanced over at the kid. He hadn't expected him to be really listening, let alone taking an interest.

'Well, I tried a few things.'

'What?'

Joe shrugged. 'Tap-dancing, a patter act.'

Sweet Thing laughed.

'You?'

'Yeah, well . . .'

Joe suddenly felt embarrassed. It was the same embarrass-ment he had felt back in his youth. He had desperately tried to overcome his awkward self-conciousness. He'd somehow imagined himself as the next Danny Kaye but the reality hadn't lived up to his dreams. The reality was awful. He had felt a clumsy fool in dance classes, horribly nervous at talent shows or try-out spots. He would stutter his vocal routines with no real sense of timing or diction.

'Well,' he coughed, 'I ended up more in the business rather than the show side of things.'

Sweet Thing nodded.

'Well, that's better, ain't it?' he said.

Joe Berkovitch smiled and nodded back.

'Oh yes, son. Much better.'

Berkovitch sighed and leant back in his seat. Sweet Thing looked out of the window. They were silent until they reached Johnny Chrome's house.

'Now look, kid,' Joe announced as the driver pulled up. 'It's going to be a long day and lots of people. If anyone asks you who you are, you say: "I'm Johnny Chrome's personal assistant." OK?'

'Sure.'

'Can you do that?'

'Yeah, of course.'

'Now, I mean. Let me hear it.'

'I'm Johnny Chrome's personal assistant,' Sweet Thing chanted.

'Good.' Joe nodded, reaching down to open the door. 'I'll go and get Johnny.'

Johnny Chrome wore dark glasses and sat between Berkovitch and Sweet Thing in the back of the car. He held Sweet Thing's hand and squeezed it every so often as Joe went through the schedule for the day. They arrived at the rehearsal studios.

'Who are all these people, Joe?' Johnny asked as Berkovitch led him in.

'They're the Chromosomes.'

'The Chromosomes?'

'Yeah, like I explained, Johnny. They're your backing band. Johnny Chrome and the Chromosomes.'

'Oh,' said Johnny.

'Yeah, here they all are.' Joe started pointing them out. 'There's Danny on lead guitar, Freddie on rhythm . . . um, what's your name, son?'

'Mungo.'

'Mungo, that's right. Mungo on bass, Floyd on saxophone, Shawn on drums and, er, Todd on drums.'

'Uh?' asked Johnny.

'What's the matter?' asked Berkovitch.

'There's two drummers.'

'That's right.'

'How come?'

'Well, that's the sound we're going for, Johnny. Heavy on the percussion. Like a tribal rhythm.'

'Tribal?'

'Yeah, but modern tribal. Urban, you know?'

'But two drummers, Joe. I don't understand.'

'Just wait till you hear it, Johnny. You'll love it.'

The band set up, got in tune and checked for sound. They started to run through 'Hey, Hey (The Gang's All Here)'.

'Hear that?' Berkovitch said to Johnny. 'It's fantastic, isn't it?'

The buzzer went. It was Adrian, the costume designer. Joe got the band to stop. Adrian was a short chubby man with a mincing gait. He was followed by a skinny blonde girl.

'Hello, boys!' he announced. 'My glamorous assistant Denise is going to measure you up for your stage outfits so let's have inside legs ready, shall we?'

He waddled over to Joe.

'So these are the cavemen you want glammed up, then, Joe?' he muttered out of the side of his mouth. 'The Chromosomes? Hmm, well, I don't know. Looks like some of them have got a few missing.'

'Yeah, yeah,' Joe retorted with a placating gesture. 'So, what do you think, Adrian?'

'Jumpsuits. Flared but tight around the crotch. Different colours. Metallic colours. It'll go with the chrome theme. And we'll have to do something about the riah.'

'The riah?'

'The hair, darling. This long shag these band boys are wearing. It looks dull. And unwashed, to be frank with you.'

'They're just session men, Adrian.'

'Yeah, but you don't want them to *look* like session men, do you? Have it layered, maybe with silver highlights, that will go with the chrome look too. Speaking of which, I've got Johnny's outfit.'

Berkovitch called Johnny over. He brought Sweet Thing with him.

'You remember Adrian?' said Joe.

'Uh,' said Johnny.

'Hello, Johnny.' Adrian looked at Sweet Thing and raised his eyebrows. 'And who have we here?'

'This is Sweet Thing,' said Johnny.

'I'm Johnny Chrome's personal assistant,' said Sweet Thing.

'I bet you are, dear,' said Adrian. 'How would you like to assist him into this?'

Adrian took out Johnny Chrome's new costume. It was a jumpsuit made up of squares of synthetic silver material.

'Wow,' said Joe. 'Look at that, Johnny. Isn't that incredible?'

'All made possible with technology from the space pro-gramme,' said Adrian.

'Uh?' said Johnny.

'Oh yes. It's what every well-dressed astronaut is wearing this season.'

'Go and try it on, Johnny,' said Berkovitch.

Johnny and Sweet Thing went into another room.

'Might need to be let out a bit,' Adrian murmured to Joe. 'He's put on a bit of weight since his last fitting.'

He was right.

'Breathe in,' said Sweet Thing as he tried the zip.

'I am breathing in,' Johnny insisted.

In the end they just left it open at the chest.

'Yeah, well, that works,' said Adrian. 'The hairy chest, the girls will just love that.'

'Yeah?'

'Yeah,' he replied, turning to whisper to Joe: 'And the paunch, well, that works for Elvis, doesn't it?'

There were boots that went with the suit. They had six-inch stacked heels. Johnny put them on and shuffled about in them.

'I don't think I can walk properly in these, Joe,' he said.

'You'll get used to them.'

'I feel like Frankenstein's fucking monster,' said Johnny as he clomped around the studio.

'Yeah,' muttered Adrian to himself. 'Exactly.'

The band began running through the number again and Johnny got changed back into his ordinary clothes. Berkovitch handed him a lyric sheet and a microphone.

'Right,' said Joe. 'From the top.'

The Chromosomes played the intro. Johnny nodded along to the beat and stared at the words. He lifted up the micro-phone on his cue. He opened his mouth but nothing came out. The band ground to a halt.

'Er, he's supposed to come in there,' said Floyd the saxophone player.

'You're a little late there, Johnny,' Berkovitch called out to him. 'Let's try it again. When you're ready, lads.'

They went through it again and the same thing happened at the point where Johnny was supposed to start singing.

'Is there a problem, Johnny?' Berkovitch asked him.

'I need a word, Joe,' he replied.

Joe beckoned him over.

'What's the matter?' he hissed.

'I can't do it yet.'

'Yet? Yet? What do you mean yet? This is costing us money, Johnny.'

'No, I mean I need to practise.'

'Well, that's what we're supposed to be doing, isn't it?'

'No, I mean . . . He nodded at the band. 'Not with them.'

'What? On your own?'

'No,' he whispered to his manager. 'With Sweet Thing.'

'With the kid?'

'I can't explain it, Joe. I just need to do it with him. He can do me better than I can.'

Berkovitch sighed. He told the band to go for lunch and cleared the studio of everybody else. 'Right then, Joe,' said Johnny. 'Play the backing track. Sweet Thing, come over here.'

'What do you want me to do?' he asked.

'You know, like you did the other day.'

'What?'

The music started.

'Show me,' said Johnny.

'Show you what?' asked Sweet Thing.

'Show me me.'

Berkovitch looked on as a strange ritual unfolded on the

studio floor. Sweet Thing started to move about as Johnny watched. It was a jerky and disjointed dance to the music. Joe couldn't figure out what he was doing at first. Then he saw that he was mimicking the Johnny Chrome act. He nearly laughed out loud but he restrained himself. Something was happening between the boy and the man. Johnny followed Sweet Thing's movements as if he were in a hypnotic trance, mesmerised by the ghost dance of his own shadow. Johnny let go and was in the moment, carried along by it. He was young again, seeing himself in the mirror once more. Sweet Thing was channelling him, invoking the spirit of Johnny Chrome in psychic choreography. He was his spirit guide, leading him into himself. There was no voice yet, but this was where the voice would come from, the dumbshow of what would follow. Johnny was possessed. First by Sweet Thing, then by a mask of his own, the mask of Johnny Chrome. Inarticulate cries came out of his tremulous body, wildly searching for the right pitch. He hit the chorus line note perfect. He found the right gestures, the right moves. He waved Sweet Thing away and took the stage on his own in a triumphant performance of sublime humiliation. It was pure kitsch, it was ridiculous, it was brilliant. He had got it. He had made a spectacle of himself. The backing track came to an end and he threw his arms out in supplication. Berkovitch found himself clapping.

'That's it, Johnny,' he called out, flooded with relief. 'You've fucking got it, son.'

The musicians came back and they started to rehearse. It all worked from then on. Johnny would sometimes look intently over at Sweet Thing to try to judge what he was doing, but he was there most of the time. The band somehow got caught up in the mood of it, even making little moves that echoed Johnny's. They enjoyed themselves, let go of their session musician haughtiness; they became the Chromosomes for a couple of absurd and glorious minutes. *This is what pop music is all about*, thought Joe.

It was six o'clock when they finally wrapped up for the day.

'Right,' said Joe Berkovitch. 'Well done, everybody. I think we're ready to record this. Tomorrow, then, gentlemen. I'll phone you your call times this evening.'

The band started to pack up their instruments. Berkovitch went over to Sweet Thing.

'I don't know what you did there, son, but it was fucking fantastic.'

'Yeah,' said Sweet Thing with a shrug. 'Right.'

Johnny was exhausted. He sat staring into space, drained.

'I've got a car coming to take you home,' Joe told him. 'You want the kid to go too?'

'Yeah,' he croaked. 'Please.'

Back at the house Johnny opened a bottle of wine and poured out a couple of glasses. He gazed at Sweet Thing, transfixed. Sweet Thing sipped the sweet wine without knowing anything of his own power. It was instinctive to him, unknowable.

'Come here,' said Johnny, pulling the boy to him.

Sweet Thing understood this. He rubbed his young body against the older man. Johnny was hard and urgent to his touch. The boy reached down and stroked his cock through the coarse material of his trousers. He started to unzip his fly. Johnny pushed the hand away.

'Uh-uh,' he groaned, and knelt down in front of the boy.

'What?' demanded Sweet Thing.

Johnny gently touched the boy's groin.

'I want to suck you,' he said.

'Yeah?'

Johnny was hungry. Thirsty.

'Yeah,' he groaned.

Johnny took out the boy's flaccid penis and put his mouth against it. Sweet Thing didn't know what to do. He tried to think of something that would make him hard as the man's lips encircled his small and undemanding dick. There was a warmth that flooded into him but not much else. He closed his eyes and tried to concentrate on something that would take him there. His own pleasure was not something that he had exploited to any real extent. He fixed on pornographic images, pictures that he had seen of the act, catalogues of a bought-and-sold world. Trade. He moved his hips and it began to work. He was playing that part, his part was being played. It was an out-of-body experience. He moved his hips, thrust his groin in and out, but he wasn't really there so it was all right. He was straight, he reminded himself. Straight in, straight out. So he thought of bodies – not real bodies, not any bodies he had known, but fetishised bodies, bent over, on their knees, subjugated, dominated, abused, just as he had been. He imagined that he had power, as his cock hardened in the soft mouth, he could shut the world up, make it gag on him, make it take what he had to give it. He grabbed hold of Johnny's uncombed quiff of hair. He started to come.

Johnny felt it pulse against the back of his throat, teeming with life; it was the essence of it. It was as if he were tasting the boy's very animus. The protoplasm tingled in his mouth – there was a currency to it. As he swallowed he imagined that he was taking Sweet Thing's very own secret inside of himself.

15

infernal machine

after the meal jesus went to gethsemene recreation ground to meditate. A couple of the disciples went with him.

– my soul is exceedingly sorrowful, he told them. stay here and watch with me.

and he went a little farther into the park. he knew that the game was up but he hoped somehow he might yet be spared.

– father, he said into the darkness. if it's possible, let this cup pass from me but I know it's not up to me, it's up to you.

and he went back to the disciples and he found them asleep and he said:

– you lazy bastards. couldn't you watch with me for just one hour? watch and pray against temptation because the spirit is willing but the flesh is weak.

and he went away again and prayed once more.

– oh father, he sighed. if this cup will not pass from me i will drink it and your will be done.

and he came back to his disciples and they were asleep once more for their eyes were heavy.

– fine fucking lookouts you turned out to be, he said to them. sleep then and take your rest for the hour is at hand when i am to be betrayed.

and sure enough a whole crowd of police arrived and all the cruisers in the park made a dash for it thinking that it was a vice squad raid. one young man rushed out of the bushes with just a towel around his naked body. and with the fuzz was judas the informer. he was to give them a sign.

– the one that i kiss, he is the one that you want, said judas.

– then we could have him for persistently importuning for an immoral purpose, one of the policemen joked.

and judas went up and kissed his boss.

– do you betray the son of man with a kiss? asked jesus.

and judas thought yes, this is an act of love. you know it. god wanted a body and someone to point the finger, to plant the smacker, the kiss of death. someone had to fit you up and i'm just the man for the job. and jesus turned to the police and said:

– when i was daily with you in the temple you did not arrest me there, but this is your hour and the power of darkness.

– are you going to come quietly? they asked him.

and jesus nodded. they cautioned him and he gave forth no more verbals and they took him away.

and judas walked through the city of night, his mind reeling with what he had done. betrayal is the most intoxicating of emotions. a rebellion against the most primal of feelings: of attachment. it makes you completely free. and completely alone.

– woe unto that man by whom the son of man is betrayed. it had been good for that man if he had not been born, jesus had said.

judas had never wanted to be born. to be dragged into this wretched life. and he was cursed with the knowledge of it. he was a loner. he could never really belong to the party, or the movement, or the gang. he had hated the establishment with all of his heart but in the end he hated the anti-establishment too. they were all part of something he felt excluded from. betrayal was in his nature. and so he would take his revenge on the whole world.

but as the morning came he was filled with the dread of what he had done. his boss had been handcuffed and led away. it was going to trial. it was serious. it had been a theoretical action at first. a matter of ideology. the poor are always with us, the boss had said. it had seemed unforgivable at the time. revisionist, reactionary even. but judas had sold him for the price of a pound of spikenard. he had been so full of anger he had betrayed the son of man. but worst of all, he had betrayed himself. sweet jesus, what have i done? he thought, suddenly knowing himself with an awful dread.

he went unto the nick where they were holding the boss.

– i have sinned, he declared. i have betrayed the innocent blood.

– what is that to us? they said. see to that yourself.

and he cast down the thirty pieces of silver and departed. they picked up the money and said it is not lawful to put this in the treasury because it is the price of blood. they got rid of the cash like they didn't want to even touch the blood money. even the police despise their own informers. no one likes a grass.

and judas walked through the streets, utterly alone. let his habitation be desolate, it was written. in his fevered mind he had his own trial, and he condemned himself to death. and he went out and hanged himself.

Pearson put the pages down. It was the end of the story. He shuffled through the pages to see whether he had missed something but, no, that was it. These were the last words of Declan O'Connell. They didn't make any sense, it was just some obscure political satire. He put the story back into its file and dropped it on the desk.

He took the typewriter and put it on one of the boxes of books in the hallway. He went back for the story. As he picked up the file, the floor creaked beneath him. He had noticed a loose board here before but had thought nothing of it. He put down the story and crouched down in front of the desk. He felt along the grooves and worked the floorboard until it came away. It had been sawn short. He reached in, under the floor, found something cold and rectangular. He pulled it out. It was a metal box.

It had a small handle on its lid and a lock on its side. It was a petty cash tin. He shook it and it rattled, but not with the sound of money. He tried to open it, first taking a knife to the keyhole of the lock, then finding a screwdriver and hammer and prising it apart by force.

There were four objects inside. A small flat tin box and three tubes of a hard waxy substance wrapped in plastic. The box had the legend John Bull Printing Set and a picture of a jovial man in a Union Jack waistcoat on its lid. He opened it and found an inkpad on one side and a loose marquetry of tiny inked rubber squares in the other. They were letters. He picked one out and a Q was imprinted on his thumb. He put the letter back and closed the box. He took one of the cylinders and looked at it. There was writing along its side. *Explosif Rocher/Société Française des Explosifs/Usine de Cugny.* He dropped it with shock then picked it up and put it carefully back in the metal box.

It was explosive material, gelignite or something. It was for making bombs, that was for sure. And the printing set? It was the same type that the Angry Brigade had used to spell out their communiqués. The workings of an infernal machine and components of a children's toy, they were both forensic evidence. One could be as incriminating as the other.

What were these things doing hidden away in O'Connell's

room? There was a fearful excitement in this intrigue. He had discovered a terrible secret. What could it mean? A strange and disturbing story began to unfold in his head. O'Connell had been involved after all. He had been one of the bombers and Pearson had been right about the reason for his behaviour, his elusiveness. He had been openly critical of the Angry Brigade and dismissive of his lover's suspicions but Pearson could see now that this had merely been a front. He had meant it when he had said that he wanted to do something serious. And knowing O'Connell, he would have been serious to the extent of covering his tracks by distancing himself from the actions of the Angry Brigade. The danger of his situation meant that he hadn't even trusted Pearson with the knowledge of it.

Pearson began to piece things together. He might not be able to know everything but at least he could start to try to understand. His mind was reeling, desperate for meaning. Here was a kind of conclusion. It appealed to his sense of drama, his need for a narrative to his grief.

The story had been about betrayal. O'Connell had been betrayed and took his own life to escape being arrested, surely that's what this meant. The Angry Brigade defendants were facing fifteen years in gaol if convicted, and this was what had made him so desperate.

He looked through the contents of the box again with dread and curiosity. Here were the props of the tragedy, instrumental in O'Connell's demise just as much as the needle and the blackened spoon they had found on the bathroom floor. An awful knowledge, but something strangely redemptive about it as well. It was evidence that O'Connell's end had not been meaningless. Proof that he had died for a cause. He had tried to take his revenge against the world and it had killed him. At least he had tried.

What was certain now was the danger of the situation. Other things fell into place in Pearson's mind. The car outside the house the night before, the knowledge that they could be under surveillance. A cold fear took hold now. He would have to do something with the evidence. Not knowing quite what, he sat in O'Connell's room and waited for Nina.

It was evening when she arrived home.

'Jesus Christ,' She gasped when he showed her the objects in the tin box.

'You know what this is, don't you?'

'Yeah.'

'It explains it, doesn't it?'

'Explains what?'

'Why O'Connell was the way he was. Why he took his own life.'

'What the hell are you talking about?'

'He was protecting me. That's why he pushed me away in the end. He didn't want me to get involved.' He gestured at the explosives. 'In this.'

'Well, he still brought this stuff into the house, didn't he?'

'Maybe he didn't have any choice. He left a story behind too. It was all about betrayal. He knew he was going to be betrayed and that's why he killed himself.'

'Pearson, what the hell is all this about?'

'What?'

'Are you trying to make him out to be some sort of hero? You know that he was in a complete mess near the end. And this? This was just fucking stupid.'

'But you support the Angry Brigade.'

'The Stoke Newington Eight Defence Committee isn't about supporting the fucking Angry Brigade. It's about defending people who've been wrongly convicted.'

'At least he was doing something.'

'He was a nihilist, Pearson, face it. Look, please, you might want to make O'Connell out to be some romantic man of action. I know it's been hard coping with what happened, trying to make sense of it. But you've got to face it, he was screwed up. This? Well, this was just bloody irresponsible.'

'So why did he do it?'

'I don't know. Some misguided sense of revenge, I suppose. He was always slagging off the Angry Brigade in public but he was angrier than the lot of them put together.'

'At least I know why he did it.'

'Why he did what?'

'Why he killed himself.'

Nina sighed. 'Yeah, maybe. But he's really dropped us in the shit now, hasn't he?'

'So what do we do?'

'Get rid of it, of course,' she snapped.

'Yeah, I'm—' Pearson muttered.

'I don't want to have anything to do with this.'

'Well, the thing is—'

'Pearson, this is fucking serious.'

'The thing is—'

'What?'

'I think the house is being watched.'

'Oh, Christ,' Nina gasped.

'There was a car parked across the road last night.'

Nina broke into a burst of pained laughter.

'This is fucking ridiculous. If they find this stuff here I'm really in trouble.'

'It belonged to O'Connell.'

'Yeah, but O'Connell's dead, isn't he? I'm the one who's involved in the Defence Committee. I'm the one that would be easiest to fit this up for.'

'I'm sorry, Nina.'

'It's not your fault. You didn't know he was involved, did you?'

'No.'

'The bastard.'

'Nina—'

'No, I'm sorry, but it's just the sort of crazy thing O'Connell would do. I mean, the Angry Brigade never had a central apparatus, you didn't have to join anything, a lot of the actions were done by people working alone. You can see how that would appeal to him.'

'Yeah.'

'But he ends up implicating us, doesn't he? Leaves this stuff behind and takes the easy way out.'

'It wasn't easy, Nina.'

'I know, I know. The poor bastard was suffering. I just don't exactly feel too sympathetic to his plight at the moment.'

'I loved him, Nina. If I had known—'

'Look, let's not talk about O'Connell just now. We need to decide what to do.'

'We'll take it away tomorrow,' Pearson suggested. 'Dump it somewhere. If we go out tonight it might look suspicious.'

Nina nodded slowly.

'Yeah,' she agreed. 'Right. Let's just hope to God they don't come tonight.'

Nina went downstairs. Pearson stayed in O'Connell's room. He locked the door. He knew that it wouldn't make very much difference if there was a raid but he did it anyway. He wanted to feel safe. He curled up in the bed and drew the bedclothes over him. He thought about O'Connell. If only he had known. O'Connell obviously didn't trust him enough. Saw him as a liability. He had taken things so much farther than the playful reprisals they had acted out together. He had not been good enough, merely a partner in the lesser crimes.

He was angry at himself. He had been useless while O'Connell had declared war against society. He felt a deadening sense of remorse, that his lover had faced all this on his own and he'd not been able to do anything to help him.

Nina paced anxiously about downstairs. She drew the front-room curtains then peered through the gap in them to see whether anyone was out there. She couldn't see anything unusual in the quiet dark street. She turned to catch sight of the lump of hashish resting on the psychedelic album in the middle of the floor and went to pick it up. They should get rid of that too, she thought for a second. Then she realised this was the least of their worries. She might as well roll a joint – she needed to calm down, that was for sure.

She sat down and started to stick three cigarette papers together. She heard the key turn in the lock and jumped up in a panic. She rushed into the hall to find Sweet Thing coming in the front door.

Sweet Thing was weary. He was spent. He had dozed off for a while in the taxi coming home. There was just a nagging feeling that he had lost or left behind something. He had kept checking his pockets but there was nothing missing.

Nina was at the foot of the stairs, staring at him with wild eyes.

'What's the matter?' he asked.

'Nothing.'

'You look a bit wired.'

'Well, you look worn out. I was going to roll a joint. Do you fancy some?'

Sweet Thing shrugged.

'Yeah,' he said. 'Why not?'

Sweet Thing watched as Nina burned the resin with a match. A liquorice scent filled the room.

'Where's, er, Stephen?' he asked.

'Gone to bed.'

'Right.'

She mixed the crumbled hashish with tobacco and rolled it up. She ran her tongue along the edge of the paper.

'How's your rich punter?' she asked him.

Sweet Thing shrugged.

'He's all right,' he said flatly.

'Are you all right?'

'Just tired.'

Nina lit the joint and passed it to him. He took a long toke and held it in his lungs, felt the warmth of the smoke. He exhaled.

'You reckon if I smoked enough of this stuff I'd become a hippy?' he asked.

Nina smiled. 'I doubt it,' she replied.

'Just as well.'

He took a few more puffs and handed it back to her.

'He's a pop star,' he declared.

'What?'

'The rich punter.'

'Really?'

'Yeah,' he drawled.

Nina's eyes widened with curiosity.

'Who?' she asked.

Sweet Thing felt the buzz of the drug. It made him feel good, but it made him feel weak as well. He grinned at her.

'You ain't supposed to be interested in stuff like that,' he told her.

'No?'

'No. You're supposed to be interested in politics and stuff like that.'

'The personal is political,' she said.

'What's that supposed to mean?'

'Everything in our lives is political.'

'That's rubbish.'

'It's true. Look at your situation. You're being exploited by somebody rich and powerful.'

'He ain't powerful.'

'Well, rich, then.'

'He ain't that rich. He's being ripped off by his own manager.'

'He's exploiting you anyway.'

'Exploiting? What does that mean?'

'It means to use someone.'

'Yeah, well, that's what I'm doing. They're paying, aren't they?'

'It's what they're paying for, though. That's being exploited.'

'Doesn't bother me.'

'No?'

Sweet Thing sniffed, shrugged.

'So, are you like him, then?' he asked, nodding upwards.

'Who?'

'Stephen. Are you gay like him?'

'Not like him, no.'

'Like what, then?'

'Well,' she said, 'I've slept with men and women.'

'Can't make your mind up, then?'

'No. It's because I have made my mind up.'

'You like both?'

'I . . .' She thought for a second. 'I suppose so.'

'Takes all sorts.'

'What about you?' she asked him. 'You ever been with a girl?'

'Of course I have,' he lied. 'I'm only gay for pay.'

'Oh yes, Stephen told me. Not bent, rent.'

'That's right.'

'Whatever you say.'

They finished the joint. Sweet Thing stood up. He looked wasted.

'Are you OK?' Nina asked.

'Tired. I'm going to bed.' He smiled. 'Got another day of exploitation tomorrow.'

'Just take care, won't you.'

'Don't worry about me.'

But she did. She couldn't help herself. There was such a stark honesty to him. He didn't believe in 'free love' or sexual liberation. There was no easy political analysis about him, just a bleak sense of survival. He was something else. Utterly ridiculous, contradictory even, but terribly, terribly real. She got up and went over to him. She put out her arms.

'What?' He frowned at her open-mouthed.

'Just want to give you a hug.'

'Oh yeah?' He grinned. 'Is this a hippy thing, then?'

'Yes,' she said, putting her arms around him. 'It's a hippy thing. Don't worry, it's not catching.' He shuddered slightly as she held him.

16

shoplifting at biba

In the morning Nina knocked on Pearson's door. He had already taken the box out from under the bed and opened it. They looked at the explosives and the child's printing set. Nina had a plan.

'We leave the house at the same time but go in opposite directions. That way if there is someone watching the house they'll have to make a decision about which one of us to follow.'

'So we divide up the stuff?' asked Pearson, holding up one of the tubes.

'No.' She shook her head. 'Don't be stupid. One of us carries the stuff, the other one is a decoy.'

'A decoy?'

Nina sighed. It was a pretty stupid idea but it was the best she could come up with. Perhaps Pearson was merely imagining that they were under surveillance, but they had to be careful.

'Look, it gives us a fifty-fifty chance at least,' she told him.

'Right,' he said, nodding.

'And once one of us has dumped the stuff we meet back here.'

'OK.'

'So, are you ready?' she asked, picking out the objects from the box.

Pearson sighed.

'Yeah,' he said. 'I guess.'

'Right,' she said, handing them to him. 'There you are.'

'What?' he demanded.

'Look, I'm under much more suspicion than you. They have watchers at the demo outside the court. They have files on everybody involved in the Defence Committee. They're much more likely to follow me.'

Pearson winced, holding the material away from his face.

'Me?' he complained.

'Yeah, you.'

'Is this stuff dangerous?'

'No. You need a, . . . what do you call it? A detonator. Come on. Let's go. Wait a minute, it'll have our fingerprints on it.'

They found a cloth to wipe down the evidence and wrapped it up in a plastic bag. Pearson put it in his jacket pocket.

'Maybe they know about me and O'Connell,' he said.

'What?'

'That would connect me. Make me a suspect.'

'Pearson, come on, you've hardly ever been that politically involved, have you?'

'Yeah, but you're asking me to make up for it now, aren't you?'

'We haven't got any choice. Come on.'

They went downstairs.

'When we get out of the house you go left, I'll go right. Find somewhere to dump the stuff, don't tell me where.'

'Nina—'

'Don't worry. They're probably not on to us. After all, they would have raided the house by now if they knew this stuff was here, wouldn't they?'

She went to open the door.

'Meet back at the house in an hour. OK?'

Pearson nodded and they made their way out. Just as they

came to the bottom of the front steps a car pulled up on the street directly in front of them. They froze. A thickset man in a suit and tie got out and came around the vehicle to confront them. It was too late to run; he had blocked the front gate.

'Mister Thing?' he asked Pearson.

Pearson stared at the man. He didn't know what to say. 'I . . . I . . . I . . .' he stammered.

'Car for Mister Thing. I have got the right address, haven't I? Pick up from here to take to Paradise Recording Studios in West London. Are you Mister Thing?'

Nina started to laugh.

'Wait a minute,' Pearson told the driver. 'I'll go and get him for you.'

For the first time in months Johnny Chrome woke up looking forward to the day. It was a bright sunny morning and he was ready. Ready to go into the studio. He had a bowl of Frosties and a cup of tea. It had been a long time since he had been able to manage breakfast.

He arrived at the studios feeling full of life. He had got his future back. He didn't know what had happened but he was revitalised. Joe Berkovitch noticed this change in him.

'Are you all right, Johnny?' he asked.

'Never better, Joe.'

'Look, are you on something?'

'No.'

'Let me see your eyes.'

Joe checked Johnny's pupils for signs of amphetamine use.

'I'm just on a natural high, Joe,' Johnny insisted.

'Good. The kid's here.'

Berkovitch called Sweet Thing over. Johnny gazed at him, his once dull eyes now sparkling. He seemed to be looking right through him.

'Hello, Sweet Thing,' said Johnny with a far-away voice.

'Is he all right?' Sweet Thing muttered to Joe through the side of his mouth.

'I hope so, son. I hope so,' Berkovitch muttered back.

Joe ushered them both into the control room. Through the huge glass panel beyond the mixing desk they could see the Chromosomes' rhythm section setting up and an engineer adjusting microphones.

'How are they going to fit two drummers in there?' Johnny asked.

'We don't need to,' Joe replied, 'we can over-dub them.'

'So why do we need two drummers in the first place?'

'It's for the live show.'

'Right.'

'Come and meet your producer, Johnny.'

A frizzy-haired man turned around in his chair at the console.

'This is Frankie Sorba,' Joe Berkovitch announced.

Johnny shook him by the hand.

'I'm going for a compressed, mechanical sound with the percussion,' Sorba explained. 'I'm going to have it really flat. The over-dub will give it a delay but I don't want it like with echo or reverb or anything. I want it the opposite of this drum-solo bullshit. I want it to sound like heavy machinery. Maybe I'll dub in some handclaps, you know, get that football terrace edge to it.'

Johnny nodded enthusiastically. He could almost understand what the producer was talking about.

'We'll do the drums, bass and rhythm. Then we'll do your lead vocal. I want to build everything else around that. OK?'

'Er . . .' Johnny carried on nodding. 'Yeah.'

'Is that all right, Johnny?' Berkovitch asked him softly.

'Yeah. Sure.'

The musicians in the studio were ready to start.

'OK,' Sorba ordered through his microphone. 'Bash it out.'

The rhythm section started to lay down the backbeat. They all sat down to watch. Johnny was transfixed, gently moving his head along to the sound. Sweet Thing slumped in his chair, already bored. Berkovitch felt the pounding rhythm, each beat a moment of studio time invoiced to his management company. He looked over at Johnny, desperately hoping that he was ready to perform. He leant towards him.

'Johnny,' he whispered.

'What?' Johnny breathed, still looking forward.

'You want some time with the kid?' Joe nodded over to where Sweet Thing was sitting. 'You know, to prepare.'

'No, Joe,' replied Johnny, vigilant and self-possessed. 'I'm ready.'

He stood before the microphone as they played the beat back. Shoulders hunched, fingertips touching the headphones that framed his shocked features. He was in a wide-eyed trance of self-hypnotism. He started to sing and a voice came through him as if it had been invoked. Trashy lyrics were delivered like a spell's incantation. Johnny Chrome was a medium, summoning up his own once dead spirit. He was back in the mirror again. He had passed through the glass darkly and was channelling his own reflected image. He had stolen himself back from Sweet Thing's impersonation, a voice like tape-loop feedback that howled out into the ether. The playback was complete. He had become the perfect pop product: the simulacrum, the copy without an original.

Frankie Sorba gave Joe Berkovitch a thumbs-up sign as Johnny came to the end of the track.

'That was great, Johnny,' he said through the microphone.

Johnny stared through the glass at the control room, his face still a mask of concentration.

'Are you OK?' the producer asked.

'I'm OK,' replied Johnny.

'One more for Frankie, then, eh?'

Johnny nodded and they wound back the backing tape. Berkovitch looked over at Sweet Thing.

'I think you can take the afternoon off, son,' he told him.

Sweet Thing's eyes smarted at the bright sunlight after the darkness of the recording studio. The afternoon off. He should have been feeling carefree. Instead he felt empty and useless. Unwanted, and at a loose end. Time on his hands that he didn't know what to do with – it made him feel anxious. There was a hungry foreboding in the pit of his stomach, a yawning fear of the passing day.

Time to kill. He might have gone to the pinball machines at Playland or checked out who was around at the Dilly. But he knew that wouldn't be enough. Something was wrong, something he couldn't pin down. The summer heat was close and oppressive. He broke into a sweat.

Everything should have been all right, he reasoned. He wasn't hungry, or broke, or out on the street. There was no apparent cause for his sense of discomfort, just a superstitious dread. He felt unlucky.

He was nervous but knew what he had to do, where he had to go. The place of sanctuary where he could find peace and calm. He told the driver to take him to Kensington High Street and drop him off outside Biba. He always felt safe there. The most fashionable department store in London. Once he had passed through its black-and-gold art deco storefront it was as if nothing could touch him. He was safe there, amid the decadent splendour, the great poem of display that chanted its many-coloured strophes. Biba's interior was tranquil and seductive, luxurious. He felt utterly at home within its soothing atmosphere of ornate commerce.

He ascended the mirrored stairway into a gallery of voluptuous kitsch. Wood panelling, stained glass, tessellated stone floors, carpets in bold geometric designs. Bronze statues of women bearing lamps, palm fronds spilling out of huge chrome plant holders, gilt mirrors, inlaid display cases. There were peacock plumes, leopard-skin lampshades, bent-wood hatstands draped with feather boas, satins and velvets. Sweet Thing moved slowly through it all; he could relax, he belonged here.

He ignored the menswear section on the mezzanine and made his way to the women's department on the first floor. With his glam style he didn't look out of place. The shop girls didn't bother him or even ask what he wanted. It was part of the ethic of Biba not to hassle the customers; in fact, if you wanted attention it would often take some time to get it. Time moved more slowly here than on the outside and Sweet Thing soon became simply part of the decoration. Some of the assistants looked as outré as he did – one girl with green hair, green lipstick and fingernails smiled over at him in quiet collusion.

This casual ambience and the low lighting conspired to make Biba the easiest place to steal clothes from in the whole of London. It was a hoister's paradise. Sweet Thing loved nicking things from shops, it gave him a buzz, but this was not the cheap thrill of fast thieving. Shoplifting from Biba was a pure, deliciously sensual experience. The art to it was to take your time.

He took a couple of items from the racks and told one of the assistants that he was going down to menswear to use the changing rooms there. He would come back, replace the clothes and take others to try on, carefully selecting his prize as the staff got used to his languid coming and going. In the end he decided on a pair of back-seamed bell-bottomed trousers in ziggurat-patterned maroon and silver lamé and a high-collared blouse with long, gathered-in sleeves in rose satin in a Japanese print. He simply took them out, walked down as if making his way to the lower fitting rooms, then surreptitiously rolled them up and walked out of the building with them.

With a broad grin he half closed his eyes against the sun and made his way to High Street Kensington Underground station. He pressed the soft material to his face for a second and sighed. He felt placid once more.

17

radical drag

News of the atrocity had come that morning. Screaming news-paper headlines and photographs of the scattered and blood-stained luggage in an airport baggage hall. On the night of 30 May a group calling itself the Japanese Red Army, said to have links with the Popular Front for the Liberation of Palestine, had launched an attack with automatic weapons and hand grenades on passengers from an Air France flight that had just disem-barked at Lod International Airport, Tel Aviv. Twenty-five people had been killed, including a dozen Christian pilgrims on their way to the Holy Land. It had been a suicide mission; two of the Japanese terrorists had been shot dead by security forces. Walker was struck by the ruthless ingenuity of the attack. It was pure terror with a barbaric logic to it. An indiscriminate spectacle of death and destruction, heedless of risk, mindless, unstoppable. Some reports used the word kamikaze: the divine wind. Suicide endowed with a higher purpose, an ethereal nihilism. Transcendental horror, a dreadful warning from the future. *Terrors appear'd in the Heaven above and in Hell beneath, & a mighty & awful change threatened the Earth.*

In comparison, the actions of the Angry Brigade seemed pretty feeble. They had been very careful not to cause any real casualties, wanting not to be seen as terrorists. Instead the bombings were like exclamation marks to a political protest. But they had lost the argument; they had already been over-taken by history. Theirs were half-measures that would be lost in the deluge that was to come.

They had played their part in the greater scheme of things. Walker's game with them was nearly over, but he had to pursue it right to the end.

Following people had always been one of his particular skills. It was a procedure that was instinctive to him. From his earliest days in plain clothes he had shown a natural talent for it. Shadowing, tailing, stalking – all the manoeuvres needed to watch a subject while on the move came easily to him. They were not merely a matter of routine but of his own personal craft. Most policemen look like policemen, talk, walk, even smell like policemen, but not Walker. He cultivated a subdued manner, never displaying the telltale swagger of power. He would move with economy, with a quiet determination. The trick was never to think of the subject as prey or quarry but rather empathise with them, enter into the mind of the hunted and see where that would lead you. One technique was not to follow at all but to go on ahead and to predict the direction in which a suspect might be moving. They would rarely think to look in front of them if they thought they were under surveillance. It was important to bear in mind that suspects, by their very nature, are full of suspicion about others.

His spectral manner helped as well. He had an almost negative presence at times. He did not merely blend into a crowd: he could almost erase himself from it. Some people have a knack of drawing attention to themselves. Walker could do the opposite. He had an anti-charisma, his cold, drawn death mask of a face drawing the eye away from it. His ghostly demeanour gave him a lugubrious cloak of invisibility.

He always preferred to work alone if possible. He got better results unencumbered by support from his more flat-footed cohorts. Fellow officers themselves would often find it hard to spot him when he was on a job. Today he had a car following him as he tracked his subject on foot, an unmarked Hillman

Hunter with a couple of Bomb Squad detectives in it. Back-up, if he needed it.

His subject was an amateur. Wary but over-alert with exaggerated gestures of subterfuge that betrayed him, a fugitive posture. He had nothing on file on this man, just a name. Not a suspect himself but incriminated by association. Walker was curious about what the man was frightened of. He was scared and Walker knew that he could use that fear to trap him. He had tailed him carefully for a while, keeping his distance but never letting him out of his sight. The man was using up a great deal of energy and Walker allowed him to wear himself out for a while. Then, when he had found the right place, he passed by him unnoticed, walked on ahead and turned to wait for him.

The man was anxiously glancing over his shoulder, as if frightened of his own shadow. He hardly noticed Walker standing in front of him as he approached.

'Excuse me,' said Walker softly.

The man jerked to a halt and looked up at him, startled. 'What?'

'Stephen Pearson?'

The man muttered something non-committal. There was an awkward attempt at a sidestep that Walker easily intercepted. He was right on top of his man, staring straight into him, trying to judge what he might do.

'Get out of my way,' Pearson said, lunging forward.

Walker blocked him again and pulled out his warrant card. 'Detective Sergeant Walker, sir. Just a quick word.'

The man stared at him, wild eyed. He was thinking of running, Walker could tell. But there was hesitation, too. Just then the Hillman Hunter drew up to the kerb behind him and a detective constable jumped out on to the pavement. Pearson turned around to see a thickset man standing by the car ready to stop him if he tried to escape that way. He looked back at Walker. He was trapped.

'What do you want?' he demanded.

'Like I said, I want to talk to you.'

'You arresting me?'

'No, no. Just a little chat, that's all.'

'And if I don't want to have a little chat?'

'Then I really will arrest you. Do you want that?'

Pearson tried to think what to do. For a moment he felt reckless. The bomb in his pocket, they would find that on him. Evidence. Proof of his bond to O'Connell, it would connect them officially. Not planted, but left like a gift, a token of their union, the perfect symbol of it.

'Come on, son,' Walker went on, gesturing at a café across the road. 'We could just have a sit-down in that caff over there.'

Walker was playing with his man. It was always best to try to get a subject to talk off the record, in informal surroundings, rather than hauling them in and having to follow official procedures. Pearson was playing too. Playing for time. He had to find a way of getting rid of the stuff in his pocket.

'All right,' he said.

'Wait in the car, Tony,' Walker told his fellow officer.

They crossed the road together and went into the empty café.

'Cup of tea?' the policeman suggested.

'OK.'

Walker ordered two teas and went to sit down. Pearson suddenly had an idea.

'I need to use your toilet,' he said to the man behind the counter.

He would get rid of the evidence there, he decided.

'Sorry, mate,' said the café owner. 'We don't have one.'

151

Walker tutted loudly.

'They really are obliged legally to have toilet facilities in a premises serving food,' he said. 'Not much I can do about it, though. Not really my patch. You nervous, son? Is that it? There's no need, you know. Just a friendly talk, that's all. Come and sit down.'

Pearson sat down opposite Walker. Two steaming mugs were brought over and set down in front of them. Walker watched his man shift nervously about on his seat. He had him just where he wanted him. He waited.

'So?' Pearson finally asked after about a minute's silence.

'So.'

'What's all this about?'

'Well, it's simple really. I'm anxious to know the whereabouts of Declan O'Connell.'

Pearson gave a strange hollow laugh. This disturbed Walker. He hadn't expected laughter.

'What's so funny?' he demanded, a little more tersely than he had intended.

'Well, it's a little bit too late for that, isn't it?'

Now his subject was playing with him. Walker didn't like that. He had lost the upper hand for a moment.

'What do you mean?'

'You can't have him now. He's safe from you.'

'What are you talking about?' Walker asked, bewildered.

'Because he's dead, you ignorant fucker. Didn't you know? Not much of a detective, are you?'

Walker narrowed his cold eyes on Pearson. He was really thrown. O'Connell dead.

'Dead?' he demanded.

'Yeah. He was desperate. He knew he'd been betrayed and he couldn't face it.'

'Betrayed?'

152

'Yeah. You were acting on information received, isn't that what you say?'

'Well, you could say that, yes.'

'Well, he's out of your reach now.'

Walker couldn't comprehend what Pearson was saying. He was still dealing with the shock. He struggled to concentrate.

'What?' he asked, bewildered. 'What happened?'

'He killed himself. He was driven to it, wasn't he?'

Walker sighed.

'I suppose so,' he murmured.

He felt an awful sense of regret and guilt. He had pushed his man too far. Now he was dead.

'You left it too late to arrest him.'

'Hang on,' Walker said, suddenly aware of a misunderstanding. 'What makes you think I wanted to arrest O'Connell?'

'Of course you did.'

'Wait a minute. You think that O'Connell was a suspect?'

'Well, he was, wasn't he?' Pearson demanded.

Walker knew then that he had regained the initiative. Pearson had known something that he was not aware of but he knew something that Pearson evidently didn't. This young man was under the impression that O'Connell had been one of the bombers. Perhaps that was what O'Connell had told him. Maybe he had learnt other things as well. Walker knew that the Mole had withheld some important information. It was his way of trying to keep some sense of control over his desperate situation. He had grassed on some people, protected others. Pearson could be one of the ones that he hadn't informed on, one of the bombers that had got away. Whatever was the case, he might know something. Walker could try to get him to talk. If he leant on him a bit. Apply some pressure then offer a way out.

'So O'Connell told you he was part of the Angry Brigade?' he asked.

'No.'

'But you knew about it?'

'Yeah,' Pearson replied quickly, without thinking. 'So?'

'So that makes you an accessory, son.'

Pearson realised that he had incriminated himself. But he didn't care. He felt impetuous, defiant.

'I was more than just his accessory,' he said.

'What?' Walker shifted forward in his chair. He was intrigued.

'I was his lover.'

Walker was caught off guard by this. He leant back in his seat. Pearson glared at him across the table.

'Does that shock you, Officer?'

'No, I . . . I . . .' he stammered.

Of course, Walker had known that O'Connell was homosexual. It was just something he had never really talked about with him. O'Connell had sometimes been provocative about it. Taunting him with comments like: *You really fancy me, don't you?* and *You're not my type, Officer*. Walker had never thought it through beyond its social and political implications. Operational procedures, Special Branch briefings on homosexuals as security risks, speculations on connections between the GLF and the Angry Brigade. He liked to think of himself as being more liberal about it than his colleagues, but he was really quite narrow minded. He had never allowed himself to see an emotional context. *Lover.* That word really did shock him. It was disturbingly intense.

'So,' Pearson went on, 'what are you going to do?'

'Listen, son,' Walker began, not quite knowing what to say. He found it hard to look Pearson in the eye, to meet the challenge of his passionate stare. This man had loved O'Connell but he had been deceived. It was obvious he hadn't known that O'Connell had been a grass. Part of him felt that he should allow Pearson his illusions but he had to know if he had been involved. There were things that still needed to be cleared up.

'Listen,' he went on, 'O'Connell wasn't a suspect.'

'No?'

'No. He was a police informer.'

'What?'

'Yes, son. He was *my* informer, to be precise.'

Walker felt bleak, referring to the Mole in the past tense like that.

'I don't believe you,' said Pearson.

'It's true.'

'No.'

'Why should I be lying?'

'Because you're fucking around with my head. You're trying to get me to say something.'

'No. O'Connell was an informer. A very good one at that.'

'Fuck!' Pearson exclaimed. 'No.'

'Yes.'

Pearson put his head in his hands. O'Connell had been a traitor. He had been the Judas in the story.

The detective looked at him, feeling slightly helpless. Walker was no good at dealing with emotional situations. But he had to keep him talking.

'I'm sorry,' he said softly.

Pearson lifted his head, drew his hands down the sides of his face.

'What do you care?' he asked.

'You'd be surprised. I rather liked him.'

'Why did he do it?' Pearson asked.

155

'He was already working for the Drugs Squad when I met him.'

'You mean he was informing for them?'

'I'm afraid so.'

Pearson felt sick at the thought of all the time his lover had been false and deceptive.

'So he sold his soul to all of you.'

'I don't think he had much of a soul left when I knew him.'

'Bastard!' Pearson hissed.

'You shouldn't be so hard on him. He was in a lot of pain.'

'What would you know about that? You're just a fucking policeman.'

'He was on my beat, you know. You can get to like people on your beat, you can't help getting to know them. It's part of the job. I got to know him quite well.'

'He was your grass.'

'Yeah, but I like to think that our relationship went farther than that.'

'Oh, please.'

'It's true.'

'What was it? The money?'

Walker shook his head.

'It wasn't that. Well, with the Drugs Squad it was so that he could have a regular supply, but with me, well, it was different.'

'I don't understand.'

'It's hard to explain. Look, the best source of information for someone in my position is a disillusioned idealist. And that's what he was. He really believed in it all once, you know? That's what made his disillusion so profound, his cynicism so deep. And he thought he was clever, he really did. He was a bright lad, one of the brightest, but not very clever. You get me? It had all gone too far before he realised it.'

'And he informed on the Angry Brigade?'

'Well, let's say he pointed us in the right direction a couple of times. These people were going to get caught in the end anyway.'

'Was he involved with them at all?'

Walker shrugged.

'He might have been, at the beginning. But I really don't think that he took their actions seriously enough. That's why he worked so well as an informer, if you ask me. He thought that they were just playing at urban guerrilla warfare, just as he thought he was just playing at being a police spy. He was aloof, contemptuous even. He thought he was above it all in some way. That's what made it easy to get him to talk about them.'

'You've really got it all worked out, haven't you?'

'Well, it is my job.'

'And did you work out that he would kill himself?'

'That I didn't foresee, no.'

'You say you got to know him well?'

'Quite well, yes. We talked about all sorts of things.'

'Personal things?'

'Sometimes, yes.'

'But he never talked about me?'

'You, son? Lord, no.'

'He said nothing about me?'

Pearson had become agitated. Walker tried to reassure him.

'Don't worry, son, he didn't pass on any information about you.'

'Yeah, but . . .' Pearson spluttered. 'He didn't mention me at all?'

It was then that Walker saw that in a strange way Pearson would have like to have been mentioned. To have been acknowledged. He had obviously been through a lot. It couldn't have been easy to have been that close to O'Connell.

Now he had to cope with all this. He wished that there was something consoling he could say but there wasn't.

'He never mentioned you, no.'

'Right.'

'I never realised . . .' Walker began clumsily. 'Well, he always struck me as a bit of a loner.'

'Well, you were right there,' Pearson said bitterly.

Walker felt uncomfortable. He wished that he could just leave this man with his grief. But he couldn't.

'Just one thing,' he said.

'What?'

'Certain items were in the possession of O'Connell.'

'Items?'

'Evidence.'

'Evidence?'

'A small amout of explosive material.'

'Oh, yeah,' said Pearson. 'We got rid of that stuff when we cleared out his room.'

Pearson wasn't quite sure why he lied about this; he just felt the need to keep something back for himself. To hold on to something.

'You sure you got rid of it all?'

'Yeah.'

'Where?'

'Where?'

'Yes. Where did you get rid of it?'

'I chucked it in the river.'

Walker looked at the man. He should really follow this up. Maybe get a warrant and search the house. But he was softened by a sense of pity. He had put this man through enough he decided. His own sadness was affecting his judgement, he knew that, but at that moment he wanted to be a little unprofessional.

'What was O'Connell doing with that stuff?' Pearson asked.

'It's best that you forget about all of this, son,' Walker said. 'For your own good.'

'Oh yeah?'

'Yes, Really.'

'And that's it, is it?'

'It is, son, it is,' said Walker, standing up. 'Thank you for your cooperation. I'm really sorry about what happened, you know. Now if you want to get in touch with me . . .' He took out a card. 'I'm on this number.'

Pearson stared at it.

'Why would I want to do that?' he demanded.

'Well, you know. Anything that might come up.' Walker shrugged, trying earnestly to appear amicable. 'If you just want to talk.'

'I wouldn't want to talk to you.'

Walker saw how Pearson looked at him and realised how appallingly clumsy his attempt at sympathy was, how ghastly he must appear to him.

'Right,' he said.

Walker held out the card. Pearson made no move to take it. In the end the detective placed in on the table.

'I'll leave it here, then,' he said, and walked out of the café.

Nina waited all day for Pearson. She came back to the house at the appointed time but he wasn't there. At first she managed to stay calm. It had taken him longer than expected, that was all, she reasoned to herself. But as the day dragged on with no sign of him her mind began to go into overdrive, multiplying the possibilities of what might have happened. She tried to distract herself but she couldn't help concentrating on their predicament with ever increasing unease. There was nothing she could do except wait and worry. At times she cursed

Pearson, imagining that he had maybe just wandered off on one of his long walks. At other moments she was convinced that Pearson had been caught and felt guilty that while she was still safe, she had let him take the blame for it all, and left him to face the consequences on his own. Her mind reeled as the clock patiently scored the minutes, the hours. She felt deranged with anxiety, an awful desperate nausea in the pit of her stomach.

It was a quarter past seven when she heard the front door slam. She rushed down the stairs with a sudden surge of hope. She met Sweet Thing in the hall.

'Have you seen Stephen?' she demanded, breathlessly.

'No.'

'Fuck.'

'What's the matter?'

'We're in trouble, that's what. Shit!' she exclaimed.

'What's going on?'

'Look, it might not be safe here. You should find somewhere else to stay.'

'What?'

'Get out, for fuck's sake,' she hissed.

'Wait a minute.'

'I mean it, Sweet Thing, I'm fucking serious.'

'You just want to get rid of me, don't you?'

'It's not that.'

'Yeah you do. You never wanted me here in the first place.'

'Jesus Christ, Sweet Thing!' she exploded. 'This isn't a fucking game!'

'Don't shout at me! I've got as much right to be here as you! You can't push me around!'

'Listen—'

'No! I ain't listening to this.'

He pushed past her and stormed up the stairs to his room. Nina sat on the stairs and sighed.

'Shit,' she said to herself as she heard his door slam.

She spent a few minutes with her head in her hands, trying to compose herself. She went up and knocked on his door.

'Go away,' she heard him say.

She opened the door anyway and walked into the room. Sweet Thing was sitting on the bed, brooding.

'I'm sorry,' she said.

He glowered at her. She was trembling.

'I . . . I . . . didn't mean . . .' she stammered.

All the tension suddenly broke inside her. She began to sob. Sweet Thing's glare became a frown as he watched her crying. He stood up and went over to her. He didn't know what to do.

'What the fuck's going on?' he asked.

She looked at him. Her eyes were bright with tears. She swiped at her face and tried to get control of her shuddering body. She grabbed hold of Sweet Thing's arms as if to support herself.

'Look . . .' she began to say, then broke into a whimper once more.

Sweet Thing reached out awkwardly and held her in his stiff arms. He felt her quiver in his embrace. She gasped and pulled back.

'We really are in trouble, you know,' she said.

'What is it?'

'Stephen found some things in O'Connell's room.'

'What things?'

'Stuff for making bombs.'

'Fucking hell.'

'He was going to get rid of it but he's not been back for hours.'

'So?'

'So he might have been caught with it. He thinks that the house was being watched.'

'Shit.'

'Yeah. That's why I was telling you to get out. We could be raided by the Bomb Squad.'

'But you said he's taken the stuff away.'

'It's just not safe here until I know what's happened.'

'Then why don't you go?'

'I've got to wait for Stephen. I can't just go. But you can.'

'I ain't got nowhere else to go.'

'Sweet Thing—'

'Look, you said yourself you don't know what's happened. Let's just wait and see.'

'But it's dangerous.'

'I want to stay.'

He forced a smile.

'Unless you really do want to get rid of me,' he went on.

She smiled back at him.

'Of course not,' she said. 'But if anything does happen make sure you get your story right. Tell them that you're just crashing here. You don't know anything about this. OK?'

'Sure. You don't have to worry about me. I'm used to lying to the police.'

She sighed. 'Well, we'll wait, then. It's been driving me crazy.'

'Why don't we have a joint? It'll calm you down.'

'I don't think I can roll one. I'm still all shaky.'

'Show me how to do it.'

He got the things from the front room and brought them upstairs. She taught him how to skin up and they shared a smoke sitting on the bed together.

'I got something to show you,' he announced when they had finished.

'What?'

'Get up off the bed,' he directed her. 'Turn around.'

With her back to him he quickly changed into the clothes that he had stolen from Biba. He checked himself in the mirror for a moment.

'Right,' he said. 'I'm ready.'

She looked around to see him shimmering in satin and Lurex. He grinned at her, his eyes sparkling with delight. She broke into a tremulous laugh.

'Wow,' she murmured.

'What do you think?'

'You look fantastic.'

'Yeah, well . . .' He shrugged, parading up and down the room.

'How much did these cost you?' she asked, inspecting his new garments.

He rolled his eyes and tutted at her.

'What do you think?'

'You nicked them?'

''Course.'

'Sweet Thing, these are women's clothes.'

'So? They fit me, don't they?'

It was true. They hung from his slim body perfectly. He looked fabulous.

'They'd probably fit me too,' she speculated.

'You want to try them on?'

She smiled shyly and shook her head.

'Don't be silly,' she said.

'Go on,' he implored her. 'You know you want to.'

'All right, then. Come on,'

'What?'

'Take them off.'

'Turn around, then.'

163

'Come on. Don't be shy.'

She pulled at the clothes and he giggled bashfully.

'Careful,' he chided her.

She started to undress herself.

'What are you doing?' he asked.

'What does it look like. I'm going to try on your clothes.'

He turned his face to one side and she pulled off her jeans and T-shirt.

'You're a funny one,' she said.

'What?' he muttered, chewing his lower lip nervously.

'What have you got to be embarrassed about?'

He looked at her. He took in her tightly curved naked body, her small breasts high and firm with dark upturned nipples. He glared at her transfixed as she unbuttoned his blouse.

'Come on,' she said. 'We're just dressing up.'

It was like a child's game. Nina felt all the fear and desperation of the day mutate into playfulness. She felt giddy and capricious. She shucked the shirt from his lean torso. His flesh was snow white, almost translucent. It quivered at her touch. She looked at his face. There was a guileless, demure look in his eyes. An awkward modesty in his demeanour and something sad and serious in his gaze. She had never seen him like this before. She took the satin blouse and turned from him.

'Go on,' she said. 'I won't look. You can put my clothes on if you like.'

He slid out of the lamé trousers, wiggling his hips; the waistband caught on the beginnings of an erection. He picked up Nina's jeans and T-shirt and quickly changed into them. He handed the Biba trousers to Nina.

Nina stepped into the flared legs of the bell-bottoms and tugged them up. They were tight around her hips, the middle seam pulled snugly into the crease of her arse and cut smoothly into her crotch. She ran her hands down the shiny material, feeling slightly turned on by the way the lamé girdled her.

She glanced at herself in the mirror. She was dressed in pure decadence. These clothes were the trappings of bourgeois exploitation, the apparel of hedonism and luxury, of course. But they felt wonderful on her. They made her feel sexy. She turned to Sweet Thing.

'How do I look?' she asked him.

'Yeah,' he said with a smile. 'You look all right.'

'I do, don't I?'

'Come on,' he told her. 'I'll make you up.'

'What?'

'I'll do your face.'

'But I haven't got any make-up.'

It was true. She had given up cosmetics in 1969.

'Yeah,' said Sweet Thing with a short laugh. 'But I have, haven't I?'

He sat her on the edge of the bed and knelt down in front of her. He took an odd collection of beauty aids from a plastic carrier bag. Lipstick, eyeliner, eyeshadow. He framed her face with his hands and looked at her thoughtfully. Then he started to work, carefully applying the stuff, murmuring to himself in concentration. For a final touch he took a vial of glitter and dabbed little star systems of silver dust on her cheeks.

'There,' he said.

She got up and went over to the mirror again and stared at her reflection. She was mesmerised by her own transformation. There was something magical about it, a metamorphosis. Radical drag. It subverted how she habitually saw herself, how she thought and felt about her own body. Now she looked alien and voluptuous, desirable. For an instant she was free of the body she inhabited. She was a different person, a disguise.

In this moment of alchemy she turned to Sweet Thing. Her T-shirt was tight against his sleek upper body. He was broader than she had expected, his baby-butch shoulders hunched slightly, his hands clenched and his wiry arms threaded with veins. He was transformed too. He had wiped the make-up off his own face and it looked scrubbed and glowing. Maybe he was blushing, she couldn't tell. A boyish man or a mannish boy, he still looked as pretty as a girl but handsome now as well. It was sublimely absurd. For a second here was everything she could possibly want. A fine down of hair traced his curling upper lip.

'You look good naturally, you know,' she told him.

'Well, you look good with make-up. I know it's not, you know . . .' He shrugged, searching for the word. '. . . political but . . .'

She laughed.

'It's personal,' she said, mostly to herself.

She didn't want to have to rationalise this moment, to explain it. That would be ludicrous. It wouldn't make sense to anybody else. It was something happening just to them. As they gazed at each other across the room there was a feeling of transfiguration, of transmission. An urgent desire overcame all her thoughts of caution or responsibility or consequence.

'Come here,' she instructed him.

'What?' he said.

'Come here,' she repeated and he came to stand in front of her.

'Kiss me,' she said.

He leaned towards her and clumsily pushed his lips against hers. Kissing wasn't something that he was particularly good at. Punters didn't usually want to kiss so he had never spent much time developing it as a skill. Nina took his head in her hands, pulled him close and showed him how it was done.

Her mouth moved with soft insistence against his. Her tongue pressed against his teeth, prising open his jaw. Her hands raked down his neck and chest. She reached down and peeled the T-shirt from his slim body. It hooded his face. He gasped as she licked his tiny nipples and he pulled the cotton from his face and dropped it on the floor.

Nina unbuttoned the satin blouse, letting her breasts fall softly towards him. Sweet Thing was mesmerised by them. With a look of wonder on his face he reached out and gently touched them. She pulled him to her and he nuzzled his face in her bosom. His mouth found a nipple and he suckled at it with a blind craving for comfort. Her body tingled with strange pleasure as he sucked at her desperately. With a shrug she let the blouse drop from her shoulders. She grabbed the metal button on the jeans and began to unzip him. She felt his hardness through the cloth as she tugged the denim off him.

He ran his hands down the warm flesh of her back and they slipped against the polished surface of the glossy fabric that tightly encased her buttocks. He cupped her smooth curves and she sighed indulgently.

'Wait a minute,' she murmured, pushing him away.

She undid the satin trousers and wriggled free of them. They stood naked before each other. Open mouthed and panting, he gazed at her with nervous fascination.

'I . . . I . . .' he stuttered, struggling to catch his breath. 'I never. . .' He shook his head.

She smiled at him. 'It's OK,' she whispered. 'I know. I know you haven't been with a woman before.'

'It's not that. It's . . .'

He couldn't explain it to her. It wasn't that he had never had sex with a woman. It was that he had never had sex without being paid for it. He had never made love, not really.

He started to try to say something but she kissed him on the mouth.

'It's all right,' she breathed. 'You don't have to prove anything.'

But he did. Up until that point he had always been in some sort of control. Often by simply blanking out what he was doing and concentrating on the transaction. He had kept all his feelings well locked up for years. He was scared of letting them free. He felt her soft flesh yielding and adhering to his own. A fearful tremor ran through his body.

They fell on to the bed. She wrapped her legs around him and brought her hips up to his. She arched her back and guided him to her. He groaned as he felt the hardness of her pubic bone grind against the soft head of his cock, then a sigh whistled through his teeth as it was swallowed by a tight sheath of wet flesh. Her breath came in measured gasps moderated by the rhythm of her thrusts. She held his haunches and watched his bewildered face as he moved inside her.

He began to push with a tight little motion, his narrow hips fitting into her perfectly for a second. She felt propelled into a heedless loss of control. Suddenly something happened. Something connected. A shock ran through her.

'Oh God!' she called out.

'What's the matter?' he huffed breathlessly, holding back for an instant.

'Don't stop,' she insisted.

She let go of herself and began to shudder frenziedly. The vehemence of her movements and sounds stunned Sweet Thing.

'Oh God!' she exclaimed again as an exquisite oscillation began to pulse through her.

Oh God, she thought, momentarily holding out against what she realised was happening to her. Why was she calling out to something she didn't believe in? Now of all times. Then she came.

Pearson walked and walked. Thoughts turning, spinning, falling through his head. He hadn't been left with much. There was hardly anything left to trust or be sure of. He had believed in O'Connell. What was there to believe in now? All those stupid things O'Connell had said. All those clever words and grand gestures. They were empty, meaningless. He had been a fraud all along. It had all been some stupid game. And this had been his final practical joke. Playing at Judas. Playing his last great trick on the world. But Pearson was the one who had been tricked. He had been O'Connell's fool. He had been taken in by his lies. He had been betrayed by him.

His mind raged at the treachery of it all. Maybe it had all been a lie, everything that had passed between them. He desperately searched in the past for something he could be certain of. Some memory to hold on to. It was all under suspicion now.

What was true and what was false? He couldn't be sure any more. He was even beginning to lose touch with what was real and what had been imagined. All the hopes and dreams he had had about O'Connell and their relationship may have meant nothing. O'Connell had just been in love with his own selfish self-pity. He had meant nothing to him, nothing really. He had been . . . What was the word the cop used? An *accessory*, yes, that was it. An appendage, a thing. An audience for his performance of self-destruction. Well, it had nearly destroyed him too. And it was driving him mad.

He reached the river as the sun collapsed behind the tower blocks to the west, its blood-red light diffused by nebulous clouds like a dying star going supernova. He walked across a bridge and looked down into the swirling brown water. This was where he had decided to dump the stuff. He hesitated for a moment. He thought briefly that he might throw himself in. Into the dirty river. But no, he wouldn't do that. That was a coward's way. His way. He would do something else. He would show O'Connell. He would show them all.

He reached into his pocket for the sticks of gelignite. He fingered the explosives gently; there was something strangely reassuring about their very weight and substance. They were real at least. This was all that he had been left with. They were evidence. These were the forensics of his attachment to O'Connell. An unexploded bomb. Love is an infernal machine, thought Pearson.

It was getting late and he started to head home. The fiery sky above, the heavy hell of evening. O'Connell was damned and he had been damned with him. It was all too much for his mind to bear. He needed help. He couldn't cope with all this on his own.

He would have to talk to someone or he would go out of his mind. He would talk to Nina. Yes, he decided. That's what he would do. She had said that he could talk to her. She would be worried, anyway, about what had happened to him. Yes, they would talk. He would tell her all about it and she would understand. It would be all right – he was just going a little crazy, that was all. It wasn't surprising given all that he had been through. A cup of tea and a chat. Maybe a joint as well. He could get it all in perspective, calm his fevered brain.

It was nearly dark when he trudged back to the squat, exhausted. He called out for Nina as he opened the front door. He went upstairs. There was no sign of her. Maybe Sweet Thing was in and would know where she was. Perhaps he could spend some time with the kid – it might take his mind off things. He could enjoy Sweet Thing's provocative beauty. His simple desire for it could make him feel real. He knocked softly on his old bedroom door. No reply. He pushed the door and wandered in. They were naked on the bed. His old bed. Nina lay with Sweet Thing curled up beside her. They were asleep.

'Right,' he said.

Nina opened her eyes and began to sit up. She stared at Pearson guiltily. He looked at them both, his eyes burning with hurt. This had been taken from him as well. It was a ghastly mockery of his unrequited feelings for Sweet Thing. She had betrayed him too. He might have known. He couldn't trust anybody any more.

'Pearson,' she whispered.

He turned around and walked out of the room. She followed him out on to the landing.

'Pearson,' she said again. 'Wait.'

He went into O'Connell's old room and closed the door behind him. Nina knocked on it.

'Leave me alone,' he called to her.

He threw himself on to the bed and began to sob gently.

18

swimming

Pearson slept fitfully, tormented by dreams. It was a humid night and when he woke at seven the sun was already up, burning down on the world. He sat up in bed. He thought that he could hear them moving about in the next room, that he could hear their voices in his head. His mind felt so crowded.

He got dressed and went downstairs to the kitchen. He lit the gas and filled the kettle. He switched on the radio. The news announced that the US bombing of North Vietnam was being intensified. President Nixon declared that he was sending more B-52 Stratofortresses to bolster a seven-hundred-strong strike force. An American air force general had declared an intention to bomb North Vietnam 'back into the Stone Age'.

He turned off the radio but voices still came. They spoke of bombs. The bombs of reason coming crashing down to earth. Pearson splashed some cold water on his face and tried to concentrate. He was tired, that was all. His mind turned again on what the policeman had told him. He should tell Nina about it. But he couldn't go up there. He thought he heard them talking again. Talking about him, laughing at him.

It was so bloody hot. He needed to clear his head. He would go for a swim, he decided. It had been such a long time. He found his trunks and a towel, stuffed them into a duffel bag and went out. As he crossed Euston Road he felt the sun blast his face. It hurt his tired eyes. There was a fresh graffito on a wall in Gower Street. NOTHING IS TRUE EVERYTHING IS PERMITTED.

'That's a stupid thing to say,' Pearson said out loud.

'No it's not,' came a voice behind him.

Pearson turned around quickly to see who had said it but they had gone, whoever they were. The changing room was cool and damp. A scent of chlorine cut through stale bodily smells that hung in the air. It was like a cleansing process coming for a swim, Pearson thought. The exercise would do him good, empty his mind. As he walked through to the poolside his eyes fixed on the sign. It was a communiqué. A message to him. WILL PATRONS KINDLY REFRAIN FROM. All the things one wasn't supposed to do. *Everything is permitted*, the slogan had said. RUNNING, PUSHING, ACROBATICS AND GYMNASTICS, SHOUTING, they were permitted. BOMBING, PETTING, DUCKING, SWIMMING IN THE DIVING AREA, SMOKING, they were permitted. THANK YOU! declared the sign

'You're welcome,' said Pearson as he waded through the foot bath.

Nothing is true. The illustration next to BOMBING showed a man curled up in a fetal position, hurling himself recklessly at the water. Bombing is permitted, thought Pearson, and he padded along the wet tiles to the water's edge. Shrill noises echoed on high against the vaulted concrete ceiling and were compressed into hisses along the walls as if in a whispering gallery. Voices. Pearson dived into the deep end, into the silence. All the screaming stopped as he swooped down. He felt tranquil, the pressure of the water tight against his body, holding him. In an arc he ascended, swimming underwater for as long as he could, until the air burned in his lungs. As he broke the surface he rolled on to his back so that his ears were still immersed in a serene deafness. He sculled along, flapping his arms like wings. The sun was streaming in through the skylights, dancing on the shifting water, molten flashes of fluid. He felt held aloft as he floated, as though he were looking below rather than above, as if he were flying. Yes, he thought, flying is permitted.

The velvet curtains glowed red, ripe and heavy with sunlight. Nina groaned at the morning, feeling Sweet Thing holding on to her. His bony frame was drawn into itself, pale skin marbled with blue veins, his blood-purple mouth suckling gently at her shoulder. She touched his face softly.

'Hey,' she breathed.

Blue eyes blinked at her, alert with amazement, his shoulders clenching suddenly with trepidation.

'What?' he gasped.

'It's OK,' she whispered, not wanting to frighten him. 'Shh.'

She sat up in the bed. *Christ*, she thought. *What have I gone and done now?* Her head was full of regret and anxiety but her body felt warm and tranquil. Sweet Thing reached out to her clumsily, like a hatchling following the first thing that it sees moving. She took his hand in hers and looked him in the face. His mouth hung open slightly, his eyes wide and curious. He looked lost. She suddenly wanted to reassure him. She kissed him tenderly on the mouth. He gave out a plaintive moan as her lips brushed against his. He ran his tongue down her neck and into the notch where her collar bones met. His mouth found her breast and closed on the clustered flesh of her nipple. It stiffened as he kissed it. She drew in a breath sharply.

'Wait,' she hissed, grabbing his hair.

She struggled for a moment, her hand making a fist in his blond scalp, holding on, holding back. Sweet Thing groaned then sucked harder. Nina felt a shiver run right through her. She let go, her fingers curling open, her mouth widening in exhalation. She felt delirious, drowsy and languid, last night's hashish still buzzing through her flesh, the lingering traces of her climax glowing embers within her. She quivered at his touch with an almost unbearable sensitivity, sensed a visceral closeness to him. She felt more than naked, as if overnight she had shed her skin and exposed raw nerve endings, sparking and charging up her desire once more.

Sweet Thing trailed his tongue down along her torso, feeling the soft lineaments of her form, pliant and yielding, drawing him in. Driven by an inquisitive lust, he wanted to know what this was, discover this secret. His mouth reached her pubis. He hesitated. He wasn't quite sure what to do. Was it the same as sucking cock? he wondered. He started to lap at her cunt. It shuddered as he licked it. It tasted musky and metallic. He found a hard nub and caught it between his lips.

Nina gasped, her hips bucking against Sweet Thing's face. She lifted herself up and pushed him back, grabbing his shoulders and and making him lie on his back. She raked her fingers over his smooth, hard body, strumming the contours of his ribcage, squeezing his haunches. His cock bobbed erect against his belly, its base wreathed with gold-wire hair. Kneeling above him, she bowed down and kissed the head of it. He let out a guttural moan. She traced her tongue along its shaft, then followed the seam of his scrotum to his perineum. She pushed his legs up, moistened a finger with her mouth and pushed it against his delicately puckered arsehole. It pulsed, contracting and then relaxing as Sweet Thing sighed out heavily and let his body collapse into submission. She straddled him, pressing her groin on his, feeling his prick slide along the groove of her cunt, slicking against it in smooth frictionless strokes.

He reached up to her and she grabbed his arms and pinned them back above her head. She moved her hips, tilting them around his hardness, finding the spot. She pushed down to take him inside her once more. He let out a short, throaty cry, looking up at her wide eyed and exposed. He let himself be taken by the urgency of her movements, possessed by her hunger. He felt her grind into him, felt helpless in a way he had never known before.

She gripped his arms more tightly, and pushed her weight forward. Her thrusts became frenzied; she could feel it coming again. She clenched her teeth and concentrated, driven by an urge to know it once more. As she started to come Sweet Thing was taken along by her desire and began to spasm beneath her. His mind darkened as she shuddered above him; he felt himself orgasm, but it was as if the pleasure didn't really belong to him.

They lay together bathed in sweat from the heat of the morning. The scent of their bodies hung heavily in the room. Nina's mind was calm and blank for a while. She tried to hold on to the still silence for as long as she could. She soon became anxious.

'Are you OK?' she whispered to Sweet Thing.

'Yeah,' he croaked. ''Course.'

'I've got to get up. You want a bath?'

'In a bit.'

She kissed him. His lips were cold, as if drained of blood.

'We need to talk,' she said.

'What about?'

'About this.'

'What's there to talk about?' he asked.

She tried to think about what she could say. She didn't know. She got up from the bed.

'Later,' she suggested.

'Yeah,' Sweet Thing replied with a shrug. 'Sure.'

She bathed and got dressed as Sweet Thing dozed in the bed. Pearson had gone out already. She needed to know what had happened, whether he had any trouble in getting rid of the stuff from O'Connell's room. He had looked so wild and strange the night before. He was angry at finding her and Sweet Thing together. It was understandable but it wasn't really fair. She went over to the bed. She patted Sweet Thing softly on the shoulder. He rolled over and looked up at her.

'I've got to go,' she told him.

'Mm,' he replied.

He looked pale and delicate. She thought about kissing him again but instead she reached down and touched his cheek, then turned and walked out of the room.

Sweet Thing lay on his back and looked at the ceiling, thinking about what had happened. He tried to calculate it as a transaction in his own terms but he couldn't. It was more than he had bargained for, but less too. There was a sense of disappointment, as if he had missed something. Something that he couldn't quite figure out. He yawned and touched himself, wondering for a moment whether he would feel anything different about his own body. There was still a trace of her warmth in the bed, the smell of her in the sheets, but it was as if she had left an imprint on his skin, his flesh marked with contact with hers.

There had been a warmth and softness that had comforted him. He now felt sickened with a need that he could not obey. He felt at a loss, helpless and scared for a moment. He blinked at the daylight and rubbed his face, trying to ease such thoughts from his head. It would never do to feel like this, he reasoned. He had to keep on top of it. After all, it didn't really matter. This was what people like them did all the time. Free love. It was all right, as long as he didn't let it fool about with his mind. He had to be in control of things, after all. This wasn't something that he could afford to mess about with. He rolled over again, heavy and lethargic, his body like left luggage. Free love, he thought with a twinge of dread, it might cost him dearly.

He got up and phoned Joe Berkovitch. Johnny Chrome was having a photo-shoot that afternoon. Joe said he would arrange a car to pick Sweet Thing up and take him to the photographer's studio.

Sweet Thing went to the bathroom and washed. He looked at himself in the mirror, studying himself. He'd had sex with a woman but it had been different to how he had imagined it. This was what was supposed to make you a man, he thought to himself. He had supposed that it would make him feel normal, but instead it made him feel odd. It was his first time, he reasoned to himself, he would have to get used to it. But he found it disconcerting that rather than making him feel hard and strong, it made him feel soft, weak.

He flexed his body before the looking glass, trying not to think about it. He shivered and rubbed a rash of goose bumps on his arms. He remembered being held by her. The consolation of her embrace. He stared hard at himself, made a tough little face. He had to go to work.

He took a long time to get ready. He stiffened his hair with lacquer spray, forming it into a spiky crown. He carefully applied make-up, delicately coating himself with a protective layer. A freckling of glitter on his cheeks. He turned his head to see how the cheap stardust caught the light. He put on his Biba drag and his red platform boots. He looked fabulous, a decorated shell. He felt empty inside. Hungry for something. But why should that matter? He looked like he meant business. He went downstairs and waited for the car to come.

19

metal guru

'The new single's being pressed,' Joe Berkovitch told Johnny in the back of the car on the way to the photo-shoot. 'It'll be in the shops next week.'

'That's soon.'

'Well, the record company have been waiting for it. We've got to get the promotion going. *Jackie* magazine wants to do an interview on Monday.'

'Oh, Christ,' muttered Johnny.

He hated being asked questions.

'Don't worry, it'll just be your favourite colour, that sort of thing.'

'Right.'

'It's just the start of it. We need to hire a publicist. We want to be in all the magazines, the music press, telly.'

'It's all happening so fast, Joe.'

'Well, the bandwagon's rolling and we're on it. Glam is where it's at. David Bowie's new album's out and he's just started a tour. Everybody's talking about it.'

'Is he the one that says he's gay?'

'Yeah.' Joe sniffed. 'Publicity stunt, I reckon.'

'I ain't saying I'm gay, Joe.'

'Don't worry. You don't have to. It's just about being flamboyant.'

'Flamboyant?'

'You know, theatrical. Bowie does all this arty stuff. With you it'll be more . . . well . . .'

'What?'

'Well, like vaudeville.'

'Comic?' Johnny winced.

'No, not comic. Er. . . .' Berkovitch mused. 'Cheerful.'

'Cheerful?'

'Yeah, cheerful. Uplifting.'

'OK.'

'And you can afford to be,' Joe told him. 'We're going places with this.'

Berkovitch sat back in the passenger seat and sighed. It was going to work, he was convinced of it now. Last week he hadn't even been sure that they would be able to deliver Johnny Chrome's second single to the record company. His act had looked burnt out then, now it was catching fire again. All sorts of plans started to take shape in his head. Johnny would record an album with the Chromosomes. They would tour late summer or early autumn to coincide with the third single. And then – yeah, of course, he thought – a Christmas record.

'Joe,' Johnny interrupted his reverie.

'What?'

'I want to talk about where we're going.'

'We're going to the photo-shoot, Johnny.'

'No.' He coughed. 'I mean our deal.'

'Not this again, Johnny.'

'Come on, Joe. We need to sort it out.'

'It's been sorted out.'

'Yeah, but I don't think I'm getting enough.'

'Enough? What are you talking about?'

'I don't know, Joe. Maybe just get someone to have a look at the contract.'

'You don't trust me?'

'It's not that, Joe.'

'So.' Berkovitch let out a loud demonstrative sigh. 'This is the thanks I get.'

'Joe—'

'I picked you up when you were just one of Larry Parnes's cast-offs. I got you work all that time when nobody else wanted to know. I looked after you, didn't I?'

'Yeah, well.'

'I made you, Johnny. And this glam thing, it was my fucking idea. You wouldn't be Johnny Chrome if it wasn't for me. You wouldn't have this success if it wasn't for me. And now it's gone to your head and you want to get rid of me.'

'It's not that, Joe. I'm grateful for all you did.'

'But now you want a new manager, is that it?'

'No. It's just the deal, that's all. Even the kid thinks I'm being ripped off.'

'The kid?'

'Yeah, Sweet Thing.'

'Sweet Thing? You've been talking about our business affairs with that little punk?'

'Well, he's a clever boy.'

'Yeah, well, maybe you should get that seventeen-year-old rent boy to represent you.'

'He does, sort of.'

'What are you talking about?'

'He does, er, sort of represent me. He understands Johnny Chrome.'

'Oh, I get it. You mean that funny little performance he did with you so that you could get your mojo working again.'

'Well—'

'And all the other things he does for you. An underage boy. The press would love that.'

'What do you mean?'

'I mean scandal, Johnny. I've kept all your naughty pro-

181

clivities nice and quiet, haven't I? Well, if I'm not needed any more the public might find out what you're really like.'

'Please, Joe—'

'Why not? If I'm being cut out of this deal why should I keep my mouth shut?'

'Please, Joe,' Johnny whispered. 'You wouldn't.'

'You think it's easy looking after you? I've organised everything. You'd fall apart without me.'

'Joe—'

'Stop the car!' Berkovitch called out to the driver. 'Pull over here.'

The car slowed down and drew up to the kerb. Johnny Chrome uttered a forlorn groan.

'Right,' said Joe. 'You want me to get out here? You can deal with everything on your own if you're not happy.'

Johnny started to sob quietly.

'What's the matter?' Joe demanded.

'I'm sorry, Joe. I didn't mean I didn't want you as my manager.'

'What, then?'

'It's just . . .' Johnny swallowed. 'It's just I thought I'd be seeing more money, that's all.'

'You will, Johnny, you will,' Berkovitch insisted softly. 'You've just got to be patient. We've got to think of the long term. It's in your best interests, believe me.'

He gently patted his client on the shoulder.

'Yeah?' Johnny sniffed and wiped his face with the back of his hand.

'Yeah. Look, what more do you want? You've got success, fame. You've got a nice place to live. You've got your little boyfriend. You know I'll get you anything you need. So what can I get you?'

'There is one thing, Joe.'

'You name it, Johnny.'

'I want to buy my mam a house.'

'What?'

'My mam. I'd like to get her a place of her own. She's lived all her life in a crappy council house in Swansea. If she had her own house it would make her so happy, and so proud of me.'

'All right,' said Joe.

Johnny blinked at his manager, his eyes bright with tears. 'Yeah?'

'I tell you what,' Berkovitch told him. 'If we get in the top ten with this single we'll get your mother a house.'

'Really?' Johnny grinned.

'Really.'

'Thanks, Joe. I'm sorry about . . .'

'Don't worry about it, Johnny. You're just highly strung, that's all. OK, driver!' he called out. 'Let's go!'

Nina arrived at the Old Bailey. She felt light-headed, her mind detached from the demonstration. There were vivid faces, voices raised in earnest intensity. She tried to concentrate on what they were saying but she was distracted. The jury had been sworn in, someone was saying. The defence had made objections that might work in their favour. Three of the eight defendants were representing themselves and would need support in the courtroom. They were allowed volunteers – 'McKenzie helpers', named after some legal precedent – to assist their advocacy. Could she help? She shrugged and shook her head. She didn't know or wasn't sure.

She suddenly felt uneasy about the demo. Finding out about O'Connell had compromised her. The protest was about defending people who had been charged with conspiracy and not about getting involved with any covert direct action. The whole point of the Defence Committee was that it acted openly, it wasn't clandestine and secretive like the Angry Brigade. She considered talking to somebody on the committee about what they had found in the house but decided it probably wasn't a good idea.

She was also aware of the high level of surveillance around the court. If something really had gone wrong she was exposed here, vulnerable. She cursed Pearson for not letting her know what had happened.

The sky was darkening. The sun raged amid the gathering clouds, which were burning at their edges, gold and purple. The heat was oppressive, the air heavy with moisture. Billowing thunderheads were forming. Some of the people in the demonstration were already furling up and taking down banners in preparation for the coming deluge.

'It's going to piss down,' someone remarked.

A man came over and talked to Nina. He told her that one of the defendant's alibis was that she had been at a GLF demonstration in Fleet Street at the time that the prosecution alleged she had gone to France to collect explosives. They needed witnesses. Had she been on that demo? Nina shook her head.

'No,' she muttered. 'I wasn't there.'

Then she thought of something.

'Wait a minute,' she said. 'I think I know someone who might have been.'

Jan, she thought. Jan may have been there. She would talk to her. Thinking of Jan suddenly made her feel guilty about Sweet Thing. She wished she didn't feel that way but she couldn't help it. She didn't want to have to explain herself or make sense of it. Not yet anyway. Instead she concentrated on the fact that she could do something useful and that she had an excuse to get away from the crowd and out of the coming rain.

*   *   *

Sweet Thing arrived at the photographer's studio as Johnny was having his hair and make-up done, ready to be shoe-horned into his stage costume. The photographer needed a stand-in to check the lighting and the backdrop. He asked Sweet Thing to pose in front of the camera tripod.

'You look fantastic,' he told Sweet Thing. 'Are you in the band or something?'

'I'm Johnny Chrome's personal assistant,' he replied, robotically.

'Well, you should be out there, you know.'

The photographer arranged the umbrella-shaped reflectors around him.

'You ever done any modelling?' he asked the boy.

Sweet Thing nodded. 'Yeah. Once.'

He'd been picked up by a guy who had done some nude shots of him. For the 'juve market', he had told him.

'I'm going to shoot a roll of you, if that's OK,' said the photographer.

'Yeah,' muttered Sweet Thing. 'OK.'

He looked frail and innocent as the lens shutter chattered away, his delicate face framed by a back-lit halo.

'I'll let you have a couple of shots, if you want,' the photographer told him.

Sweet Thing shrugged, listlessly. 'OK.'

'You should really think about modelling. You've got the looks for it. Something special.'

Johnny Chrome felt anxious. He was still a little shaken from his argument with Berkovitch in the car. He took a couple of Mandrax and swilled them down with a glass of tap water. He emerged from the dressing room staggering across the floor on his six-inch platform boots.

'Good Lord,' the photographer muttered under his breath.

Johnny froze in the centre of the studio.

'What's the matter, Johnny?' Joe asked him.

'I want the kid,' he croaked.

Berkovitch beckoned to Sweet Thing to come over. Johnny reached out to him as if to steady himself. He stroked the boy's arm gently.

'You look lovely,' he whispered.

Johnny stared at the boy. Sweet Thing found it hard to meet his gaze. He didn't usually feel this uncomfortable. It was as if he were looking right into him.

'How do I look?' asked Johnny.

'You look . . .' The boy coughed. 'You look great, Johnny.'

Johnny smiled and nodded.

'Right,' he announced. 'Let's get started.'

Joe Berkovitch went over to Sweet Thing once the photo session had started.

'All right, son?' he asked.

'Yeah.'

'So what's this you've been talking to Johnny about?'

'What?'

'About his management contract.'

'I ain't said nothing.'

'Well, you made some clever comments in my office the other day. And now Johnny tells me you reckon he's being ripped off.'

'Well, he is, isn't he?'

'No, he's not.'

'He never seems to have any money on him.'

'I take care of it for him.'

'Yeah,' said Sweet Thing. 'I bet you do.'

'Look, son, don't wind things up. Your job is to keep Johnny happy.'

'So?'

'So, keep your mouth shut. Look . . .' Joe took out a wad of money and handed it to the boy. 'Here's next week's fee.'

'Right.'

'No more discussions about his career, OK?'

'OK,' said Sweet Thing, and pocketed the cash.

'And another thing.'

Joe pulled out an LP and handed it to Sweet Thing. The boy looked at it. It was David Bowie's *The Rise and Fall of Ziggy Stardust and the Spiders from Mars.*

'Smooth,' muttered Sweet Thing with a smile as he fingered the cover.

'It's just been released. Everybody's talking about it. Have a listen to it. Tell me what you think.'

'What do you mean?'

'You know. Ideas. Anything we might borrow. You know better than anyone what this glam thing's supposed to be.'

'OK.'

'So I want some instant market research. Know what I mean?'

'Yeah,' replied Sweet Thing, still staring at the album cover. 'I guess.'

The storm was building, charging up in the sky. Pearson felt the suffocating intimacy of the day. He had been calm after his swim. His mind had cooled down for a while. Then the heat and humidity bore down on him once more. Heavy clouds swagged low over the horizon, pressing down on the city, brooding over him. He felt clammy and restless, feverish in his thoughts. He had to work out what to do now; all he felt was nervous excitement, an awful anxiety in his febrile brain.

A vein of lightning pulsed through the bruised sky. He felt a palpable relief as the pressure fell suddenly and the first fat drops of rain spat on the hot pavement at his feet. Thunder followed quickly, its percussion rolling through the streets. *It sounds hungry*, he thought. *Like a huge stomach rumbling. It could eat the whole city*. The atmosphere was already cooler, with a smell of washed tar, a hint of ozone in the air. The sky earthed itself once more and a discharge of light froze the city for a second in a ghostly image. *Shock treatment*, thought Pearson, *that's what's needed*. The whole ugly sprawl convulsed with electric therapy, cured of its madness.

Thunder came again and Pearson imagined explosions, bombardments. A sign from above. It was marvellously dramatic. It soothed him. The rain came down in a torrent. People ran to doorways for cover. Pearson kept on walking, drenched by the cloudburst, feeling calm, determined.

Sweet Thing went back with Johnny after the photo-shoot. They sat in the car together. Johnny looked drawn and tired.

'I reckon those Red Indians are right, you know,' he said.

'What?'

'About photographs. They reckon if you have your picture taken it steals your soul.'

'Yeah?'

'Yeah. That's how I feel after all that.'

Johnny leant back and tried to relax. The rain drummed insistently on the roof of the car, sounding like distant applause. White noise. He clutched the boy's knee. Sweet Thing winced slightly. He looked at the back cover of the album Joe had given him. Bowie was in a phone box staring out at the night, looking beautifully lonely, one hand on his hip, the other gently touching a glass panel of the booth. Sweet Thing tapped the image lightly with his fingertips as if he were making contact with it.

When they got back to Johnny Chrome's house they sat and watched *Top of the Pops*. Johnny opened a bottle of white wine and poured them both a glass. He took the pills from his pocket and swallowed two of them.

'What are they?' Sweet Thing asked.

'Downers,' replied Johnny. 'Want some?'

'Yeah, all right.'

Johnny handed the boy a couple and Sweet Thing chased them down with the sweet wine. T.Rex was number one with 'Metal Guru'. Sweet Thing's eyes brightened as Marc Bolan came on to the screen, tossing back his mane of corkscrew curls, screwing up his painted elfin face as he howled the screeching ululation of the intro. Johnny noticed Sweet Thing gazing intently at the performance.

'You like him, don't you?' he asked moodily.

'Yeah,' murmured Sweet Thing absently, staring all the time at the telly. 'He looks good.'

'You think he's pretty?'

Sweet Thing turned and frowned at Johnny.

'I said he looked good,' he replied indignantly. 'I didn't say I fancied him.'

'Just asking.'

'Yeah, well.'

The programme came to an end. Johnny got up and switched off the box. He sighed. Sweet Thing held up the album.

'Let's put this on,' he suggested.

'All right,' Johnny agreed.

Johnny sat back in the white leather sofa and closed his eyes. He drifted off for a bit, the opening drum pattern like a heartbeat in the womb, soothing his head. Lyrics spoke of a coming apocalypse and the thought of it all drawing to an end comforted him.

When the fourth track, 'Starman', came on Johnny opened his eyes and looked at Sweet Thing.

'Go on,' Johnny implored. 'Dance for me.'

Sweet Thing got up and began to move to the music. Johnny got off the sofa and clumsily joined in. At the chorus Sweet Thing casually draped his arm around Johnny's shoulder. Johnny misinterpreted the gesture and pulled Sweet Thing into an embrace. The boy pushed the man away and he fell back on to the sofa.

They listened to both sides of the album. Johnny cried softly at the end of 'Rock 'n' Roll Suicide'. That was the way to go, he pondered sadly. It was a beautiful record; the emotion of it touched him but he couldn't really understand it. The kid could get it but it was beyond him. It was full of secret messages transmitted on a frequency that was way out of his range. His own songs were just a joke in comparison, but Joe Berkovitch was right, they could cash in on it somehow.

Johnny Chrome felt empty. He could never be as good as Bolan or Bowie. He was much farther down the food chain. He was absurd. He knew what he needed. He stood up and went to the middle of the room.

'Come here,' he whispered to Sweet Thing.

The boy came over and Johnny knelt before him in supplication. Like the condemned man before his executioner. Sweet Thing shuddered as the man took him in his mouth. He couldn't block things out as well as he had done before. Sex with Nina had messed up his head. It hadn't mattered so much before, it had just been an act. Now if seemed real. He closed his eyes and tried to think about her but it didn't work. It felt raw and painful, like he was being swallowed whole. Awful memories of what had been done to him flashed in his head. Johnny pulled back his head and looked up at him.

'Your hands,' he whispered hoarsely.

'What?' said Sweet thing, bewildered.

'Give me your hands,' Johnny insisted.

He took the boys hands and put them around his neck. 'That's it,' he panted. 'Squeeze.'

He did what he was told and Johnny put his mouth around Sweet Thing's penis once more. The boy started to thrust at Johnny's head as he gripped his throat. The violence of it helped him concentrate. He tried to give Johnny Chrome all his pain, cursing and gritting his teeth.

Johnny's head swam. He wanted oblivion. He wanted the tape wiped clean. He wanted to be obliterated, just the kid's energy pulsing inside him, possessing him. He was trash but this would be spectacular. He would take Sweet Thing inside him, become him and shrug off Johnny Chrome like a snake shedding his skin. He would become glam, kitsch but spectacular. He was on stage, the orchestra pit empty, like an open grave. A gallows beneath the proscenium arch. He started to choke. He saw stars, flashes of glitter behind his eyelids. His head exploded, vaporised into stardust. He blacked out.

'Shit!' Sweet Thing exclaimed as Johnny went limp on the floor.

The boy crouched over the prone form. He slapped his face.

'Come on,' he implored. 'Wake up!'

Sweet Thing went into the kitchen and filled a glass with cold water. He came back through to where Johnny lay. He threw the water in his face.

Johnny sputtered back into life. Consciousness flared up in his head like a sunburst. He blinked at the light and his head strobed with energy. He felt revitalised, resurrected. He looked up at Sweet Thing and grinned.

'That was great,' he drawled.

Sweet Thing stood above him. He shook his head.

'Fucking hell, man,' he said. 'I thought you were dead.'

'Maybe I was. Just for a bit.'

'Yeah, yeah,' Sweet Thing muttered, and picked up the phone. 'I'm calling a cab.'

Johnny sighed, lifting himself up from the floor. 'It felt wonderful.'

'You're fucking weird,' the boy said as he dialled. 'You know that?'

'You don't have to go, you know. You can stay if you want.'

Sweet Thing frowned. 'Nah, I'm going.'

Johnny collapsed on to the sofa, dazed and trembling. When Sweet Thing had gone his head began to throb and his tired flesh ached. His old self was flooding back into his body. The high he had felt was over and he was back down to earth. He groaned softly and reached for the Mandrax.

20

the wise old queen

Nina sat in the kitchen and watched the rain against the window. Rivulets of water snaked down the glass. The house was empty, just her and the cat. She had placed a saucepan underneath the brown patch on the ceiling of the upstairs landing where they had never managed to stop water coming in. She could hear the drops tinking against the metal, echoing like sonar through the hallway. *This squat is going to get damp in the winter*, she thought.

She had checked the street periodically to see whether anyone was watching the house. There was no sign of anyone out there but how could you really tell whether you were under surveillance? They could be anywhere. She had phoned Jan and arranged to meet her at a Stoke Newington Eight benefit gig on Saturday night. She thought again about moving into the commune. It would make sense. She was exhausted from all that had happened in the house in the past few weeks.

Pearson came in at about six o'clock, drenched from the storm. He was bright eyed and shivering, his mouth curled in a rictus of a grin.

'Jesus, Pearson,' she said. 'You're soaked through.'

He chuckled through chattering teeth.

'I'm all right,' he declared.

'Where have you been?'

'I've been for a swim,' he said with a cackle. 'Good day for it, don't you think?'

'What's the matter with you?'

He frowned.

'Nothing's the matter,' he replied.

'Pearson—'

'Don't worry, Nina. It's OK.'

'But what about the stuff?'

Pearson looked puzzled.

'The stuff?'

'Yeah. You know, the stuff we found in O'Connell's room.'

'Oh, that.'

'Yes, that. Did you get rid of it?'

'Yeah.'

'And you didn't have any trouble?'

Pearson thought for a moment. No, he wouldn't tell her. He couldn't trust her. He couldn't trust anyone any more. He had to be careful what he said.

'No,' he replied flatly. 'No trouble.'

'And do we know if we're being watched?'

'Watched?'

'You know, you saw that car outside the house the other night.'

He shrugged. 'Yeah, well, maybe it was just a car.'

'What?'

'Maybe I just imagined we were being watched.'

Something was up with Pearson, she thought. He was being elusive. Maybe he was being off with her about Sweet Thing, about seeing them both in bed together.

'Look,' she said, 'about last night—'

'Last night?'

'You know . . .'

His face suddenly darkened as he remembered seeing them naked together. He recalled the hateful jealousy he had felt. But he couldn't let it get to him. Not now.

'That?' he said. 'That? That doesn't matter.'

'Look, I'm sorry.'

'You're sorry?' he said indignantly. 'You're sorry for me?'

'No, I just meant—'

'I'd rather you weren't sorry for me, Nina.'

He was sick of all the pity that people felt for him. The pity he had felt for himself. He had had enough of that. He turned and walked back out into the hall.

'Pearson,' she called after him.

But he ignored her and slowly mounted the stairs.

Sweet Thing sat in the back of a taxi as it drove through the city. His head throbbed as streetlights strobed past the passenger window. Night was coming down. The rain had stopped but the streets were still wet and slick, like black vinyl. He didn't want to go back to the squat, not yet. He told the driver to drop him at Piccadilly. The Circus, the pagan circle of Eros, the Dilly. He felt at home here beneath the blazing advertising hoardings, ENJOY COKE and CINZANO. A firework display. He shivered slightly as he emerged into the cold air; there was a chill in the luminous evening. He went to Playland, its slot-machine calliope rattling through his head discordantly. He felt dull and weak; the downers Johnny had gave him deadened his will but sharpened his senses to the dissonant noises and the harsh scintillance of illumination.

He went over to Fire Queen and slotted a couple of florins into the pinball machine. His hands shook against the flippers and he lost the first two balls without much of a score. The clatter of the machine rattled him, he couldn't concentrate. He gave up after the third ball. He had lost the knack somehow. It was a bad omen.

He staggered out back into the night. He felt that he had to keep moving. If he were to stop and turn around, he might see something unbearable. The grim shadow of his memory was

195

following him. He mustn't look back. A shudder of sadness ran through him. Just the cold, he told himself. He wrapped his thin arms around his body. He had to hold it together. Feelings that he couldn't understand were spilling out of him.

No pinball to concentrate on, no Biba to shoplift from, what could he do? He was tired and empty. He felt a hunger without appetite. He wanted to get away from where he was. Speed, that was what he needed. That would take him somewhere else fast, give him an escape velocity to break free of the awful gravity he felt in the pit of his stomach.

He saw the boys at the meat rack. He recognised some of them. Angel was there, Chick and B.J. The silly names they called themselves, their posturing display and exaggerated mannerisms. He had once thought that he was cleverer than they were. But they knew more about themselves than he did. His lack of self-awareness had worked in his favour before. Now a dim trace of knowledge glimmered somewhere and it unnerved him.

'Hey, Sweet Thing!' Angel called out to him.

'Where have you been?' asked Chick. 'We haven't seen you for ages.'

'Haven't you heard?' Angel cut in. 'He's got a sugar daddy.'

'Wow,' Chick murmured. 'Is that right?'

Sweet Thing shrugged. He was in no mood for chatting.

'What's the matter, baby?' Angel asked him.

'I'm just tired.'

'Been working hard?'

'Yeah. I need some speed. Is Tony the Dealer around?'

They found Tony and Sweet Thing bought a bag of amphetamine sulphate for them all. They took turns to snort it in the toilets of a late-night café. Sweet Thing cut out two long fat lines on the top of the cistern and sniffed them up with a rolled-up fiver. He felt the corrosive drug sear into the membrane of his nostrils, burn into the synapses of his brain. He tilted his head back and snuffled; bitter mucus trickled down the back of his throat. He swallowed and licked his lips. He felt the rush coming on, the buzz through his skull as he clenched his jaw. Yeah. This would give him the edge he needed, accelerate the deadly kerb-crawling hours, the vagrant minutes. Fast forward. Street-life time travel.

The boys were sitting huddled in a booth at the front of the café, jabbering away on the sulphate. Sweet Thing went over and stood by their table. So many things he wanted to say, to try to explain, but they were telling stories, rumours and gossip, punters they'd conned, the endless misadventures of their young lives.

'What's up?' Angel asked, looking up at him.

'I got to go.'

'Why?'

'Something I got to do.'

'Oh yeah?' Angel enquired archly.

They called after him as he walked out of the café, stupid comments, gestures and laughter. Then they turned back to their furtively animated conversation.

The lights of the Dilly looked extra sharp now he was speeding. He felt their coruscating iridescence. Constellations of somnambulant pleasure. The myriad burning filaments had drawn him in once. The glitter of the signs that had once signalled some sort of hope. Hope that seemed a cheap thing now.

Drunks and tourists, tarts and dirty old men. Junkies in a huddle outside the twenty-four-hour chemist's. Sweet Thing wandered through them, his head throbbing with a dull insistence. He saw it all clearly now, his night vision keen but indifferent. A state of numbed lucidity. He'd seen it all before. And he didn't care. His mind was sparked up, bright as neon. He was ready to work.

Faces passed slowly by. A flicker of eye contact here and there. He saw how they looked at him, how they saw him. He returned their stares with a listless gaze and a sullen flare of his nostrils.

'You want a cup of coffee?' a middle-aged man asked him.

Sweet Thing knew what this meant.

'Yeah,' replied Sweet Thing. 'Why not?'

'Come with me, then.'

The man led him to his car, which was parked in a side street. He drove them to a mansion flat in Earl's Court.

'Here we are, then,' the man announced as he opened the front door and turned on the lights.

He wore a purple cashmere V-neck, white flared slacks and brown loafers. He looked older than he had under the street lamps.

'I'm Walter,' he announced.

'Sweet Thing.'

'Charming. Shall we have a proper drink?'

'If you want.'

Walter went to get a bottle of brandy and two tumblers.

'Make yourself comfortable,' he implored.

Sweet Thing slumped on to a sofa. Walter handed him a glass and poured out a couple of inches of spirit. He sat down next to him, one hand holding his own glass, the other snaking around the upholstery to rest on the nape of the boy's neck. Sweet Thing's shoulders spasmed. The man patted him gently. Sweet Thing leaned forward and took a gulp of brandy.

'Are you OK?' asked Walter.

Sweet Thing swallowed and sighed, breathing the spirit's vapours. Another gob of speed-phlegm trickled down his throat. He felt the brandy glow inside him, his face blushing with its infusion.

'Yeah. What do you want to do?' he demanded.

'Well,' said Walter, stroking Sweet Thing's curved back, 'we can talk for a bit, can't we?'

'If you want.'

'You seem a bit out of sorts.'

'I'm fine.'

'I know what it's like, you know.'

Sweet Thing turned to look at the man.

'What do you know?' he asked.

'I used to be, um, well, a professional.'

'A what?'

'You know.'

Sweet Thing squinted at the man incredulously.

'You?'

The man gave a bitter little laugh.

'Well,' he mused, 'it was a long time ago. I was quite a looker in my day.'

'Yeah?' Sweet Thing mumbled.

'Oh yes. But you know what they say: today's trade is tomorrow's competition.'

'What's that supposed to mean?'

'What you used to sell when you were young, you end up buying when you're old.'

'I don't know about that,' Sweet Thing muttered, picking up the brandy once more and draining it with a slurp.

Walter sighed. 'Of course not. Another one?'

He picked up the bottle. Sweet Thing nodded and held out his glass.

'I'm not predicting your future, you know,' Walter went on as he poured. 'You have to find your own way.'

'I just do it for the money, mate.'

'Of course.'

'I've got a girlfriend,' The boy announced. 'I live with her.'

Sweet Thing liked the idea of this. It made him feel secure.

'Good for you. Does she know what you do?'

'Yeah. She's cool about it.' Sweet Thing took another sip of brandy.

'Well, that's good.'

'Yeah. So what do you want to do?'

Walter put his glass down and stood up. He held out his hands.

'Come here,' he said, and he pulled Sweet Thing up from the sofa.

'You really are a sweet thing, Sweet Thing,' he said, stroking the boy's hair. 'You think I'm just an old queen but I'm a wise old queen. I can see right through you.'

'What?'

'You're a lost boy. You think you're tough and you're clever but you're lost. You've got to find yourself, Sweet Thing.'

'Look, mate, shall we just get down to business?'

Walter sighed. 'If we must. I just want to touch you. To lie with you. I need the company. I'm so fucking lonely.'

Sweet Thing shrugged.

'If that's what you want,' he said.

Walter led Sweet Thing into the bedroom and undressed him. He took off his own clothes and got into bed. He lifted up the covers and patted the mattress.

'Come here,' he whispered, and Sweet Thing got into bed beside him.

Walter groaned mournfully as he pawed at Sweet Thing, as if palpating the tactile memory of his own lost youth. He craved contact with something irretrievable, murmuring soft words in the darkness, counting out the spent years in his mind as he touched the boy.

Sweet Thing lay supine and inert and tried to detach his mind from the attentions being paid to his body. Walter soon drifted off into sleep and Sweet Thing turned away from him and curled up on the edge of the bed. He wanted to rest for a while, but his head reeled with speed and reverberated with the words Walter had said to him. He was used to punters talking, they would come out with the most ridiculous things, but the old queen's comments had disturbed him. They interfered with his mind, and that was much worse than someone just messing about with his body.

He had to find himself. What did that mean? That he was queer after all? It takes one to know one, that's what they always said. Sex with Nina hadn't been what he had expected. It wasn't like those gleaming images he'd focused on in the past to concentrate his mind when he had done it with men. He had wanted the affection, the comfort of being close to her, but it was a distant yearning. The act itself had a desperate urgency that he couldn't connect with, a ferocity he hadn't expected.

He could understand a man taking his pleasure, the easy currency of that, but he couldn't imagine being in command of it himself. It had been so simple when it had been for money. It had made sense. But without that he was lost. And maybe Walter was right, one day when he was old and ugly he would pay for it himself. There was a dreadful logic to this equation, an auditing even – the books would one day have to be balanced. The thought of it appalled him.

He got out of the bed and padded about the room, retrieving his clothes. He found a wallet in the back pocket of Walter's trousers and pulled out a sheaf of notes. He let himself out of the flat and crept out into the night.

* * *

Nina couldn't sleep. She had begun to worry about Sweet Thing as it got late and there was no sign of him. She realised that she felt protective towards him. She cared about him but she didn't know what to do with this feeling. It was a ridiculous situation. She had acted impulsively, overcome by the passion of it. She felt mocked by her own desires.

She was concerned about Pearson as well. He had been behaving erratically on and off for some time, but now he seemed in such a strange mood. Maybe he was having some sort of breakdown. She turned in her bed, trying to slow her mind down and submit to her own tiredness, trying to find a way into sleep.

She heard the front door slam at three in the morning. She slipped into a pair of jeans and a T-shirt and went downstairs. Sweet Thing was standing on the landing, wraith-like and trembling. He stared up at her, his wide eyes glimmering in the darkness.

'Sweet Thing,' she whispered, descending the last few steps to stand in front of him. He reached out to her and stumbled forward. She caught him and held him in her arms. He started to rock to and fro in her embrace and gave out a strange animal whimpering.

'Hey,' she murmured, holding on to him.

His breath came in heaving sobs, as if he was struggling for air. Nina pulled back from him. His eyes glistened with tears.

'Can I sleep in your bed?' he gasped.

Nina sighed.

'Sweet Thing,' she said. 'Look—'

'Please,' he implored.

She didn't think that she could deny him, given the state he was in. There was a weary resentment of the sense of responsibility that she now found herself burdened with.

But it was her own fault. She would have to deal with it somehow.

'OK,' she agreed, and took him upstairs.

He burrowed into the bed next to her, as if he were trying to hide.

21

life drawing

Sweet Thing had slept heavily, dreaming away the anxieties of the previous night. His ability to blank things out from the past was a necessary skill he had learnt. So many things he had to forget. He always had to think of the future, of the next main chance. It was another day, he was rested and ready for it. He felt calm and warm, curled up tight in Nina's bed. She had left him there, alone in its refuge. Her absence allowed him to speculate on luxurious possibilities. Restful thoughts of an easy life, a bit of peace and quiet. He could relax for a while, but he was already working out in his mind how he could make this situation work for him. Instinctively calculating what the trade was. He had a vague notion of her looking after him, taking care of him. He had no idea of quite what he would have to do in exchange for this, just a simple sense of opportunity.

He stretched out on the bed, enjoying the acquisitive pleasure of occupying somebody else's space. For a moment he had a thought that was peculiar for him: that he could be safe here. He so rarely felt like this, and then only in transient situations, like when he was in Biba. He could settle for a while. He could even give up the street, he thought. He was getting too old for it, after all. Maybe he could try something else. Modelling perhaps – that photographer had said that he had the looks for it.

He got up and looked through his clothes, searching for his money. He counted out the two stashes he had carefully secreted. Eighty-four pounds and twenty pence left from the ton Joe had given him and forty-five pounds that he had taken from the queen last night. Near enough a hundred and thirty quid. He saw a dressing gown hanging on the back of the door. He put it on and checked himself in the mirror. He looked rather good in it, he decided. He stuffed the cash in one of its pockets and went downstairs.

As he wandered into the kitchen he pulled the gown tight around his skinny hips and let it fall open slightly at the front. He affected a sultry expression, hooding his eyes and curling his lips.

'Hi,' he said huskily.

As Nina looked up at him her face creased into a frown.

'Sweet Thing, that's my dressing gown,' she complained.

'Yeah,' he replied, caught off guard. 'Well –,'

'Don't you think you ought to be getting dressed in your own clothes?'

'I just thought . . .'

With a shrug he arched his torso and put his hands on his haunches.

'What?'

She seemed tetchy and impatient. This wasn't working, he realised. Maybe women were different from men in how they responded to a come-on. He really didn't know. He sat down at the table next to her.

'Well?' she demanded.

'Nothing. Is there any tea?'

She gestured abruptly. 'There's some in the pot. Help yourself.'

He poured himself a cup then held up the pot.

'Want some more?' he offered.

'No thanks.'

He added milk and shovelled in four spoonfuls of sugar. He ventured a grin in her direction. She smiled thinly back at him.

'I'm starving,' he declared.

'Well, there's nothing in the house. We've run out of kitty money.'

'That's not a problem,' he said with a hint of triumph.

He pulled out his wad of cash and peeled a few notes from it.

'Here you are.'

Nina stared incredulously at the thick sheaf of bills in his delicate hands.

'Sweet Thing, for goodness' sake.'

'Goodness has nothing to do with it,' he retorted. 'Go on, take it.'

He pushed the money across the table towards her. He felt good handing the cash out like this. It gave him a sense of power.

'Sweet Thing, really.'

What was the matter with her? What did her sort of people have against money, for God's sake? What did they think, that they could get through life for free? He suddenly felt resentful. He was the only person who seemed to be doing any work in this house, after all. He left the notes on the table and stood up.

'What's wrong?' he asked. 'You think it's bad money, don't you?'

'It's not that.'

'Yeah it is. But you've got to make it somehow, you know.'

'I'm sorry,' she said. 'I'm just not in a very good mood this morning.'

What did that mean? he wondered. Had he done something wrong? She had been so tender towards him, now she was so awkward and cold. He couldn't work it out.

'Right,' he said with a nod. 'I'm going to get dressed.'

*　　*　　*

Johnny Chrome woke up at ten in the morning with an awful barbiturate hangover. The phone was ringing, hammering away at the inside of his skull. He groaned and reached across blindly, trying to grab the shrill device on the bedside table. The handset clattered to the floor and he crawled to the edge of the bed, feeling for it among a pile of dirty clothes.

'Johnny?' He heard Joe's voice emitting from the receiver, tinny and distant. 'Hello? Johnny?'

Johnny followed the faint drone with his hand. He found it and pulled it up to his face.

'Yeah?' he grunted.

'Johnny?'

'Yeah.'

'It's Joe.'

'Yeah.'

'Are you OK?'

'Yeah.'

'Did I wake you up?'

'No,' replied Johnny. 'Well, er, yeah.'

'It's good news.'

'What?'

'We're on the playlist.'

'What?'

'"Hey Hey" is on the playlist. Radio One and Capital Radio. They love it. We're on our way, Johnny.'

'That's great,' Johnny croaked, trying to muster some enthusiasm into his voice.

'Yeah, it is. The record company's happy. They think we could go top ten on advance orders alone. I'm hoping for the new-release spot on *Top of the Pops*.'

'Yeah?'

'Yeah. We've got a busy week ahead of us. Lots of promotion and that. Get some rest this weekend, yeah?'

'Sure.'

'Are you all right?'

'Yeah, I'm fine.'

'You want me to get the kid to come over?'

Johnny thought for a moment. His mind felt like lead, his body old and sluggish. He just wanted to blank the day away, get back to the warm void of sleep.

'No,' he said to Berkovitch. 'I'll be OK on my own.'

'Well, you rest now, eh?'

'Yeah, Joe.'

'See you Monday, then.'

The phone clicked dead and purred a dialling tone. Johnny put it back on its cradle. He sat up in bed and rubbed his face. He would have to try to take it easy with the pills. He would need to keep it together; he'd got it now, what he had to do. His great spectacular performance. He would need all the energy he could muster for that. Then he could have a long, long rest.

He got up and took a shower. The hot jet hissed into him, bringing him back to life. He towelled himself down and looked in the mirror. His eyes were puffy and bloodshot. He brushed his teeth and rubbed some cold cream into his face. There was something that he had to do and he needed to look his best for it.

He got dressed and did his hair. He took his time over it, grooming it lovingly. He liked the soothing rake of the comb against his scalp. He worked the top into a high pompadour and teased the sides and back so that they flared out around his neck and shoulders. He was ready.

He picked up the phone and dialled. It rang three times and then came the voice, plaintive and familial:

'Who is it?'

'It's me, Mam,' Johnny said softly.

She sighed. 'Johnny. It's you.'

'Yes, it's me.'

'It's been a long time, son.'

'Sorry, Mam. I've been busy, see? Got a new record out.'

'Oh, Johnny. Are you all right?'

'Yes, Mam.'

'They treating you well?'

'Yes.'

'So when am I going to see you?'

'You might see me on the telly again.'

'Yes, but when are you coming home, Johnny?'

Johnny felt a melancholy spasm in the pit of his stomach.

'Soon, Mam,' he replied, holding back a sob. 'Real soon.'

Pearson felt a lot calmer than he had the day before but he was still full of energy. His mind had entered an organised state of madness. Everything around him conspired to make some sort of sense. He felt imaginative, inspired. It hadn't been like this for such a long time. He felt creative. He wanted to start work on something.

Sweet Thing wasn't in his room that morning so he took the opportunity to sort out some of his materials. A stack of his canvases was leaning against the wall. He pulled a few of the smaller ones out. He might as well get rid of the rest, he reasoned. He hardly had any room for them, after all. There was a portfolio of drawings and a few sketchbooks. He pulled them on to the floor of the bedroom and started to leaf through them. He hadn't looked at this stuff for months.

It had been a while since any of this had meant much to him. It had all been so important once. O'Connell had dragged him down, made him feel cynical about things. He had once had a higher purpose. It struck him that he could return to that now. That what he was planning was a work of art. He just wasn't quite sure how he would execute it yet.

He was curious to look at some of his early stuff, as if to remind himself of something, and was surprised by the boldness of some of his juvenalia. There were ideas here that he'd completely forgotten about. Studies for some notion or image now lost and unrealised. Art had been so exciting and engaging then. A way to affect things, he had thought, to change them. He had believed too that it was a medium that he could apply to his own life, that it would somehow make him free. He had tried to rough out his own future, draw an outline of it. These time-weathered scraps of paper were a smudged record of the past now. They had once been his plans, he remembered wistfully. It had all been so innocent then. Now he would embark on a bold and shocking work. Something conceptual. A real happening.

He found the first sketch he had made of O'Connell, in that life-drawing class when they had first met. He smiled dolefully and shook his head. He had got him wrong even back then. He had enhanced O'Connell's proportions slightly, idealised his features to make him a little more handsome than he actually was. What had he been thinking as he drew this? he wondered. Had he already been dreaming of the man rather than trying to capture the truth? Had he, right from the start, wanted the person to resemble the drawing rather than the other way around?

He was so absorbed for a moment that he hardly registered the sound of footfalls in the hallway. He looked up. Sweet Thing was standing in the doorway with Nina's dressing gown loosely wrapped around him.

'What are you doing in here?' the boy muttered suspiciously.

'Just sorting out some of my stuff.'

'Oh.' Sweet Thing yawned.

Pearson started to gather up the work. Sweet Thing looked down at the floor.

'You an artist, then?' he asked.

'Not really,' replied Pearson. 'I went to art school.'

Sweet Thing bent down and peered at the drawing of O'Connell.

He pointed. 'Who's that?'

Pearson felt an embarrassed urge to cover the picture. He didn't want to talk about him to Sweet Thing. He didn't want to betray his vulnerability. Besides, he reasoned, the kid got freaked out about dead people.

'No one,' he said, a little too hastily. 'Just a model.'

'He's naked.'

'Yeah, well, life models usually are.'

'How much do they get paid for that?'

Pearson tried to remember. Thirty shillings an hour was the rate that O'Connell used to earn back in the sixties.

'Oh, about one pound fifty an hour, I think.'

'One pound fifty an hour?' Sweet Thing exclaimed, his sleep-lidded eyes suddenly opening wide. 'For nude work? You've got to be kidding.'

'It is in the interests of art, you know.'

'Yeah?' The boy shrugged, pulling the gown around his shoulders. 'Well, art's cheap.' Pearson burst out laughing.

'What's so funny?' Sweet Thing demanded, walking over to the bed.

Pearson shook his head.

'No,' he said. 'It's good. You're right. Art is cheap.'

The boy sees it all, Pearson thought. He sees how cheap the whole world is. Sweet Thing perched himself on the end of the bed and rubbed the back of his neck. He looked drowsily ethereal, as if softened and lightened by sleep. Pearson gazed at him, for a moment entranced by his languid radiance.

'What?' Sweet Thing quizzed him with a delicate squint.

'I could draw you,' Pearson suggested.

'Oh yeah?' Sweet Thing retorted with an impudent pout. 'You gonna pay me?'

Pearson sighed and began scooping up his drawings.

'No, Sweet Thing. I'm not going to pay you.'

'Hey,' the boy said gently, 'I was only kidding.'

Pearson looked up again.

'You want me to draw you?' he asked, tentatively.

'Yeah. Sure. I ain't going to take my clothes off, though.'

Pearson smiled at him.

'Don't worry,' he said. 'You're fine as you are.'

Pearson dragged a chair over, found a pencil and sharpened it. He sat with a sketchbook on his lap and studied the boy. He asked him to turn slightly to the right. He lined up his aim on Sweet Thing's half-profile. The stub of wood and graphite trembled in his hand. He chewed his lip. It had been such a long time he wasn't sure he still had the knack for it.

'Turn your head a little bit more,' he said. 'That's it.'

The light caught the edge of the boy's cheek, casting his face in softly hued contours, illuminating his flesh. Pearson started to mark out shape and proportion on the pad. Sweet Thing was a better model than he had imagined. He thought that he would fidget but he maintained a marvellous stillness. Pearson suspected that this was due to exhaustion rather than patience, but the kid looked serene. Pearson roughed out an image, working quickly in a trance of transfiguration.

A mood of tranquil concentration descended upon the room. Sweet Thing felt unusually calm. He wasn't used to being observed in such a steady and detached manner. He knew so well the reptilian scan of trade, the furtive ogling of the punters. This was different. There was a gentle attentiveness that was somehow soothing. In the quietude of repose he lost track of time. It was a long while before he felt the need to adjust his position.

'Can I move for a bit?' he asked.

'It's all right,' Pearson replied. 'I'm done.'

'You've finished?'

'Yeah.'

He put down the pencil and looked at his work. He had caught something precious. He had neither embellished nor exaggerated Sweet Thing's looks. He hadn't needed to – the drawing had seemed to map itself out without any kind of intention on his part. The kid looked angelic, iconic.

'Let me see,' Sweet Thing insisted, jumping up from the bed in a sudden spasm of movement.

Pearson handed him the pad.

'Cor,' Sweet Thing cooed.

'You like it?'

'Yeah.'

Sweet Thing held the sketchbook carefully in his hands as if it were a sacred object. There was something magical about how he had been transformed into the image on the paper. He was seeing his own beauty for the first time. Pearson smiled again, feeling a simple affection for the boy. He had an urge to touch him, to hold him. To love him. But he had captured his likeness. There was something pure about that. It was enough.

'You can have it,' Pearson told him. 'If you want.'

'Can I?'

'Sure.'

Pearson took the sketchpad and carefully tore out the page. He handed it to Sweet Thing.

'There you are,' he said.

'Er, thanks,' Sweet Thing said, his eyes glimmering with delight. 'Thanks a lot.'

'Well,' Pearson said, turning to the scattered pieces on the floor, 'I've got to get on.'

22

the benefit

'What's this?' Pearson asked, picking up the money on the kitchen table.

'It's Sweet Thing's,' Nina replied.

'What's it doing here?'

'It's his contribution to the kitty.'

'Wow.' Pearson counted the notes. 'There's ten pounds here.'

'Look, it wasn't my idea. I didn't want to take it.'

'Why not? We're skint, after all.'

'Yeah, but—'

'You know what it means, though, don't you?'

'What?'

'We're living on immoral earnings.'

'Pearson, please don't joke about this.'

He fixed her with a cold stare.

'Who's joking?' he demanded.

'Don't give me a hard time.'

'I'm not.'

'Please.'

'All right.'

'Things just got a little crazy, that's all.'

Pearson gave a flat laugh.

'You can say that again,' he said.

'Look, Pearson, I've been thinking. It's all got a little too strange.'

'What do you mean?'

'I mean I'm thinking about moving out.'

'Right.'

'This place has got too much for me.'

'I see.'

'I'm sorry.'

'That's all right. Where will you go?'

'There's a place going at Jan's. I feel bad about leaving you on your own but—'

'I'll be all right. What about the kid?'

'I don't know, Pearson. I'll talk to him.'

'When are you going?'

'Well, I'm meeting Jan later. There's a benefit gig tonight.'

'A benefit gig?'

'Yeah. For the Stoke Newington Eight.'

Pearson frowned.

'I'd like to come to that,' he said.

'Really?'

'Yeah. I'd like to get involved, you know.'

'Well, this is new.'

'You could say I'm already involved. You know, with what happened.'

'You mean because of O'Connell?'

'Yeah,' he replied, nodding slowly. 'Something like that.'

In the evening they all went out. Sweet Thing declared that he wanted to come along too. They walked up Hampstead Road to Camden Town. The Stoke Newington Eight benefit was held in a dilapidated dance hall on Camden High Street. The band was still setting up on the stage when they arrived. Groups of people were milling around the dance floor. There were political stalls set up around the edges of the auditorium.

'Let's get a drink,' Pearson declared, and led the way to the bar.

'I'm buying,' Sweet Thing offered, and pulled out a sheaf of notes.

'Jesus, Sweet Thing,' Pearson muttered.

'See?' the boy said proudly. 'I'm flush.'

Nina and Pearson each had a pint of bitter and Sweet Thing got himself a double Bacardi and Coke. The auditorium began to fill up and they filed in to watch the proceedings. There were speeches and announcements and then the band came onstage. They launched into a bluesy intro, with screeching guitars and busy drum patterns.

'Christ, this is boring,' complained Sweet Thing. 'Let's have another drink.'

They went back to the bar and Sweet Thing insisted on buying another round. Pearson spotted someone in the crowd. Nina noticed his intent stare.

'What's the matter?' she asked.

'Nothing.'

'Seen someone you like the look of?'

'Yeah,' he said absently. 'I'll see you later.'

She watched him weave his way through the throng and spotted Jan. Nina smiled and made a little wave.

'Good to see you,' Nina said as Jan approached.

They hugged each other and Jan kissed her gently on the cheek.

'How have you been?' Jan asked.

'OK.'

'You mentioned something about a GLF demo.'

'Yeah. In Fleet Street, on the nineteenth of August. Were you on it?'

'Yeah, I was.'

'Do you remember Angela Weir being there?'

'Angela Weir? She's a defendant, isn't she?'

'Yeah, and the prosecution are saying she was in France that day with two other defendants picking up explosives to smuggle back into the country.'

'She was on the demo, yeah.'

'Are you sure?'

Jan thought for a moment.

She nodded. 'Yeah. She was there.'

'And you could swear to that?'

'I could.'

'That's great. Her defence might want you as a witness. Maybe there's someone here tonight we could talk to.'

Nina looked around the dance hall. Jan reached out and touched her arm.

'It's good to see you.'

Nina turned to look at her.

'I've been thinking,' she said.

'Yes?'

'If the offer still stands . . .'

'What?'

'I'd like to move into your house.'

Jan grinned, her eyes sparkling.

'That's great.'

She grabbed Nina with both hands and brought her face up close to hers. Nina felt a momentary sense of relief. She kissed Jan on the mouth. Jan pulled her close and held her in an embrace. Nina let Jan's lips press urgently against hers for a couple of seconds, then she gently pulled away from her. As she did so she saw Sweet Thing standing a few yards away, watching them. Her face clouded with anxiety. Sweet Thing's features twisted into a scowl. He turned and walked back towards the bar.

'What's the matter?' Jan asked.

'I'm all right,' Nina replied. 'Things have just been a bit mad lately.'

'I know,' Jan said with a smile.

Nina wondered whether Jan would ever understand what she meant. She could hardly comprehend it herself. Things would never be simple for her. But it had all been too much. If she made some sort of decision about her life it could be easier for her. She could make a choice.

Sweet Thing leant on the counter and waved a five-pound note to try to get the attention of the barman. He glanced around the bar as he waited. There was a man with shoulder-length hair and a moustache looking over at him. Sweet Thing stared back at him for a second then turned away.

'Hey, mate,' he called to the barman. 'Over here.'

'Hello,' came a voice.

The man with the moustache was at his shoulder.

Sweet Thing nodded tersely. 'All right.'

'Let me buy you a drink,' the man said.

'I'm fine, mate.'

'I insist.'

'Oh, you insist, do you?'

'Yes.'

The drink had gone to Sweet Thing's head. He wasn't used to it. It made him belligerent.

'Why don't you fuck off,' he spat out at the man.

Pearson made his way over to the person he had spotted. It was Phil, the man Pearson had seen with O'Connell from time to time. That casual acquaintance of his lover who had often turned up, apparently by chance, at places they had been together. Meetings that appeared coincidental, inexpedient even. 'Hang on, I've just got to see yer man over there,' O'Connell had said when he had spotted him standing by the bar when he and Pearson had been having a drink at Henekey's on Portobello Road. No encounter with this man ever seemed planned or pre-mediated, and O'Connells's acknowledgement of his appearances was always signified by their contingency. He would affect an air of mild annoyance, of inconvenience, and deliberately deny any hint of interest that he had in the man. One night, when they had been at Ward's Irish Bar in Piccadilly, O'Connell had alluded to the uninvited guest who nodded obliquely in their direction with a pint of Guinness in his hand by saying: 'Sure, here's your actual enemy of the state.' Pearson was used to O'Connell ridiculing political activists among the underground, but as he watched him walk over with a weary shrug he had noticed not the habitually confrontational demeanour of his lover but rather a quiet accommodation that he seemed to have with the man. Not much ever seemed to be said, just a mundane exchange of words, but they were accompanied by an intimate dance of gesture, a language of signs that spoke of some tacit agreement.

This was the man with whom Pearson had thought O'Connell had been cheating on him. O'Connell had always denied that anything was going on and had explained briefly that Phil was connected with some article or other O'Connell had written, but Pearson had never lost his suspicions.

Now Pearson realised how wrong he'd got it, just as he had been wrong about O'Connell being a covert bomber. Odd little details flickered into meaning, rough outlines in the shadow of his memory. He felt a certain clarity amid all the confused thoughts he'd been having. He wasn't imagining this. It had been another kind of conspiracy, he was sure of that. Phil had been involved in some way – maybe he had been an informer too. He hoped not. He sidled up to him.

'Phil,' he said.

The man turned to look impassively at him.

'What do you want?' he demanded.

'I was a friend of O'Connell's. Remember?'

'Oh yeah,' Phil said with a slight nod. 'An awful shame about him.'

'I need to talk to you.'

'What's there to say?'

'I know what he was involved in.'

'I don't know what you're talking about, man.'

'Look, I know.'

Phil looked Pearson up and down as if he were inspecting him for the first time.

'There's nothing to say,' he insisted. 'It's all over now.'

'No it's not,' replied Pearson. 'We need to talk.'

'I don't know.'

'It's important. It's unfinished business.'

The man glanced around furtively. Pearson picked up on the nervous energy of the man. He was buzzing with paranoia. Pearson could feel it – it was like a vibration in the air around them. Bad knowledge. Pearson felt that he had to tune into it. To find out what it was.

'Well, we can't talk here,' Phil told him.

'Where?'

'Come and see me tomorrow. I'll give you the address.'

Pearson searched in his pocket for a piece of paper. He found the ticket for the gig and pulled it out.

'Have you got a pen?' he asked.

Phil shook his head.

'We don't write anything down, man. I'll tell you it and you remember it. OK?'

Phil told him a number and a street name.

'You got that?' he demanded.

'Yeah.'

'Don't write it down anywhere. That's how people got caught. Fucking address books.'

'Don't worry, I won't.'

'Right,' Phil said. 'I'll see you tomorrow.'

'OK.'

'Go,' Phil told him, looking around again. 'It's best you're not seen with me. We can't be too careful.'

Pearson walked away slowly. He made his way into the hall and stood at the back, listening to the band. Nina found him there twenty minutes later. She tapped him on the shoulder.

'Hey,' he greeted her.

'Come on,' she ordered him. 'You've got to give me a hand.'

'What's the matter?'

'It's Sweet Thing. He's drunk. We better take him home.'

They found him propped up at the bar.

'Fucking hippies!' he was calling out.

'What's the matter with you?' Pearson asked him.

'Nothing. I want another drink. You want another drink?'

'I think you've had enough. Come on, let's go home.'

They grabbed an arm each and steered him out of the dance hall.

'I want another drink!' he shouted as they took him outside.

'Let's get a taxi,' Nina suggested.

'We haven't got any money for a taxi,' Pearson reminded her.

'Yeah,' she said. 'But he has. Have you seen how much money he's got on him? It's ridiculous.'

They hailed a cab and bundled him in. When they got back to the squat they pulled him out and steadied him up the stairs. They got him into his room and lowered him on to the bed. He looked up at them and grinned. The ceiling began to spin above his head.

'Not bent,' he jabbered. 'Rent. But there's no rent in a squat, is there?'

'Shh,' shushed Nina. 'Go to sleep.'

He groaned and rolled over.

23

the last communiqué

In the morning Pearson made a pot of tea and some toast and sat at the kitchen table, flicking through a tabloid newspaper. There was an item on the Stoke Newington Eight trial on the comments page which caught his eye.

These so-called urban guerrillas are violent terrorists hell-bent on revolution. They are the ugly face of the permissive age, determined to destroy all the values of normal society. Trade union militants, student extremists, dole scroungers, drugged-up hippies, homosexuals and bra-burning women all striving for liberation. They are all angry. Whenever you see a demonstration or a sit-in, a picket line or even a public library stocked up with socialist literature, you might find them. They have spread like a disease throughout the nation. There's no telling where they might be or where they might strike next.

There was something direct and powerful about the style of the piece. It was vulgar and explicit but it made more sense to him than all the Angry Brigade communiqués put together. It was like a direct command. Another sign, he thought.

Nina came down and poured herself a cup of tea.

'You going to take one up for Sweet Thing?' Pearson asked.

'What?'

'He could probably do with one after last night.'

'I don't know.'

'All right. I'll do it,' he said, standing up and grabbing a mug from the draining board. 'How many sugars does he take?' he asked, shovelling in spoonfuls. 'Three? Four? He's like an ant that boy. He lives on the stuff.'

Nina watched Pearson move jauntily around the kitchen. His mood had changed completely in the last couple of days. He wasn't morose any more. There was a kind of manic energy to him now.

Sweet Thing felt a grinding pain in his head, a hollow nausea in his stomach. He'd never had a proper hangover before. He heard a knock on the door. He whimpered and pulled the covers over him. Pearson came in.

'Hey,' he said softly. 'I brought you a cup of tea.'

Sweet Thing emerged from the sheets bleary faced and shock headed.

'What happened?' he moaned.

'You got drunk, man. You were out of it.'

'Shit.'

Pearson placed the mug he was carrying on the floor by the bed.

'You should take it easy, you know.'

Sweet Thing groaned.

'All this rushing about, getting out of your head. You're burning yourself out. You need to cool out a bit, you know?'

'Uh,' Sweet Thing replied.

'Did you have a good time last night?'

'Not really.'

'What do you think about what it was in aid of?'

'What?'

'You know, the Stoke Newington Eight, the Angry Brigade.'

Sweet Thing groaned again.

'Why are you asking me all these questions?'

'I'm curious. What do you think about it?'

Sweet Thing took a sip of tea and rubbed his face.

'I don't know,' he said. 'They set off them bombs, didn't they?'

'Yeah. What do you think about that?'

'Well, they planted one in Biba. What did they want to do that for?'

Pearson thought for a moment.

'As a protest against consumerism,' he said.

'What does that mean?'

'Making money out of people. Forcing them to spend money on expensive clothes.'

'But they're beautiful clothes. And they don't have to be expensive.'

'What do you mean?'

'Not if you hoist them. And Biba is the easiest place to shoplift in the whole of London.'

Pearson laughed.

'They didn't think of that, did they?' Sweet Thing went on.

'Well, you've got a point there. So, where would you plant a bomb?'

'Me? Why would I want to do that?'

'Say you did. Where would you blow up?'

'I don't know.' Sweet Thing mused for a second, thinking of all the places that he could take his revenge on. 'I reckon I'd blow up the Dilly.'

Pearson laughed again and Sweet Thing joined in.

'Yeah,' he went on. 'I'm sick of that place.'

'I'll bet you are.'

'Yeah.'

Sweet Thing stopped laughing. It was hurting his head.

'I'll leave you to it, then,' Pearson said as he walked out of the room. 'Have some more of that tea. It'll make you feel better.'

Sweet Thing leant over and took another glug of the hot sweet tea, then fell back on to the bed with a sigh. He felt on edge, twitchy. He was trembling; he felt tired but restless at the same time. A nervous agitation ran through his quivering body, a strange, delirious impulse of arousal. He had a hard-on. He touched himself, began to stroke his cock with feverish stimulation, then gave up. He didn't quite know what to think about, what to concentrate on.

'How is he?' Nina asked.

Pearson smiled.

'He's suffering. I don't think he's used to the booze.'

'I guess not.'

'Well, I'll leave you to it.'

'What?'

'I'm going out.'

'Where to?'

'Oh,' he said, 'just to see a friend.'

The address Phil had given him was a flat above an electrical goods shop on the Holloway Road. He pressed the buzzer.

'Who is it?' came the voice on the intercom.

'The friend of O'Connell's.'

'Right,' said the voice, and the door buzzed open.

The flat was barely furnished; there were boxes and a couple of suitcases on the floor. It looked as though the occupants had just moved in or were getting ready to leave. Phil showed him through to a small dreary kitchen. They sat down.

'O'Connell was a good man,' said Phil.

'Yeah?'

'Oh yeah. You and him were . . .' Phil shrugged, not knowing what word to use.

'Yeah,' replied Pearson.

'A good man,' Phil repeated. 'Someone you could trust.'

'Really?'

'Oh yeah. A lot of people involved never knew how to keep quiet and that got us into trouble. Declan always knew how to keep his mouth shut and his head down.'

It was then that Pearson realised that Phil wasn't an informer. Nor did Phil seem to be aware that O'Connell had been one. He had been tricked like so many others. He could be tricked again. Then he could be useful. Pearson had to play a part, to dissemble. He had to give off the right vibes.

'I feel guilty, to tell you the truth,' Phil went on. 'About the Stoke Newington lot. I mean most of them are being fitted up for things they were never directly involved in while some of us who were more on the heavy end of things never got caught. It's like we left them behind.'

'And were you on the heavy end of things?'

'I'm saying nothing, man. But you know, I mostly feel guilty about O'Connell. It was terrible what he did. He must have really felt desperate.'

'Yeah,' said Pearson, biting his lip. 'I think he was.'

'It must be tough for you, man.'

'Uh-huh.'

'You knew he was involved?'

'Yeah,' he lied, 'I knew.'

'Well, you know how good he was at keeping things safe, don't you?'

'You're telling me.'

'Must have been a shock, though.'

'Yeah.'

'I don't know what to say, man.'

Pearson's mind was racing. He had to concentrate. He had to focus his thoughts so that he could convince this man.

'I want to do something,' he blurted out, full of conviction.

'Yeah, sure.'

'I mean, really do something.'

'What are you saying?'

'I want to get involved,' Pearson declared. 'You know, take action.'

'Oh, man.' Phil closed his eyes and lowered his head.

'Come on, help me,' Pearson urged.

'I can't help you, man.'

'We've got to do something.'

'It's too late now. It's all over.'

'You mean the Angry Brigade is finished?'

'Look, man, there never was an Angry Brigade. It wasn't some structured organisation. It was an idea. And it didn't work.'

'But—'

'Those people in the dock, they're just scapegoats mostly. We worked individually or in autonomous cells. There was no leadership or hierarchy. It was a state of mind.'

A state of mind, Pearson thought. That was it. His state of mind. It was all here in his head.

'Listen,' Phil said, grabbing a pile of papers and rifling through them. 'It's here somewhere.'

'What?'

'The last Angry Brigade communiqué.'

Phil found a dog-eared copy of *International Times* and thumbed through its pages.

'Here it is,' he announced, flattening the paper on the kitchen table. ' "*It's time to weigh the balance between revolutionary advances and the gains of oppression*," ' he read out. ' "*No revolutionary group can carry on regardless.*

We are not military generals or a ruthless elite. The more Angry Brigade bombs, the more innocent people are framed, then revolutionary solidarity demands second thoughts and different actions." See,' he declared, folding up the paper, 'we're supposed to regroup, plan a new strategy.'

'Admit defeat, you mean.'

'Well, some of us were for carrying on.'

'You?'

Phil shrugged.

'To tell you the truth, man, I don't know,' he sighed. 'I'm getting out of London, that's for sure.' It's got too heavy. I'm going up North for the duration.'

'I want to do something. You can help me.'

'How?'

'You know about . . .' Pearson lowered his voice. 'Bombs.'

'I never said that.'

'But if you—.'

'Even if I did, there's nothing left. We got rid of everything.'

'But if there was some way—'

'Let's not even talk about this.'

'All I want is your expertise. Your knowledge. I'd do the rest.'

'This is fucking dangerous, man. Even talking about it counts as conspiracy these days.'

'So let all those people left behind take the rap for it while you get out of town.'

'Don't play some mind trip on me.'

'O'Connell. He was left behind.'

'You want to do something because of him?' Phil asked. 'Because of Declan?'

Pearson thought for a moment and then nodded.

'Yeah.'

'Then that's personal. We're talking about putting more people at risk here.'

'I'll be taking the risks.'

'Yeah. You and anybody connected to you.'

'All I want is some knowledge. Then I'll be acting alone.'

'This is just some revenge trip, right?'

'Maybe it is.'

'Then as I said, it's personal.'

'Let me tell you about what is personal and what is political,' Pearson announced, full of unexpected rage and fury. 'I found my own lover dead by his own hand. Because of them. Because of what he believed in. We loved each other even though society would never accept us. They oppressed us and drove him to suicide. They took him away from me. So, yeah, I want my revenge.'

'Easy, man.' Phil held up his hands.

Pearson caught his breath. He was enjoying this, almost carried away by it himself. And it was working. Phil bore an expression something like shame, as if humbled by this display of passion. Pearson felt sure that he was close to winning him over.

'Please,' he whispered imploringly. 'You owe it to him. We both owe it to him.'

Phil gave a long, heavy sigh.

'OK,' he agreed.

His face suddenly hardened into a steely gaze.

'You've got to be fucking careful, man,' he muttered through clenched teeth.

'I know.'

'There's nothing we can do now. Give me a couple of days. I'll phone you. I'll use a coded message. Something me and O'Connell worked out when we needed to make contact.'

24

skylight

Nina sat on the lip of the skylight and looked across the rooftops. The sun hung low over the city, still sharp and bright, catching the spires of St Pancras station, making them sparkle. A jet slowly cut its way high across the firmanant, leaving a thin white scar in its wake. This was a part of the house she would miss, she thought. It always seemed so calm up here.

She heard a knock on her door and called out in response. Sweet Thing came into her room and looked around. Nobody was there; he was confused.

'Nina?'

'I'm up here.'

He heard her voice above his head and looked up to see her in silhouette against the deep blue sky.

'What are you doing up there?' he asked.

'Just taking in the view,' she replied. 'Come on up.'

He clambered up the ladder and she reached down to help him up through the skylight. He manoeuvred himself to perch on the ledge opposite her. He looked out across the vertiginous diorama of the city.

'Wow,' he breathed.

'Good, isn't it?'

'Yeah.'

'I come up here to get away from it all.'

'From what?'

She shrugged. 'You know. Everything.'

The sun was in his eyes. He screwed up his face. It looked like he was smiling.

'You feeling better?' Nina asked him.

'Yeah,' he replied. 'A bit.'

They sat for a while not saying anything. He reached out and took her hand in his.

'Sweet Thing,' she said. 'We need to talk.'

He didn't like the sound of this. There was something about the tone of her voice that made him uneasy.

'Yeah,' he said, not knowing what else to say. 'OK.'

'We better go back down,' she told him.

Back in the room they stood facing one another, each waiting for the other to say something.

'Sweet Thing,' she began. 'Listen.'

He stepped forward and held on to her. He leant his head against her breast and nuzzled against it, his mind urgent with need. If only he could connect with her again, everything would be all right. He felt weak and helpless, brimming with emotions that he could neither control nor understand. He just wanted so much to be held by her. But she pushed him back firmly, holding him at arm's length.

'What's the matter?' he demanded.

'We need to get things straight.'

'Yeah?'

'Yeah. This can't go on.'

'What can't?'

'What happened, well, it happened, but—'

'It didn't just happen. You wanted it.'

'Yeah, but I wasn't thinking straight. It was all mixed up.'

'You saying it was wrong?' he asked her.

'Not wrong, no, just . . .' She struggled for what to say. '. . . inappropriate.'

'What does that mean?'

'It's just not a good situation.'

'You mean I wasn't any good? Is that what you're saying?'

'Christ, Sweet Thing, it's not about the sex, it's—'

'But it was good, wasn't it?'

'That's not the point.'

'Then what is?'

'We've got to be sensible about this.'

'Why?'

'Because I can't have a relationship with you. We've got to work this out.'

Sweet Thing felt a terrifying sense of emotional dispossession. The brief warmth of safety he had known was being snatched away from him. He struggled to understand what had happened. He could only make sense of it in his own terms. He had lost out. He should never have done it for free, he knew that now. He might have known that would get him into trouble. It had never been free for him. It was either bought or sold. Or taken. Free love, that was a joke. He had been taken advantage of. She had taken what she had wanted and left him with nothing.

'You think I'm dirty, don't you?' he demanded.

'What?'

'You don't want me because I'm just a dirty rent boy, that's it, isn't it?'

'No, it's not.'

'You hate me for that, don't you?'

'I don't hate you Sweet Thing,' she insisted. 'I . . . I . . .' She stumbled. 'I really like you.'

'You pity me more like.' He spat the words at her. 'Well, don't pity me. I don't need pity. I can look after myself. I'm all right, me. I pity the world and everyone in it.'

He glared at her, his blue eyes cold and steely.

'Sweet Thing,' she implored.

234

He turned away from her and walked out of her room.

Pearson came back into the house and went to his room. He locked the door. He could hear the voices above, muffled by the ceiling. He strained to work out what they were saying. Then there were thundering footsteps on the stairs and the sound of the other bedroom door being shut firmly.

He sat down on the bed. The house was suddenly quiet but it seemed to reverberate with nervous tension. He closed his eyes and breathed slowly until he began to feel calm and detached. He knew what he was going to do now.

He stood up and walked over to the desk. He crouched down and rubbed his palms together in a sort of meditation. There was a knock on his door. He sprang out of his reverie and went to it.

'Nina?' he said as he unlocked it.

Sweet Thing was standing there.

'Oh,' Pearson commented, 'it's you.'

'Can I come in?'

'Sure,' said Pearson.

He stepped back to let Sweet Thing into the room. The boy closed the door behind him and stood there glowering at Pearson.

'What do you want?' Pearson asked.

Sweet Thing needed someone to want him, to make him feel wanted. It was the only way he could feel real. Seductiveness was the one certain skill life had taught him. It was a matter of survival; he didn't know how to exist without it. If he couldn't make this work then he was lost. He moved towards the man.

'Well?' Pearson demanded.

Sweet Thing reached out and put his hand against Pearson's chest.

'What's all this about?'

'You know,' Sweet Thing murmured, flaring his nostrils and raking his fingers along the furrows of Pearson's ribcage.

'For God's sake, Sweet Thing.'

'You know you want it,' The boy purred through pouted lips.

'No.'

The hand slid down to encircle the outline of his hardening cock. Pearson's lust was mixed with panic. He had to stop this. It was as if Sweet Thing had been sent to tempt him from his purpose. Something terrible was making the boy behave like this. A ghastly force controlling him that must be destroyed. Pearson grabbed his wrist and pulled it away.

'No,' he repeated.

Sweet Thing shook his hand free of the grasp.

'What's the matter with you?' he asked.

'You've got to stop it.'

'What do you mean?'

He looked at the boy. Sweet Thing glowered back, his beautiful face quizzical, provocative. Pearson felt weak with desire. He had to stop it getting to him. He had to get the boy away.

'Look, just go. Please,' he told Sweet Thing.

'What?'

'Just get out!' Pearson hissed at him.

Sweet Thing stared at him with a look of hurt and bewilderment. Then he turned on his heels and stormed out of the room. Pearson closed the door after him and locked it. He pressed his head against the frame and put a hand to his cheek.

He turned and walked back to the corner of the room. He stooped before the desk again. He could hear Sweet Thing stomping about next door, throwing things about. Pearson pulled up the loose floorboard.

Sweet Thing was out on the landing, then there was a clattering of platform-heeled steps down to the front door. He heard it slam. He sighed. He pulled out the sticks of gelignite and held them in his hands. He felt a waxiness as he rolled them between his fingers. They were like large crayons. His medium, he mused, his materials. And he would be able to use them now. He would have to. It was meant to be so. He was destined to do this work. It was his duty as an artist to show them. To make them see.

25

timing

Sweet Thing didn't come back to the house that evening, and after three days there was still no sign of him. Nina began to worry. She was supposed to be moving out but she delayed things. She spent more time than she really needed in sorting out stuff and packing things into boxes. She found unnecessary difficulties in arranging for a friend with a van to move her into Jan's place. She was stalling for time. She wanted to know what had happened to Sweet Thing. She wanted to be there if he came back to the house.

Disturbingly she felt guilty about what had happened. Her feminist logic insisted that it was men who exploited women, but this was a more complex situation. Sweet Thing had been so damaged by life. He was emotionally vulnerable and she had taken advantage of him. She hadn't meant to but her impulsiveness had messed about with his head. She should have been more careful. All she had given him was confusion. She thought that he might be with his 'rich punter', but there had been anxious phone calls to the house. Whoever they were, they didn't seem to know where he was either.

The squat became very quiet. Pearson seemed self-absorbed, working on something in his room for most of the time. He told Nina that he was getting back into his art, that he was preparing a new piece. She wasn't sure what he meant by this. She saw him scribbling in a sketchbook, muttering to himself, making strange notes and drawings, clearly focused on something. She was no longer concerned about leaving him on his own. He looked occupied, inspired even.

She continued to be involved with the Defence Committee. It gave her something to concentrate on. There hadn't been any apparent repercussions from the discovery of explosives in O'Connell's room, so she felt reasonably safe going to the picket outside the Old Bailey. She tried to feel positive about what they were doing. The committee had a clearer sense of purpose than the clandestine actions and the arcane communiqués of the Angry Brigade. They were finding creative ways to organise, developing new strategies, tangible skills that could be used against the power of the state.

But she felt numb to the defiance and righteous indignation around her. Bereft of conviction, light headed and heavy hearted, lost, without a cause. There was a sadness that ate away at her hope. She felt a tremor of regret as she remembered how Sweet Thing had clung to her with such desperate eagerness through the night. The crowd called out its certain protestations and urged her to join in. The chants sounded mournful now. A lamentation came from within her in response. No, she thought. There would be no revolution. No liberation. No equality. No justice. No end to war, to poverty, to oppression. Just the endless spiral of it. Passion and suffering, that was all there was.

She made an excuse and left the demo. She thought about going back to the squat but then found herself walking in the wrong direction, past St Paul's and along Cheapside. She was suddenly taken by an impulse to go somewhere else. She reached Bank station and took a Northern Line train bound for Mill Hill East. The Tube was crammed with the rush-hour swarm, herding themselves homeward.

She got off at Finchley Central and walked to her father's shop. It was a calm, warm, suburban afternoon, full of tranquil memories. She wasn't sure what had brought her here. She had just felt the need the find a way back. The chemist's hadn't changed. The same outsized carboys on display in the window, the translucent rotund flasks filled with green and amber liquid. She had thought them magical when she was a child; *the giant's medicine*, she had called them.

She stood outside the pharmacy for a while, wondering whether she would go in. It had been two years since she had seen her father. She had kept in touch, writing to him and phoning occasionally to let him know where she was, that she was all right. She had blamed him for his lack of understanding, but it was she who had cut herself off from him.

The same bell rang as she pushed the door open, a tintinnabulation of lost time. Her father was at the dispensary in his starched white coat, taking the prescriptions from customers, deciphering their cryptic scrawl, handing out bottles and boxes, wrapping them in little paper bags. He gave instructions on dosages and their frequency. She noticed that he took time to enquire after a regular customer's health in a gentle, consoling voice. She waited among the small throng of sufferers until he had dispensed the last medicine. She stepped forward and he looked up, his face widening with surprise as he saw his daughter.

'Nina,' he gasped, beaming at her.

'Dad.'

His smile narrowed into a frown.

'What are you doing here?' he demanded.

'I just wanted to come and see you.'

'So you don't phone to let me know you're coming? You just turn up?'

'I'm sorry. I just thought—'

'What's the matter?' he asked.

'Nothing's the matter,' she insisted. 'I just wanted to see you. If this isn't a good time—'

'No, no, it's fine,' he said. 'Well, I've got to shut up the shop.'

He pulled down the shutters on the shopfront and they walked home together.

'Are you in some sort of trouble?' he asked her.

'I'm all right, Dad,' she replied.

The semi-detached house was just as she remembered it. They went through into the kitchen. A drug company's calendar on the wall, a copy of *The Morning Star* folded on the table. He made them a pot of tea and they sat down.

'So are you still staying at that place?' he asked disapprovingly.

'The house is fine, Dad,' she lied.

'Even so.'

'I'm moving soon. I'll give you the new address.'

'Right. So, what have you been doing with your life?'

'I've been busy, Dad.'

'Really?'

'Yes, really. I've been involved politically.'

'Hmm.' He shrugged.

She didn't want to tell him how disillusioned she felt, how burned out by it all she was. She wanted to find hope.

'I've been working to try and make things better. Surely you can understand that.'

'Yes, but dropping out . . . In my day we didn't have the luxury of that. You couldn't really drop out of the Depression, you know.'

'Yes, I know, Dad. But you've got to appreciate that we see things differently now.'

He nodded grimly.

'Unfortunately so,' he muttered.

'I'm just trying to find my way through the world.'

'Yes, yes,' he said. 'But what about the future?'

'The future?'

'Yes. Your future. Without qualifications.'

'Dad.'

'I mean, you had opportunities.'

'I'm sorry, Dad,' she declared sharply.

'What?'

'I'm sorry. I'm sorry that I disappointed you.'

'Don't say that.'

'But it's true, isn't it?'

Her father winced at this, as if in chronic pain.

'Please,' he said softly. 'Don't say that.'

'I was never good enough for you.'

'Nina . . .'

He shook his head, his face all creased up.

'Dad?'

A tear squeezed out of his screwed-up eyes. He swiped at it with the back of his hand.

'What's the matter?' she asked.

He released a couple of sobs. His expression loosened, his lips trembling. Nina reached across the table to take his hand. He looked her in the eye.

'I just wanted things to be all right,' he said. 'I know I said the wrong things, did the wrong things. It's just that when your mother died I was . . .' He sniffed. 'I was so scared.'

Nina squeezed her father's hand.

'I'm sorry, Nina,' he said.

'It's all right, Dad. It's all right.'

'I just worry about you so much.'

'Hey,' she said, 'it's all right. I'm going to be all right.'

And in telling him this she almost convinced herself of it.

The phone rang in the squat that afternoon. Pearson picked up the receiver.

'Every night and every morn,' came a voice. 'Some to misery are born.'

It was Phil. Pearson had memorised the required response to this call sign.

'Every morn and every night,' he replied. 'Some are born to sheer delight.'

They were on. Pearson left the house and made his way to the Holloway Road. Phil let him into the flat and made a pot of tea.

'Well?' he said.

Pearson pulled out the explosives and placed them on the kitchen table.

'Hm,' Phil mused, picking up one of the sticks and examining it. 'Where did you get this from?'

'O'Connell left it behind.'

'It's the real thing, all right. Part of the French consignment. Probably the last of it.'

He took out a cloth and wiped it down. He carefully lined it up with the others.

'So,' he said.

'Can you do something with it?' asked Pearson.

Phil laughed flatly.

'Oh yes,' he declared. 'I can do something, all right. Just need to be sure of something.'

'What?'

'What you're going to do with it.'

'Well—'

'Look, I don't want to know the target. But I have to know

that it's not going to hurt anybody. Property, yes, but we're not the IRA or the Baader-Meinhofs. We made a lot of mistakes but we never killed anybody. It would only take one outrage to discredit everything.'

'Don't worry.'

'Don't worry? Look, I shouldn't be doing this. This part of the struggle is supposed to be over now. Though I'm glad that somebody's still prepared to do something. Let's do this for O'Connell, yeah? We owe him that much.'

'Yeah,' Pearson agreed.

'So you're not going to hurt anybody.'

'Of course not.'

He didn't even know what the target was himself yet, but he knew that it would come to him soon. He was just waiting for a sign.

Phil went and retrieved a canvas bag from under his bed. He put it on a chair and started to pull things out of it. A coil of wire, a roll of insulating tape, a battery, an electric travel alarm, a pair of wire-clippers and what looked like a set of watchmaker's tools. He started to assemble something, talking softly all the while, explaining what he was doing, pointing out the meaning and implications of every element and how they connected.

'Timing,' he said with a grin. 'With bombs as in comedy, it's the crucial thing.'

He showed Pearson how to set a specific time for detonation. He went through the procedure laboriously, checking again and again that Pearson understood how to work the thing.

When he was finished he wiped everything down and cleared all the equipment away back into the bag.

'Well,' he sighed wistfully, 'that's the last bomb. Be bloody careful with it. You're on your own now.'

'Right.'

'I'm getting out now, man. It's a bit too warm for me around here.'

Pearson gingerly wrapped up the device. He stood up to leave.

'Good luck, man,' Phil said as he showed him to the door.

26

the teenscene discothèque

Joe was anxious to know where Sweet Thing was too. He couldn't track him down. He hadn't phoned or replied to the messages he had left. Johnny was complaining. All the interviews, appearances and photo-calls were taking their toll. He looked burnt out already, and it was only Tuesday.

'I need the kid,' he croaked.

'Don't worry,' Joe tried to reassure him. 'He'll turn up.'

'If I'm going to do *Top of the Pops* on Thursday I'll need Sweet Thing. I can't face it on my own.'

'But you're not on your own, Johnny, you've got me. And the band.'

'It's not the same, Joe. I need him.'

'I know.'

'I need his energy. It won't work otherwise.'

'Come on, Johnny, you'll be all right. It's just nerves.'

But Joe knew that it was more than that. He had to make sure that Johnny could pull himself together for his big television moment. He'd be miming, so he wouldn't have to worry about his voice, but the performance meant everything. He had to keep Johnny going somehow. He had an idea. He phoned Carl Dunstan, who ran the Teenscene Discothèque in Surrey, and arranged for Johnny to make an appearance that evening. The Teenscene had been running since the fifties as a venue for adolescents and a draw for queer pop impresarios keen to do some 'market research' on what young people were into. Joe had been there himself a few times to try to get some ideas on what the teenyboppers were up to. The professional regulars were quite clearly preying on the teenage talent there, ogling the pretty youths on the dance floor, grooming the star-struck ones with stories of fame and fortune and the occasional slug of whisky in their Coca-Colas. Maybe he could set Johnny up with somebody there or at least draw him out of his anxious state.

At first Johnny wasn't keen.

'I don't want to do an appearance tonight, Joe,' he complained.

'Come on, Johnny. It'll be fun. There's plenty of pretty young lads at the Teenscene.'

Johnny brightened up a bit at this.

'And it'll be a chance to see what they think of the new record,' Joe went on. 'A big star like you at a place like that? They'll love you. You never know, you might get lucky.'

'Lucky?' Joe mused. 'Yeah. OK.'

They drove down through South London and arrived at the place at seven thirty in the evening. The Teenscene was held in a drab municipal theatre. There was a queue of teenagers at the front entrance. As they made their way to the stage door they noticed a white Rolls-Royce in the car park. It had a personalised number plate: TR 45.

'Look,' said Joe, pointing it out. 'Timothy Royal's here.'

Timothy Royal had had a hit in the mid-sixties with 'Under the Sun' and had gone on to make a series of novelty records under various pseudonyms. Public school and Oxford educated, Royal cultivated a casually aloof manner about the deliberately tacky nature of his product, but he had a sharp and knowing sense of how to manipulate the business. Everything he did was conducted with a calculated air of frivolity.

Joe and Johnny went in through the side entrance and were greeted by Carl Dunstan.

'Johnny!' he exclaimed. 'So glad you could come. Great record, by the way. Joe, good to see you, you're on to a winner here. Come through, come through.'

He ushered them into the backstage area. There was a space in the wings to the right of the stage where a group of men were sitting. Timothy Royal was talking intently to Kenny Morton, a Scottish band manager. He looked up as they came in.

'Johnny Chrome!' he called out, standing up and shaking Johnny's hand. 'Fantastic! But you simply must let me produce your next single. Tell me I can do that, Joe.'

He turned to Berkovitch. Joe always felt intimidated by Timothy Royal. He was never sure whether he was being played with.

'I guess,' he said.

'Promise me, Joe,' Royal insisted with a mischievous smile.

'All right,' Joe replied with a forced laugh. 'I promise.'

They all sat down. Their vantage point was partially hidden by a curtain but they had a clear view of the stage where the DJ desk was set up and the cleared auditorium beyond which served as the dance floor. As the teenagers filed in, Royal, Dunstan and Morton talked furtively among themselves, commenting lewdly about boys they recognised, pointing out newcomers they liked the look of. Johnny watched intently too but sat in silence.

Joe started a conversation with Kenny Morton.

'I've got a great bunch of lads,' Morton said of his new band. 'They're going to be big, I'm sure of it. I mean, if I fancy them they're sure as hell going to appeal to teenage girls, you know?'

'I'm afraid I haven't quite got your expertise, Kenny,' said Joe.

'That's a pity. Not so many perks for you, then.'

248

The music had started and the teenyboppers began to jerk about in an awkward hormonal ritual. Timothy Royal leant forward and spoke to Johnny, all the time keeping his eyes on the dance floor.

'Lot of talent here tonight, Johnny,' he murmured salaciously.

'Yeah,' Johnny replied. 'I guess.'

'So who do you like the look of?'

'What do you mean?'

'Who looks good? You know what's good about this place? It's a way of seeing how fashions and trends work, I mean really work. It's like a testing ground.'

'I suppose so.'

'And useful for you. I mean, you can see what your fans look like close up.'

'Yeah.'

'So.'

'What?'

'Which one do you like?'

Johnny scanned the crowd. There was a red-haired youth in the middle of the dance floor, stomping around with all the elegance his platform shoes would allow him. He wore a rounded-collared shirt, an ice-blue tank top and baggy beige trousers.

'That kid looks good,' he said, timidly pointing him out.

Timothy Royal told one of the staff to bring the kid backstage.

'Well, now you can meet him. It's as easy as that.'

'But maybe he doesn't want to meet me.'

'Don't worry, Johnny. You're famous, for God's sake. Everyone wants to meet you.'

The red-haired boy shuffled nervously into the inner sanctum.

'Hello, son,' Royal purred at him. 'Come on in. Don't be shy. What's your name?'

'Peter,' the youth mumbled.

Royal plucked a bottle from the crate on the floor, topped it up with whisky and handed it to him.

'There you are, Peter. Coke with a kick.'

Peter took the bottle and gulped from it.

'This is Johnny Chrome,' Royal told him. 'Come and meet him.'

Johnny reached out and shook the boy's hand clumsily.

'Nice to meet you, Peter,' he croaked.

Peter stared at him.

'Johnny's a real star,' Royal went on. 'And he thinks you're a really good dancer.'

'Thanks,' said Peter, taking another swig from the bottle.

'Maybe you could be a star, Peter,' said Royal.

'Yeah?' said Peter, wide eyed and open mouthed.

'You've got the looks for it,' Morton chipped in.

'If you like you could do an audition for me,' said Royal.

'What would I have to do?'

'I'd just need to see how you perform. Give me your phone number and we can set it up. And Johnny will give you his autograph, won't you, Johnny.'

'Yeah, sure.'

'I haven't got anything to write on,' Peter said.

'He could write it on your arm,' Royal suggested.

'Or anywhere else you'd like,' Morton added.

Johnny suddenly felt sick. He stood up.

'I got to . . . got to go,' he stammered. 'To the bathroom.'

And he stumbled out to the dressing rooms.

When he came back Joe was waiting for him.

'Are you all right?' he demanded.

'Yeah. I'm not sure if this was a good idea, Joe.'

'Well, you're on.'

'On?'

'Yeah. Carl's going to introduce you, play the single and then you can sign some autographs. OK?'

'OK.'

Carl Dunstan's voice came over the PA.

'OK, boys and girls, we've a treat for you tonight! We've got Johnny Chrome here to say hello and play his new record!'

The crowd broke into applause and little squeals of delight.

'So here he is! Johnny Chrome!'

Johnny stood transfixed in the wings. Joe gave him a push.

'Go on, Johnny,' he whispered urgently.

Johnny staggered on to the stage, looking lost and bewildered. Dunstan beckoned him over to the microphone. He stared down at the sea of eyes glaring up at him expectantly. Faces filled with hope and dreams that would never come true. Dunstan handed him the mike.

'Um,' he started, trying to concentrate on something. 'It's great to be here. I hope you like the new record and I hope, er, I hope you all have a wonderful evening.'

They cheered.

'Johnny!' a girl's voice rang out through the hall. There were whistles, cat-calls. He stumbled off the stage, waving at the crowd. 'Hey, Hey (The Gang's All Here)' started up and the boys and girls started to dance to it.

'Well done, Johnny,' Joe murmured, and patted him on the back.

'They like the tune, Johnny,' Timothy Royal remarked, peering out at the dance floor.

'Have a drink, Johnny,' Morton suggested.

'I want to go home, Joe,' Johnny said.

'You've only just got here,' the Scotsman retorted. 'Have a drink.'

'I want to go.'

'We were hoping that you could judge the David Cassidy lookalike competition later,' said Royal.

'Hmm,' said Morton. 'I'm looking forward to that.'

'Take me home, Joe.'

'Are you sure?' asked Joe.

Johnny nodded.

'I'm sorry, gents,' Joe said. 'Johnny's very tired. A busy week and all that. Got to keep his strength up.'

Royal sniffed. 'Suit yourself.'

Johnny pushed through the fire exit and walked quickly through the car park as Joe made hurried farewells to everybody. He caught up with Johnny and unlocked the car.

'What's the matter with you?' he demanded.

Johnny slumped into the passenger seat.

'Just take me home,' he replied.

They drove for a while in silence.

'I didn't like those guys,' Johnny announced finally.

'They're just parasites,' Joe told him.

'I'm not like them,' Johnny muttered.

'Of course you're not,' Joe reassured him.

Joe dropped Johnny at his house and told him to get some rest.

'Don't worry about tonight,' he insisted. 'You were fine.'

Johnny poured himself a glass of wine and took a couple of Mandrax. There was an awful feeling in the pit of his stomach. The nasty, predatory lustfulness. He was just as bad as they were. He would have to be punished for it.

It was getting dark when Nina got back to the squat. She was glad that she had gone back home. She felt a sense of quiet resignation. She realised that she had spent too much of her life worrying that she wasn't good enough – whether it was for her father or for the causes that she had been involved in. Maybe there could be some stability in her life from now on. But as she came in through the door of the house she remembered that Sweet Thing was still missing.

'Is he here?' she asked Pearson.

'Who?'

'Sweet Thing, of course.'

'No. He hasn't been back.'

'Shit.'

'What's the matter?'

'I'm worried about him. Rushing off like that. He was in quite a state. Maybe something's happened to him.'

'Yeah, well.'

'And it was my fault.'

'No.'

'Well, I didn't act very responsibly with him, did I?'

'It's not your fault, Nina. They are controlling him. You know that, don't you?'

'What?'

Pearson saw that Nina was frowning at him, as if she suspected something. He had to be careful.

'Nothing,' he muttered.

'No. What did you say? Who's controlling him?'

'It doesn't matter. We could go and look for him,' he said, quickly changing the subject.

'Where?'

'Well, we could start at the place I first found him. Piccadilly. We could go there tonight.'

Nina thought for a moment.

'You go. I'll stay here in case he comes back.'

'OK.'

'Let him know that he can come back here. If he wants to. I just want to know that he's all right.'

He walked into town. It gave him time to think. He went through Bloomsbury towards the West End. It was a pleasant evening. He crossed Russell Square and gazed at the buildings that loomed up out of the foliage of the park. Senate House and the British Museum. He could bomb these places, he mused. He felt a power of possession over the city. It was his. Anywhere could be a legitimate target. He would know soon, he felt sure of that.

Twilight in Piccadilly, always twilight at the Dilly, never nightfall. Bright lights that polluted the darkness with a sickly fuzz and blotted out the miserable sky. Pearson walked along the meat rack, a line of youths in the shadows, fiery eyes twitching with street luminescence. A boy was leaning against the railings, a cigarette hanging lazily from his lips. He caught Pearson's stare.

'Looking for somebody?' the boy asked him.

'Yeah. Sweet Thing. You know him?'

'What's wrong with me?'

'It doesn't matter.'

Pearson entered the raucous din of Playland. One-armed bandits pumping, greedily feeding with mechanical cackles. Here. It suddenly came to him: the sign he had been waiting for. Of course. Here. The harsh chimes of fortune, of misfortune. Catch-penny lights, the buzzing games, the hustle of chance, the gamble of life. Here. Boys touting their bodies in a wanton hoopla of lust. Fruit machines of automatic pleasure. Insert coin here. Here was the stock exchange of cheap thrills. Here was the love market. The sideshow, the joke parade for the main event. The absolute locus of evil fun time. The shooting-gallery firing squad. Targets and fluffy toy prizes. Here: the target. Amusements, a gimcrack parody of pleasure, an insect hum of entertainment, the idiot grin beneath the skin. Skull-rings and plastic juju trinkets waiting to be won.

Death on holiday. Here was the worst spectacle of all. *Here*, he thought.

He watched the boys milling around the games. The machines were controlling them, that much was clear to him. They must be destroyed, he knew that now. Everything before had led up to this. That's what had drawn him here in the first place.

He thought of what Sweet Thing had said. *I reckon I'd blow up the Dilly*. He knew. The boy knew that this was the only way he could be set free. Then he remembered that he was here to look for Sweet Thing. He had to concentrate for a moment. He nodded at a saturnine boy who stood next to the arch of orange bulbs that framed the change booth. He came over.

'I'm looking for Sweet Thing,' he said.

'Yeah? Who wants him?'

'A friend.'

'I ain't seen him, mate.'

'You know anyone who might know where he is?'

'Angel!' the boy called out to another youth. 'You seen Sweet Thing?'

The youth shook his head nonchalantly.

Pearson went back out into the street. He made a trawl of all the all-night cafés and coffee bars in Soho. He checked every haunt and street corner he could think of. He couldn't find him.

When he got back to the house it was past midnight. Nina was waiting up for him.

'No luck?' she asked.

He shook his head. *No luck*; he thought of the gambling machines of Playland. They were all fixed. No luck. No odds. No chance. No pay-out.

'You should go, Nina,' he said.

255

'What?'

'Sweet Thing isn't coming back here. There's no point hanging around waiting for him. You want to move, so move.'

With Sweet Thing and Nina gone he would be on his own. That was how he wanted it to be.

'Wait a minute,' Nina said. 'What about the guy who was phoning up for him?'

'Yeah, but he didn't know where he was.'

'But Sweet Thing said he had a rich punter. A pop star.'

Pearson remembered the first time he had seen Sweet Thing with the guy in a plum-coloured suit. He was a manager for someone. *A household name*, he had said. Johnny something.

'His name's Johnny,' he told Nina.

'Johnny what?'

'I don't know. But there's a number on the wall by the phone.'

'Right,' she said.

She would try the number tomorrow, she decided.

27

low-intensity operations

He could close the dossier now, file it with his other records, index it under information received. Walker faced the morbid conclusion that O'Connell's death had cleared up his case very neatly. No need for a full report for his superiors. No need for any final comments or conclusions. No space for any marginalia of feelings on the matter. O'Connell was a finished document now. All that he had known of the man could be consigned to an archive of cold intelligence.

On an operational level he was blameless. He had followed official procedure with regard to the handling of informants. The fact that he had known that O'Connell was in possession of evidence that could have been used as a plant to incriminate others, that had been bending the rules a little. But there was nothing that could connect Walker directly to this, and besides, the material in question had been disposed of.

Deep down he realised that he had handled his informant very badly. He had been negligent. The man was unbalanced and he had used this very instability to needle him. Walker had driven him too far. He knew that he would never have to account for this to anyone else in the job. Only he would know. It was a guilt that he would have to live with.

He felt a contrite grief for O'Connell and a sense of the loss of something else. It was the end of his contact with all these wild theories and flamboyant concepts that he had been able to discuss with the Mole. There was still a lot of work do be done on the Angry Brigade case. But it would be dull from now on. Presenting the police evidence, keeping an eye on the demo outside the Old Bailey, endless amounts of paperwork. It was going to be a long trial, that was for certain. For him it would be a return to routine. For a while he had been challenged to think in bold and imaginative ways. Now his enthusiasm was gone. He felt uninspired, disillusioned even. *For the man has closed himself up, till he sees all things through the narrow chinks of his cavern.*

There was a knock on his door.

'Come,' he announced gloomily.

It was the commander.

'Eric, we need a top-level briefing on any links between the Angry Brigade and the Provisional IRA,' he said.

'Well, I can tell you now, sir, there aren't any,' Walker replied.

'Are you sure?'

'Oh yes. The Angry Brigade were libertarian, the IRA are authoritarian. They're poles apart ideologically.'

'Well, maybe you could explain some of this. Not all of us are up to speed on the political theory behind these groups.'

'Yes, sir.'

'And don't they share some common goals? What about the Post Office Tower bomb? There was a theory that it was a joint operation.'

'Never substantiated, sir. I suggest it was highly unlikely.'

'What's the matter, Walker?'

'Sir?'

'You don't seem very keen, that's all.'

'Sorry, sir. I'm a bit tired, that's all.'

'Well, put something together, will you? We need all the leads we can get. The mainland campaign has already started. Intelligence has it that there's already at least one Provisional

IRA active service unit operating in London. The Paddies are on the warpath. It's going to get pretty bloody.'

'I suppose it is, sir. Yes.'

'Not like your lot.'

'My lot, sir?'

'You know what I mean. You got close to them and we appreciate that. But you quite liked hanging about with the hairies, didn't you?'

'I was only doing my job, sir.'

'Quite. Well, it's not going to be the same again. We've got to keep the upper hand. Subversion, industrial unrest, Irish terrorism, and God knows what else. The new squad is going to be busy from now on.'

'Yes, sir.'

'Oh, and did you sort out that little problem of yours?'

'Problem, sir?'

'Something about losing contact with an informant.'

'That's all dealt with now, sir.'

'Good. Well then, I'll leave you to it,' said the commander.

He left the room. It was over now, thought Walker. The end of idealism. It would be brutal from now on. Real terrorism. The Angry Brigade had just been a rehearsal for it.

Later that day a detective constable attached to photographic surveillance came into his office. He had a buff foolscap envelope in his hands.

'The latest on the Phil Sanderson plot-up, Sarge,' he said, handing him the envelope.

Walker opened it and pulled out two glossy enlargements.

'Subject seen entering and leaving Sanderson's premises on Saturday the third of June and again on Tuesday the sixth.'

Walker held the photographs up and narrowed his eyes at them.

'And Sanderson?' he asked. 'Is he still under surveillance?'

'Was until yesterday, Sarge. He's left the flat. He's no longer at that address. We're terminating that plot-up, with your permission, Sarge.'

'What?' Walker said absently, still focusing on the pictures in front of him.

'Well, we're supposed to be back to low-intensity operations with this lot. Now the trial's started.'

Walker looked up at him.

'Hmm.' He looked back at the pictures.

'Resources are being reallocated. You know. The Irish are our priority now.'

'Yes.' Walker nodded. 'Of course.'

Sanderson had been an important suspect but Walker had never been able to pin him down. O'Connell had flatly refused to implicate him, but he knew the man had been involved. He had just managed to cover his tracks. The detective constable noticed how intently Walker was looking at the photographs.

'Know who this body is, then, Sarge?'

'Yes,' Walker replied, thinking that maybe it wasn't all over just yet. 'Yes, I do.'

The receptionist buzzed through to Joe Berkovitch. 'There's a woman here from *New Musical Express*.'

'I told you Johnny's not doing any interviews today.'

Joe had had to cancel a whole day of appointments and appearances. Johnny had had a panic attack that morning and he had to be taken home and and fed Mandrax to calm down. He was racked with anxiety.

'I can't do it, Joe, I can't do it,' he kept repeating in a hyperventilated stutter until the barbiturates started to work and put him into a catatonic trance.

Joe didn't know what he was going to do. *Top of the Pops* was a day away.

'She wants to see you,' said the girl on the front desk.

Joe groaned. All this grief was bound to give him an ulcer.

'Show her in, then,' he said, clicking off the intercom.

Nina walked into the office. She had called the number on the wall that morning. It was a for a management company called Diamond Music, with an address in Wardour Street. She decided on a direct approach, and so had concocted a story about being a music journalist. Joe looked up.

'What can I do for you, love?' he asked

She saw the poster of Johnny Chrome on the wall behind Berkovitch's desk.

'Johnny Chrome.'

'Look, Johnny's not doing any interviews at the moment.'

'But you represent him?'

'Yeah.'

'So you know about Sweet Thing.'

Joe's eyes narrowed on her.

'I don't know what you're talking about, love,' he said in the most off-hand manner he could muster.

'I think you know exactly what I mean.'

Oh sweet fucking-Jesus, thought Joe. This could ruin everything.

'I didn't realise the *NME* was into muck-raking now,' he said. 'I thought you were serious journalists.'

'Well, I'm not actually from the *NME*.'

'What?'

'But it would be quite a scandal, wouldn't it?'

'Are you trying to blackmail me?' Joe folded his arms.

Nina laughed.

'To be honest, I hadn't really thought about it.'

'Because you can fuck right off if you are.'

'I just want to know where he is.'

Joe sighed.

'I wish I knew,' he told her. 'He's unpredictable is that one.'

'Yeah, well, it's understandable in the circumstances. He is being used, after all.'

'Spare me your bleeding heart. The boy's a clever little hustler.'

'Even so.'

'What's he to you anyway?' Joe asked.

Nina thought for a moment.

'I just care about him, that's all.'

'Well, that's very charitable of you. And if I had any idea where the little hooligan was I'd tell you. But I don't.'

'But—'

'Now if you'll excuse me, I'm a busy man.'

'Wait,' Nina said. 'Promise me you'll do something for me.'

'I don't like the sound of this.'

'Well, if you want to protect the precious reputation of your client you'd better.'

'Well?'

'If you find out where he is, tell him . . .' Nina paused, struggling to come up with a suitable message to give. 'Tell him Nina's sorry. And to come back to the house. Or phone. If he wants to.'

'Nina.' Berkovitch nodded. 'Right. Well, I'll be happy to oblige if I ever see him again. Now if you don't mind . . .'

Nina shrugged and left the office. Berkovitch clicked on the intercom again.

'Cancel everything for this afternoon. I'll be out of the office.'

He had to go to see to Johnny. Try to coax him into some sort of intelligible shape. He drove down to his house and rang the doorbell. Johnny was shaking as he let Joe in.

'You feeling any better?' Berkovitch asked him as they went through into the front room.

'Not really, Joe,' Johnny replied, and curled up on the sofa.

'You've got to pull yourself together.'

'I've lost him, Joe.'

'Sweet Thing will be back.'

'No, not just him. I've lost Johnny Chrome.'

'You can't have lost him. You are Johnny Chrome.'

'No, he's . . .' Johnny struggled to explain. 'He's someone else. I have to find him.'

'It's just nerves, Johnny. You'll be all right.'

'You don't understand. I . . . I have to become him. I need Sweet Thing.'

'What do you mean?'

'He's got the secret, see? He can make him appear.'

'Now you're not making any sense.'

'I'm so tired, Joe. So tired of it all.'

'I know, Johnny.' Joe patted him on the shoulder. 'Try to relax. We'll have a fresh start tomorrow.'

'I need my Mandies,' Johnny said, pointing at the bottle of pills on the coffee table.

'All right,' said Joe. 'I'll get you a glass of water.'

Johnny gulped down a couple of pills and chased them with the water. Joe poured himself a stiff drink. The doorbell rang.

'Who can that be?' Johnny asked nervously.

'I'll go and see,' said Joe.

It was Sweet Thing.

'Well, thank fuck,' Joe declared. 'Where the hell have you been?'

Sweet Thing was dazed. He couldn't really recall.

'Here and there,' he muttered, staggering into the hallway. He had wandered the city, sleeping rough or sitting on a park bench and watching the dawn. In an all-night cinema showing apocalyptic science fiction films. *The Earth Dies Screaming*. All that he could really remember was running out of money and making his way to Johnny Chrome's place. There seemed nowhere else to go.

Johnny sat up on the settee.

'Sweet Thing. Is it really you?'

'Yeah,' he muttered. 'I guess.'

'Isn't he wonderful?' Johnny asked Joe.

'Well, he looks a bit rough to tell you the truth.'

'No,' Johnny insisted. 'He's fantastic. He's a star, Joe. Don't you think?'

'I don't know about that,' Joe muttered.

'You could make him a star. Couldn't you, Joe?'

Berkovitch smiled. Maybe he could do something with the kid. He'd need some sort of pay-off in the long run to avoid any scandal.

'Yeah,' he said. 'Maybe. What do you think, kid?'

'I don't know. I just want paying for now.'

'It was supposed to be a retainer you were on. You haven't exactly fulfilled your part of the bargain, have you?'

Sweet Thing stared at him sullenly.

'I'll go now, then, shall I?'

'Wait up, son. You'll get your money. Tomorrow. Johnny's got to be at Television Centre in the afternoon. There'll be a car for him. Come with him and I'll pay you there.'

'Right.'

'What the fuck happened to you anyway?'

'Nothing.'

'You nearly gave me a heart attack. Someone else has been looking for you too. They're worried about you.'

'Who?'

'Some bird called Nina? Yeah. She says she's sorry and for you to go and see her at the house. Or phone.'

Sweet Thing nodded, blank eyed. *Nina*, he thought. It had all seemed such a long time ago.

Joe figured that it was probably best to leave them to it. The whole thing still seemed precarious but there was a sparkle in Johnny's eyes now.

'Tomorrow, then,' he said, and went to the door.

'Sweet Thing,' Johnny cooed at the boy when Joe had gone.

'What?'

'Dance for me.'

'Dance?'

'Yeah, you know, do me. I need you to do me.'

Johnny Chrome leapt up from the sofa, suddenly possessed by a borrowed energy. He went to the stereo and took out a copy of his new single. Sweet Thing knelt down and cleared a space on the coffee table. He cut out a couple of lines of what was left of his amphetamine sulphate. A crackle came over the speakers as Johnny lowered the needle on to the vinyl. Sweet Thing snorted up the speed, stood up with a defiant sniff and began to jerk about robotically to the inane song.

28

top of the pops

Joe Berkovitch watched as Johnny had the final touches to his face done. Sweet Thing was slumped on a chair in the corner of the dressing room. Johnny chatted to the make-up girl.

'You all right, love?' he asked her.

'Yeah,' she said, dusting his cheeks with glitter. 'Never had so much work. All the blokes want to be tarted up these days. It's great. There. You're done.'

'Thanks,' said Johnny, gazing at his image in the mirror. Joe patted him on the back.

'You ready, Johnny?' he asked him.

Johnny took a deep breath and huffed.

'Give me a couple of minutes,' he replied.

'Right,' Joe announced. 'Everybody out. Johnny needs a moment to himself. No, not you, Sweet Thing. You stay here.'

When they had all left Johnny stood up and called Sweet Thing over. He held his hands and looked into the boy's eyes, tuning in to him.

Johnny Chrome was on first. He stood waiting on the stage as the *Top of the Pops* theme tune, CCS's big-band rendering of 'Whole Lotta Love,' blared out on playback. A camera craned over the studio audience, zooming in on the presenter. Johnny saw Tony Blackburn's face flash up on the monitor. He waited intently, hardly hearing what the DJ was saying, concentrating on his cue.

Transmission. Camera 1 panned across the two drummers as they began the mechanical stomp of the intro and then pulled out to take in the whole band. The power chord riff started up and the buzzsaw sax blared out its fanfare. Camera 2 picked up Johnny, standing with his back to the crowd, arms outstretched, then went tight in on his face as he spun around to start the song.

Johnny Chrome's eyes were agog with intensity. That strange and compelling look of wonder beamed into millions of sitting rooms. Spastic kabuki theatrics, exaggerated gestures and mock-shock expressions, as if he were reacting to an unknown and irresistible force that oscillated in the airwaves. On the chorus, Camera 1 picked up the band as they joined in on the 'heys' of the refrain, then back to Johnny on Camera 2, the studio mixing following the banal rhythm of the tune. Johnny never lost it for a moment; he was utterly possessed by his gaudy persona. The garish spectacle, a flashy exhibition of cheap glamour, was a perfect *Top of the Pops* performance. As the song ended the crane swooped over the audience, swaying moronically to the beat, some holding aloft silver scarves with 'Johnny Chrome' emblazoned on them.

Playland was crowded, buzzing like a hive around him. Pearson felt the drone of it in his head. The whole place was throbbing with evil. He walked slowly to the far end of the hall, keeping his head down. He stood before a one-armed bandit. He put in a coin, pulled the lever and looked around. Nobody was looking. He was ready. Nina had moved out of the squat that morning. He was on his own now. Now was the time. He crouched down and carefully placed the device behind the slot machine.

He walked out and phoned a warning to the premises. He then dialled the number Walker had given him. He spoke quickly as the line was picked up.

'This is the Angry Brigade,' he announced, muffling his

voice with a handkerchief. 'There's a bomb in the Playland amusement arcade in Piccadilly.'

He waited by the statue of Eros for ten minutes. Nothing was happening. He started to panic.

Twenty minutes left before the bomb went off and the arcade was still full of people. He rushed to a phone box and dialled 999. As the operator answered he heard the police cars' sirens tearing up Piccadilly.

Johnny sat in the back of the limousine between Berkovitch and Sweet Thing, staring out in a dazed stupor as they drove back from Television Centre.

'You were fantastic, Johnny,' Berkovitch said to him softly.

'I'm just glad it's all over, Joe.'

'Over? We've just started, Johnny. There'll be more telly. I think I can get you on *Lift Off with Ayshea* next week. Then there's the tour to organise.'

Johnny felt a groaning sense of dread. He was all played out. He just wanted to go home. Joe pulled out a wad of cash, peeled off some notes and handed them across to Sweet Thing.

'There you are, son,' he said. 'A job well done. Just try not to run off again without us knowing where you are, eh?'

'It's all right, Joe,' Johnny said, patting the boy's knee. 'Sweet Thing's staying with me now, aren't you?'

'Yeah,' Sweet Thing mumbled, pocketing the money and staring blankly ahead.

The limousine dropped Johnny and Sweet Thing off.

'Goodbye, Joe,' Johnny Chrome said to his manager.

'I'll see you tomorrow,' Berkovitch replied.

Inside the house Johnny phoned his mother.

'Did you see me on the telly, Mam?' he asked her.

'Yes, Johnny,' she replied. 'You were very, er, extravagant.'

'I'm coming, Mam.'

'What?'

'Home. Soon.' He hummed the words like a mantra.

'Are you all right, son? Have you had a drink or something?'

'I'm fine, Mam. Really.'

'I expect you'll be having a bit of a celebration.'

'Yeah. Something like that. I love you, Mam.'

'I love you too, son.'

She put the phone down. For a while Johnny kept the receiver to his ear and listened to the soothing purr of the dialling tone. His head was full of warm fuzz. He was ready.

He went back into the front room. Sweet Thing was sitting on the sofa with his feet up on the coffee table.

'Come here,' Johnny murmured.

Sweet Thing got up and walked over to him. Johnny Chrome knelt at the boy's feet. He took his belt off, snaking the leather through the loops of his trousers. He put it around his neck, pulling the tongue of it through the buckle, tightening it into a noose. He held the end of it up to Sweet Thing.

'Now,' he said.

Sweet Thing began to tug with one hand, while pressing the other against the buckle. The boy gritted his teeth with exertion, suddenly possessed by a burning rage. He was taking it back. All that had been stolen from him. His whole life. Every violation of his self, his being, his very soul.

Johnny's head began to burst with the dark tight pleasure of asphyxiation. A deep blood-red warmth in his eyes, a dying sunset. The leather dug into his neck, separating his mind from his body. He would get there this time. Transmission. The glimmering light came once more, flickering at the beckoning night. He was floating now, looking down at his shuddering body. He was free. White light shot through his mind like an atomic pulse, then he swooned down into the yawning void.

*   *   *

The infernal machine blitzed through the empty arcade, shattering fruit machines and spitting out a bombshell jackpot of shrapnel and small change. The plate-glass windows disintegrated into diamanté splinters; the illuminated sign at the entrance collapsed in a shower of sparks. A glittering cloud of debris confettied out on to the street. A pall of white smoke drifted across Piccadilly Circus.

'Wow,' Jan gasped, holding tightly to Nina's trembling body. Her flesh was hot and slippery with sweat. Nina sobbed, shuddering out the last spasms of her orgasm. Jan grinned up at her, reaching out to hold her breast and feel her fluttering heartbeat. Nina let out a long groan of relief. She rolled over Jan's body to lie next to her.

'Nina,' Jan whispered.

'Shh,' she replied, gently touching Jan's face with the tips of her fingers. 'Please. Don't say anything.'

Nina snaked her arm under Jan's neck and rested her own head on the bed. She didn't want to talk. She felt at peace for the moment and she wanted to hold on to that. She could be at home here. She might not fit in completely, but where would she anyway? Here was a sanctuary.

She had decided that she would stop worrying about whether or not she was good enough for other people. What mattered now was what was good enough for her. Nina felt happy as she looked at Jan. She was so beautiful next to her. Nina loved her, she knew that for sure. She wanted to be with her, to live with her, to share a life with her. This was enough. What did it matter that it was Sweet Thing she was thinking of when she came?

Pearson still felt shell-shocked when he got back to the squat. Aftershocks reverberated through him. He felt propelled by the event; it spun like a centripetal force in his consciousness. His mind raced on and on. He had been slightly deafened by the blast. The voices in his head sounded muffled now. He couldn't quite work out what they were saying.

What was he going to do now? He needed further instructions. He wandered about the house in an agitated state. He needed to know whether it had worked. His head was full of static.

He heard the front door being unlocked and somebody letting themselves into the house. He went out on to the stairwell and looked down into the gloom of the hallway. He could just make out Sweet Thing, shimmering with the feral terror of a hunted animal.

What was Sweet Thing doing here? he wondered. Then he realised and a wave of relief flooded through his insane mind. It had worked. He had destroyed the controlling machines. Sweet Thing was free.

'Hey,' he called down at him.

Sweet Thing climbed the stairs quickly and came up close to him. He was shaking.

'What's the matter?' he asked the boy. 'It's all right now. You're free.'

'What are you talking about?' Sweet Thing muttered through trembling lips.

'I've broken the spell. Don't you see?'

Sweet Thing looked at Pearson. He was wild about the eyes. Stoned or something, he thought.

'Where's Nina?' he asked.

'Gone.'

'Gone?'

'Gone to live with the sisters.'

'You're not making any sense.'

'She left a number. It's on the wall by the phone.'

'Right.'

Pearson went into his room and sat on the bed. He yawned and his ears popped. He could rest now. It had worked. Sweet Thing went downstairs to the hall. He picked up the phone and began to dial.

The whole area had been cordoned off. Eric Walker stood by a line of uniformed officers, surveying the scene. The commander walked out of the wreckage of Playland and came over to him.

'You say the phone call claimed it was the Angry Brigade?'

'Yes, sir.'

'Well, preliminary forensics indicate it could be a similar device to ones used in their bombings.'

'Sir.'

'This could make us look bloody stupid. We're supposed to have caught them.'

'Well, it never was a centralised organisation, sir. It's bound to have disparate elements.'

'Yeah, well, have you seen the communiqué?'

'No, sir.'

'We just got it from *International Times*. It's bloody odd. Here,' he said, handing Walker a sheet of paper. 'See if you can make sense of it.'

Walker took the page and read:

Brothers & Sisters

Playland is not an amusement arcade, it is a slave market where runaway boys are lured by false pleasures and turned into donkeys, beasts of burden for the hidden desires of a sick society. The evil machines that control them must be destroyed! We are not mercenaries. We attack property not people. And people are not property. Young bodies are not slot machines for greedy lusts that lurk in the closet, they belong to the children of the revolution. We demand their liberation. We are not terrorists, we are an army of lovers.

We are also in Arcadia.

LOVE & REVOLUTION

The Final Communiqué
Over & Out

'What do you make of it?' the commander asked. 'Some sort of gay liberation rant, is it?'

'Something like that, sir.'

'Bunch of fucking fruitcakes, that's for sure. So come on, Walker, you're the expert.'

Walker sighed. He understood the communiqué. It was strange and rambling but it spoke to him clearly. A personal attack on the spectacle. A final gesture of idealism. Playland was a notorious haunt for male prostitution. West End Central regularly ran juvenile sweeps of the place.

Pearson, he thought. O'Connell's lover. The surveillance photographs with an Angry Brigade suspect. Maybe he hadn't got rid of the gelignite after all. He had felt sorry for the man. Guilty about what had happened to O'Connell. It had made him soft. It had affected his professional judgement. Part of him still felt a kind of sympathy. He thought for a second. He could let this pass. It had been partly his fault that the explosives had been in Pearson's possession. There could be trouble if the whole story came out into the open.

'Walker?'

He looked at the commander's face. Reassuringly stern, the expression of authoritative expectancy. Then Walker knew that he couldn't let them get away with it. He couldn't pretend to be something he was not. He was a horse of instruction. This was his job. His duty.

'I think I know who did this, sir,' he said.

'Really? Do you know where we might find them?'

'Oh yes.'

'Then get an operational team together and go after them.'

Nina saw the light on in Sweet Thing's room when she arrived at the squat. He had sounded desperate on the phone. He was in some sort of trouble, he had said. Jan hadn't been pleased when she said that she had to go back to the house.

'Don't leave now,' she had said. 'Not now.'

'I've got to. There's some sort of emergency.'

'You're always leaving. What's the matter with you?'

'I'm not leaving,' she had insisted. 'I'll be back later.'

She let herself into the house and went upstairs. Sweet Thing was sitting on the edge of the bed.

'What's happened?' she demanded.

'I'm in trouble,' he said. 'Real trouble.'

'Where's Pearson?'

'He's in his room. He's in a weird fucking mood.'

She sat on the bed next to him.

'So?' she asked.

He hissed in a breath and turned his head to the corner of the room.

'Fuck!' he spat out.

'What is it?'

'I didn't mean to do it.'

'Do what?'

'You know the punter I was talking about? The pop star.'

'Johnny Chrome?'

'How do you know?'

'I found out.'

'How?'

'I was looking for you. I was worried about you.'

'Why would you be worried about me?'

'Sweet Thing—'

'I killed him.'

'What?'

'I killed him,' Sweet Thing replied with a strangely melodious catch in his voice. 'I killed Johnny Chrome.'

'Jesus,' Nina said. 'What happened?'

'I strangled him. He was into that, see? He liked to be throttled. He wanted me to do it. But I lost it, didn't I? I went too far. And now . . . now . . .'

'What?'

'Now he's dead.'

'Shit.'

'What the fuck am I going to do? When they find out, I'm fucked, aren't I?'

'When did this happen?'

'I don't know, an hour ago.'

'Where?'

'At his house.'

'So nobody knows about this yet?'

'No. Except you.'

'But it was an accident. It was an accident, wasn't it?'

'Yeah, of course. But they're not going to see it like that, are they?'

'Who knows that you were there?'

'Joe Berkovitch. His manager.'

'Oh, yeah. Him.'

'Yeah,' Sweet Thing said. 'Him. What am I going to do?'

'I don't know,' Nina replied. 'If you explained to the police that it was an accident—'

'I ain't going to the police.'

'No.' Nina tried to think. 'Right.'

There would be a way out of this, she reasoned, there must be. Joe Berkovitch wouldn't want this scandal over his client's demise. Johnny Chrome was as valuable to him dead as he had been when he was alive. But he would want to preserve his precious reputation. Maybe she could make some sort of deal with him.

There was a commotion in the street outside. The sound of vehicles pulling up at high speed. The screeching of brakes and the thump of car doors slamming. Footsteps clattering up to the house. They were banging on the door.

They knocked the door off its hinges with a sledgehammer and it collapsed on to the hallway floor. Sounds from the street rushed into the house.

'Police!' a voice called up at them.

There was a clamour of footfalls on the stairs. Nina and Sweet Thing went out on to the landing. Pearson came out of his room.

'The machines!' he shouted. 'The machines are coming!'

Walker's ghostly face looked up at him. He nodded slowly, mournfully, gesturing at Pearson to the officers who followed.

'Take him,' he said bitterly.

'Don't say anything, don't say anything until I get you a lawyer,' Nina said, turning to Sweet Thing. But the boy had gone. He was rushing up the stairs to her room.

She followed him up. As she got to the loft she saw his legs on the ladder. He was going up to the roof. She looked up. He had climbed the ladder to the skylight.

'Sweet Thing!' she shouted. 'Wait!'

She mounted the steps herself. She grabbed hold of the frame as a police officer burst into the room. He shouted up at her.

'Oi! Come down here!'

Sweet Thing had pulled himself through the window and had started to edge himself out on to the rooftop, clinging to the slates which overlapped like scales on the back of a huge beast. He pushed himself up and crouched hunched against the incline. Swaying against the pitch, he started to walk up the tiles. Nina's head emerged from the skylight.

'Sweet Thing!' she called out

The boy began to laugh. He looked up and felt that he was above the whole world. Stars were burning against a canopy of electric blue. A sickly yellow fluorescence tinged the rim of the sky. Sweet Thing reached out to a chimney stack. He laughed out loud once more, his head giddy with escape. Fleet and fugitive, he stepped nimbly out along the roof. He gazed in wonder at the swirling sequined sky.

Nina sat on the edge of the skylight.

'Careful!' she called to him.

He looked back at her.

'Come here,' she beckoned to him. There were shouts from below. Insistent demands. He wanted to get away from them.

'I'm fucked,' he said, spitting the words out across the rooftops of Somers Town.

'Look,' she said, feeling the cool night air against her face, everything suddenly clear to her — what she had learnt from the Stoke Newington Eight Defence Committee, all her political involvement, becoming practical in this moment. 'Don't say anything. I'll get a lawyer. We'll deal with this.'

'Yeah?' he asked.

'Yeah. Come back down.'

He started to edge his way back to the skylight. He suddenly felt fear take hold of him. Nina sensed he was scared.

'Don't look down,' she told him.

And he knew she was right. If he looked down he would fall. This had always been the way. He mustn't look down. If he did, gravity would claim him. The dull solid earth would swallow him up.

'I'm frightened,' he said to Nina.

'It's all right,' she told him. 'I'm frightened too.'

'Oh shit,' he said.

'Tell me something,' she said, wanting to take his mind off the danger.

'What?'

'What's your real name?'

'What?'

'Your real name. I'll have to know that now, won't I?'

He closed his eyes as he clambered across the tiles. It had been such a long time.

'Stewart,' he blurted out, suddenly sounding like a school-boy at registration. 'Stewart Laing.'

Nina climbed up on to the ledge of the skylight. She reached out to him as he came closer.

'Here,' she said. 'Give me your hand, Stewart.'